A
FAMILY
Secret

Libby Ashworth was born and raised in Lancashire, where she can trace her family back to the Middle Ages. It was while researching her family history that she realised there were so many stories about ordinary working people that she wanted to tell. She has previously written historical novels – *The de Lacy Inheritance* and *By Loyalty Bound* – as well as local history books.

Libby currently lives in Lancashire with her son.

Also by Libby Ashworth

The Cotton Spinner
A Lancashire Lass

A FAMILY *Secret*

Libby Ashworth

arrow books

1 3 5 7 9 10 8 6 4 2

Arrow Books
20 Vauxhall Bridge Road
London SW1V 2SA

Arrow Books is part of the Penguin Random House group
of companies whose addresses can be found at
global.penguinrandomhouse.com

Penguin
Random House
UK

First published in Great Britain by Arrow Books in 2021

www.penguin.co.uk

A CIP catalogue record for this book is available from
the British Library

ISBN 9781787463585

Typeset in 11.5/15.7 pt Palatino
by Integra Software Services Pvt. Ltd, Pondicherry

Printed and bound in Great Britain by Clays Ltd, Elcograf S.p.A.

The authorised representative in the EEA is Penguin Random
House Ireland, Morrison Chambers, 32 Nassau Street,
Dublin D02 YH68.

Penguin Random House is committed
to a sustainable future for our business,
our readers and our planet. This book is
made from Forest Stewardship Council®
certified paper.

For my Mum

Acknowledgements

Thanks to my editor Jennie Rothwell and all the team at Arrow, including my copy editor Richenda Todd, for her close attention to detail. Thanks as well to Amy Musgrave, the cover designer and Silas Manhood, the photographer who tracked down the all-important kid-skin gloves, Isabelle Ralphs, my publicist, and everyone who has worked so hard under difficult circumstances to bring this book to fruition.

Also, huge thanks to my agent, Felicity Trew, and everyone at the Caroline Sheldon Literary Agency for all their support and professionalism whilst everyone is working from home.

And also thanks again to the Tuesday Reading Group. We may not have been able to meet in person, but hearing your voices has helped keep me from becoming a total recluse.

Chapter One

1842

It was still dark when she woke, but Bessie could hear the knocker-up making his way down the street, rapping on the windows until he heard an answer from the sleepy occupants inside. She pulled the blankets tight around her neck and hoped for a few more minutes' sleep.

Beside her, Peggy was breathing deeply as she lay with one hand tucked under the flock bolster and the other curled into a tight fist near her face. She'd slept like that since they were children, for as long as Bessie could remember.

It was no use, she thought, she couldn't wait a moment longer. Not needing a candle or rushlight to find her way, Bessie swung her feet over the edge of the mattress and felt for her clogs with her toes. They were icy cold and a shiver ran through her. She reached for her shawl from the bedpost and pulled it around herself, over her red-flannel nightgown. She was bursting for a wee and knew that it would be perishing cold outside. She went down the steep stairs, resting her hand on the wall where they curved midway, glancing back as she heard her mother getting up. She'd be in trouble if she was caught going out in her night clothes. Her mother didn't approve of her going down the yard until she was properly dressed, but Bessie couldn't wait and she hated using the chamber pot.

She unbarred the door slowly, trying not to let it squeak and wake Grandma Chadwick who had her bed in the parlour now that she couldn't climb the stairs any more. Bessie could hear her snoring and knew that she'd be lying on her back with her mouth wide open, and probably a dribble of spittle running down her chin. She hated that her grandma had grown old. She remembered her when she lived in the cottage at Ramsgreave, when they would walk up there to visit her and Grandad Chadwick. Bessie had always enjoyed that. She'd liked the way that the skies cleared to let the sun shine through and the scent of the air changed as they left the town and its dozens of smoking chimneys behind. The stench of the Blakewater was replaced by the clear streams that ran down from the hills, and the incessant noise of the engines gave way to the sound of sheep calling to their lambs and the gentle thud of the handloom weavers at work.

Her grandad had been a handloom weaver. She remembered watching him as he sat at his loom, working the treadle with his feet as the shuttle flew back and forth. He'd tried to teach her to weave, but her legs hadn't been long enough and her feet couldn't reach the pedals. He would laugh and kiss the top of her head and call her his grand little lass. She missed him.

It was cold in the house and there were frost patterns on the inside of the back kitchen window, but the chill that struck her as she stepped outside was even more fierce. Her feet slipped on the ice as she made her way down to the little brick building at the bottom of the yard that housed the privy. She lifted the latch and pushed open the door before sitting down with relief on the wooden board, her teeth chattering as she emptied her bladder.

The knocker-up had moved on to the next street and in the distance she heard the noise of the engines starting up in the mills for another day's work. Her day began at six and it would be six this evening before she was finished – and her father would work another couple of hours after that. She supposed they were lucky. The mills were working full-time at the moment and the money was welcome, although there was always the fear that they would be put on short time again if the mill owners decided they had more cloth than they could sell.

When she went back inside, her mother was down and had lit the fire. She was helping Grandma Chadwick get up and Bessie managed to close the door quietly and creep back up the stairs unseen. Her teeth were still chattering as she took off the nightgown and replaced it with a petticoat, followed by her skirt and blouse with an indoor shawl crossed at the front and fastened around her waist. She'd take it off later because even if she was cold now it would be hot in the mill. She welcomed the thought of beginning her work, even though it would be difficult to mend the threads at first until she got the feeling back into her fingers.

Peggy was still in bed. She didn't begin her work at the school until eight o'clock and Bessie often felt jealous of what she regarded as the privileges her elder sister had. But, she reminded herself, her sister didn't bring home the wages that she did as a four-loom weaver at the Brookhouse Mill.

She went back down to get her breakfast. The parlour was growing warmer and she tried to stay near to the fire, even though her mother kept calling her into the back kitchen to carry through the bowls and cups to put on the table for their porridge and tea.

Her father came yawning down, scratching his head, and sat in his rocking chair by the hearth.

'It's a cold 'un this morning,' he observed. 'They say as when the day lengthens, the cold strengthens. And it's true.'

'I'll be glad when it comes lighter in the mornings,' said Bessie as her mother dished out the oatmeal. 'I hate starting work in the dark and finishing in the dark. And the smell of the gaslight makes me feel sick.'

'It's better than oil lamps and candles,' her father told her. 'In my day that's all we had, and there's many a mill gone up in flames because of it. Lives lost too,' he added as he blew on his tea to cool it before taking a long sup from his pint pot. 'Things have changed a lot since I were a lad. But not always for the better.' He frowned. 'The Chartists are right when they say we should have a fair day's pay for our work every day instead of being subject to the whims of yon mill owners.'

'Don't be startin' on politics at this time of the morning,' her mother warned him. 'We've heard it all before anyroad.' She sliced a thick crust off the end of a precious loaf of bread and spread it

5

with butter for him. 'Let that stop thy mouth for a bit,' she said.

Her father was always talking politics, thought Bessie as she ate. And he was always out at some club or meeting after he'd come home from work and had his tea. Her mother sometimes complained that they hardly saw him, but Bessie preferred it when he was out. She liked it best when only she and her mother were at home. Her father … Well, she found him difficult, and he'd never made any secret of his favouritism for Peggy, who, if it was to be believed, never did a thing wrong – unlike her, who never seemed able to please him.

Her mother poured a cup of tea for Grandma Chadwick and took it to her. She was sitting up in bed with a couple of pillows propped behind her, and her shawl tight around her shoulders. Her mother would move her to the rocking chair by the fire once her father had gone to work and she'd sit there all day, nursing a little rag doll that used to be Peggy's and singing it lullabies as if it were a real babe. They were the same songs that her grandma used to sing to her and it made Bessie feel sad. Grandma Chadwick had not been the same since Grandad died three years ago. It was the shock, her mother said, that had done something to her mind.

'Time we were off,' said her father and drained his cup. He took his jacket and cap from the peg by the door and Bessie got her outdoor shawl and put it over her head and shoulders. She kissed her mother goodbye and followed her father out on to the dark street to join the other workers who were coming out and slamming their doors behind them before making their way to the mills – some to the Dandy Mill, some to Quarry Street, but most, like them, to the Brookhouse Mill.

'Good morning!' The street was filled with early greetings: some heartfelt, but most perfunctory as folk, still sleepy, trudged to their jobs. Her father soon fell in with friends and Bessie walked behind until they reached the gates. As the hooter blared across the town, joined by those of the other mills until it sounded like a fanfare, her father and the other men clattered up the iron stairs to the spinning rooms while she followed the women into the weaving shed. She hung up her shawl, slipped her feet out of her clogs, checked the looms and set them running. Two were weaving Blackburn Check for shirts and the other two were weaving a fine calico that would be sent up to Darwen to be printed in bright colours for summer frocks.

Her friend Ruth, who worked beside her, greeted her with a smile. It was too noisy to hold any conversation but they managed to convey their thoughts with sign language, Ruth making it plain she was cold and tired, and wished it was already time to go home.

Bessie had worked hard to progress to being a four-loom weaver, but running four looms took a lot of concentration and she was kept busy all day knowing that the cost of any mistakes or flaws would be docked from her wages and make her father cross. It was very different from her grandfather's handloom that she'd been thinking about earlier. There was no chance to take ten minutes for a breath of fresh air and a cup of tea here. Once the engines began to turn, the looms worked without stopping until dinnertime.

Bessie was a conscientious worker and she prided herself on her skills. She found it difficult to hide her jealousy of her sister though. All her life she'd seemed to live in Peggy's shadow, with their father telling everyone that Peggy was the clever one, the quick one, the pretty one. There'd been no question of Peggy leaving school at thirteen to work a twelve-hour day in the mill. Their father had been adamant about that. No, Peggy was to be a schoolteacher and so she'd stayed on at the Girls' School as a pupil-teacher. At first Bessie had enjoyed the reflected esteem. The other girls had admired her for having a big sister who was their teacher even if Peggy had sometimes

8

been intolerably bossy. Bessie had hoped that her father would do the same for her. But as her thirteenth birthday had approached, he'd made it very clear that she was to go into the mill to learn to weave.

'Book learnin' won't suit her,' he'd told her mother as Bessie had hidden behind the kitchen door listening to them discuss her future. 'She's good with her hands. Weavin'll suit her better.'

Her mother hadn't argued. Not much anyway. And no one had asked her what she wanted. Once she was old enough, she'd had no choice but to leave the calm of the classroom for the frantic, deafening world of the cotton mill.

Chapter Two

Peggy pulled the door shut behind her and took the familiar route to the Girls' School on Thunder Alley. It was the route she'd walked since she'd begun at the charity school as a little girl, in the days when her mother used to take her.

Since the age of seven or eight she'd always walked through town alone. She enjoyed it. She liked to see people hurrying out of the doors of their cottages, the men with their caps pulled low and the women clutching their shawls at their throats. She liked to see the horses hauling the heavy wagons to the doors of the mills, delivering bales of cotton and collecting stacks of cloth. She watched the early coaches arrive at the market square, with their bugles sounding and the horses snorting, delivering the mail and taking away the businessmen who had meetings in other towns – Preston, Lancaster and even Liverpool.

When she reached the top of Church Street she saw the man coming, dressed in his black jacket and grey cravat. She passed him at almost exactly the same spot every morning and he always exchanged the time of day with her. She knew who he was, of course. Her Auntie Hannah had told her. He was John Sharples, the son of Joe and Nan Sharples from Paradise Lane where her family had lived when she was a baby. Auntie Hannah had warned her to have nothing to do with him. When she'd asked why not, her auntie had said that there'd been a falling-out, but even when pressed had refused to say more.

'Ask thy mam,' her auntie had told her. 'I don't really know the details.' Though Peggy was sure that she did.

When Peggy had mentioned it, her mother had simply said, 'Have nowt to do with him. We don't want any more trouble.' And then she'd got that look on her face, with her lips pursed together, that meant she didn't want to talk about something. It almost drove Peggy mad. John looked such a nice person and she couldn't believe that he'd ever done anything bad enough to her family that she wasn't even allowed to speak to him. So she continued to exchange a word with him each morning, and she was disappointed and unsettled all day on the few occasions when their paths didn't cross.

'Good morning!' he said as he reached her and touched his cap. His smile was friendly and she returned it.

'Good morning,' she responded, wishing that he would pause and talk to her properly rather than hurrying by and turning in at the door of the ropemaker's where he worked.

She reached Thunder Alley and walked past the Boys' School where her uncle, James Hindle, was the master. She waved towards the window of the schoolhouse next door in case her Auntie Hannah was looking out.

Her auntie was said to have gone up in the world when she married a schoolmaster, and it was partly their influence that had allowed her to stay on as a pupil-teacher at an age when most girls went to work in the mill. She knew it was a privilege. Her father told her often enough, especially when times were hard and she had nothing to give to her mother for food and board. It was at those times she sometimes wished she could work as a weaver like Bessie did. Even when the mill was on short time Bessie could contribute something towards the household. And when they were working to full capacity she earned good money and was allowed to keep some of her wages as spending money, which meant she sometimes had cash for nice material to make herself new clothes. She might wear her shawl and clogs to work on a weekday, but on a Sunday she dressed like a lady and it made Peggy feel shabby beside her. But, she reminded herself, her own learning was an investment for her future. If she could qualify as a teacher she would never be short of work with all the new schools that were opening. The mills might fall on hard times, but there was never a shortage of children.

She lifted the latch on the Girls' School door and went into the classroom where Miss Parkinson already had the fire blazing. The teacher was sitting close to it, warming herself as she unravelled some knitting.

'Good morning, Margaret!' she called. 'Close that door quickly. It's chilly out there.'

Peggy hung up her shawl and went to warm her hands at the fire. Even though she'd had her thick gloves on, her fingers were numb with the cold and she rubbed them together vigorously as she held them as near as she dared to the flames.

'You'll get chilblains,' warned Miss Parkinson as she wound up the wool into a tight ball and dropped it into the basket. 'Have you spoken to your father yet about the Queen's Scholarship?' she asked her. 'You would like to have a try for it, wouldn't you?'

'I would,' said Peggy, although she hardly dared hope that she might be successful. The places were limited, but it would be a way to leave this dirty northern mill town with its belching chimneys and filthy streets and go to a school in London or Oxford where she would study for a teaching certificate. 'My father's been working long hours,' she explained. 'They're busy at Brookhouse at the moment.' It sounded like an excuse, and it was. She hadn't asked him yet because she was afraid that he might say no to her going away from home and tell her that when she finished her apprenticeship she would be qualified enough for a job as an assistant teacher in Blackburn.

'You did so well in your last exam I'm sure you would be successful,' said Miss Parkinson as she picked up the handbell to go and ring it at the door for the girls to come in. 'Don't leave it too long or you'll lose your chance.'

'I'll ask him tonight,' promised Peggy.

A fierce draught made the fire smoke as the door was opened and the girls lined up outside. The voices of children in the alley fell silent as the boys' bell rang as well. Peggy went to stand by the door to supervise the girls as they came in, making sure they were quick to hang up their shawls and take their places at their desks.

Miss Parkinson led the morning prayers and hymn singing. Then it was time for the Bible lesson. Peggy sat on a stool whilst Miss Parkinson read the story of the Good Samaritan to the whole school. It was Peggy's job to watch the pupils and reprimand anyone who appeared to be fidgeting or daydreaming. Then it was time for dictation. Miss Parkinson read out a few lines of the story they'd just heard. She used simple words at first, ones that the younger girls should be able to spell. Then it was time for Peggy to check the slates of the younger class whilst Miss Parkinson continued with harder spellings for the older girls.

When dictation was done they moved on to arithmetic and Peggy moved between the rows correcting the numbers on the slates as Miss Parkinson called out the sums to be calculated. Then it was dinnertime. The pupils hurried home for their meal whilst Peggy took the hand of her little cousin Emily, who had recently started at the school, and they went next door where Peggy ate her dinner with her auntie and uncle on school days.

Auntie Hannah had the meal on the table ready for them and they were soon joined by the older two boys, Henry and George, who went to the Boys' School. Auntie Hannah had the youngest two at home: little Julia and baby Albert, named

15

for the prince, who was sleeping in a crib near the range.

With Uncle James as well, it was a crowd of them around the table, but Auntie Hannah always made something good and wholesome to eat and today it was a stew, made with the leftovers from their Sunday dinner. It was a particular favourite of Peggy's.

They said grace and ate quietly. When they'd finished, her uncle went back to his desk in the schoolhouse and the boys went into the back yard for half an hour to kick a ball about until it was time to resume their lessons.

'Miss Parkinson's been asking me again if I mean to go for the scholarship,' said Peggy as she helped her auntie wash up.

'Uncle James'll give thee some help if tha's worried about not passing,' said her auntie as she put a basin to dry on the draining board. 'I'm sure he will.'

'It's not that,' said Peggy. 'I'm not sure my father will let me go.'

'Oh, I think he will,' her auntie reassured her. 'He's been set on thee being a schoolteacher ever since tha were a little girl and used to give lessons to Bessie in front of the fire on a Sunday afternoon. It was because of that I learned to read and write myself,' she told her. 'I'd always thought it would

16

be too hard, but reckoned that if a little lass could do it then I should give it a go.' She dried her hands on the towel. 'Is it what tha wants to do though?' she asked. 'It's a big thing, goin' so far away from home. Tha's bound to be a bit worried. It's only natural.'

'I'm not worried about that. I'll be glad to get away,' said Peggy. She'd read about what it was like in the south of England, how the sky was always blue and the air was sweet and clear and you could hear the birdsong. It would be like heaven compared to the filthy, crowded streets of Blackburn with their incessant noise and belching chimneys that meant there was a permanent haze over the town which the sun rarely penetrated.

'I know how tha feels,' said her aunt. 'I was the same when I were younger. I went away to Mellor to work in a big house and I thought it were paradise when the sun shone on my face. Then Mr Sudell went bankrupt and I had to come back here. Still, I met thy uncle here. I'll not regret that!'

She went to pick up baby Albert who had begun to cry and laid him on the rug to change him. A smell even worse than the mill chimneys wafted through the parlour and Peggy made her excuses and went back to the girls' classroom early.

Chapter Three

Bessie glanced up at the high windows when the looms powered down. She guessed that it was only around four in the afternoon – not quite dark.

'Master says we're to finish for today,' the overlooker told them.

'Aye, he's saving money on gas and on our wages,' grumbled Ruth as she tied off some threads. 'I thought we were done with short time.'

Bessie folded a length of finished cloth and went to fetch her shawl. It would be nice to walk home early, but it was surprising. Folk had been saying that trade was booming and that there was more work than there'd ever been now that the markets had opened up in China. But it seemed it wasn't true and the workers were all grumbling as they left. Although short time working and closures gave the mill owners the chance to spend more time with their families, it came at a higher cost for working folk. No money coming in meant there was nothing to buy food with and there was a difference between driving around the country-side in a carriage, visiting the sights, and trying to scrape together a dinner for six on half a green potato and a mouldy crust.

As she followed the workers spilling from the door on to the street, Bessie saw a huge wagon trying to turn into the yard. The driver was attempting to back up the horses so he could take a wider sweep and come in straight, but the animals were agitated by the crowds and seemed to want to go in every direction except the one he intended. On the back of the wagon was a huge iron barrel. Bessie stared at it, unsure what it was.

'It's one of them new steam boilers,' Ruth told her. 'My father says all the mills are installing them and Hornby doesn't want to be left out.'

They watched as the heavy load was hauled slowly through the gateway into the yard with the horses snorting and tossing their heads and the driver threatening them with his whip.

'It must be why we've shut down early,' Ruth went on, 'so as they can put it in.'

By the time Bessie got home her father was already there, sitting at the table and complaining to her mother who was trying to finish off some ironing.

'They'll not have it installed for weeks! Mark my words,' he was saying. 'There's nowt been said about workers being laid off, but mill'll be closed in t' morning! It's bound to be. They just wanted folk to go home quiet tonight! If they'd told 'em t' truth they'd never have been allowed to get yon boiler into t' yard!'

Her mother put her cooling flat-iron back on the hearth to heat and picked up the hot one with a cloth.

'And when there's no work, there's no money,' she said as she carefully pressed the starched lace collar of a blouse. 'I hope it won't be for long … now that we have another mouth to feed.' She glanced at Grandma Chadwick, who was rocking in her chair, oblivious to what went on around her.

'Hast tha got owt put by?' asked her father.

'A bit,' she said. 'And I'll get paid for this laundry when I take it back tomorrow. We'll manage.'

'There's always the Friendly Society,' he said.

'Hush!' Her mother glanced towards the door as if she feared there might be someone listening. 'Tha knows better than to talk about that!'

'There's nowt amiss with it now.'

'I don't want thee in trouble with the law again,' she said.

20

'That were goin' on for twenty years ago!' he replied. 'And it were never my fault as tha well knows.'

'I know tha were arrested for being in the wrong place at the wrong time,' she told him. 'And tha knows what I thinks of thee meeting up with Chartists and radicals and unionists and suchlike all the time. There's many a night I've not a minute's peace until I hear thee come safe home.'

'Tha worries too much,' he told her.

The door opened and Peggy came in, surprised to see them home early.

'What's happened?' she asked, taking off her hat.

'Mill's closed for a new boiler,' her father told her. 'Nowt for thee to worry about.'

Bessie went into the back kitchen to fill the kettle for tea. She looked to see what there was to eat and found half a loaf of bread, a scraping of butter and a bit of fatty bacon. It would just about stretch between them all with some oatcakes, she thought. Her mother came through with the finished basket of washing for one of the families on King Street that she did laundry for.

'I hope t' mill won't be shut for long,' she said. 'Thy father will drive me half-mad if he's at home all day. I'll hear about nowt but steam boilers from morning to night.'

'He'll be off to one of his meetings later,' predicted Bessie. 'Give him a shilling for beer and he'll be setting the world to rights with someone else 'til bedtime.'

'Aye, tha's right,' replied her mother as Bessie sliced the bread as thinly as she dared. 'It'll be worth it to get a bit of peace.'

'Peggy says as how Miss Parkinson has recommended her for a Queen's Scholarship!' her father told them as they sat around the table to eat. He looked swelled up with pride and Bessie was glad that her sister had the sense to look a bit embarrassed by him. 'I always knew she were a clever lass, and now she has t' chance to become a proper teacher, with a certificate an' all!'

'I'd have to pass the exam first, and do well,' Peggy told them. 'Places are limited and they only take the best.'

'Tha's one of t' best!' said her father. 'They'll be lucky to have thee.'

'So you don't mind?' asked Peggy.

'Mind? Why would I mind?'

'Well, you know it means me leaving home. I'd have to go away to a school.'

'But tha said as there's a grant. It won't cost me owt, will it?'

'No. But I won't be here to help out with wages,' she said, glancing apologetically at Bessie. 'And if the mills go on short time—'

'Tha's not to worry about that,' he interrupted her. 'We'll manage. Besides, yon mill's bound to be up and running again soon. Hornby wouldn't be spending his cash on a new boiler if there wasn't plenty of work.'

Bessie stood up and began to clear the plates. She knew he was only saying it so that Peggy would be reassured and she tried not to be jealous of the fact that Peggy was never allowed to have any concerns. She told herself that Peggy was clever and it was right that she should do well for herself, but the way their father praised her to the skies always rankled with her. It wasn't fair. She knew it wasn't. She'd done well at school too and she would have liked a chance to better herself rather than being sent to the mill.

Her mother followed her into the back kitchen. 'Tha's done well too,' she said. 'Tha worked up to being a four-loomer in next to no time and we'd be struggling without thy wages coming in.'

Bessie knew she was trying to be kind, but it made it worse. She wished that her mother would sometimes speak up for her and tell her father that he was being unfair, but she never did. And although she offered some sympathy when they were alone, Bessie thought it wasn't enough. She felt that she'd been let down and she fretted about what it was that she'd done to make her less loved than Peggy. She tried to be a good lass. She brought home a wage. She pulled her weight around the house. She didn't complain. And yet she felt that she was never appreciated.

She began to wash the cups and dishes and her mother picked up a cloth to dry them. As they worked, her father called that he was off out and there was a blast of cold air as he opened the front door and slammed it behind him. It shook the house, rattling the windows and made her mother frown.

When everything was cleared away Bessie went back into the parlour where Peggy was sitting opposite Grandma Chadwick with a book in her hand, turned to the light of a candle.

'I'll need to study hard if I'm to pass,' she said. 'Would you like me to read aloud to you?'

'Not tonight,' said Bessie. She was interested in what Peggy was reading, but she preferred to read things for herself, quietly, so she could reread anything that interested her or that she found hard to understand. She hoped that if there was no work tomorrow Peggy might leave her book behind and she'd have a chance to borrow it.

Chapter Four

The mill gates were shut and chained when they arrived at work next morning. No hooter sounded although hammering echoed from the engine house. Workers were milling about, their angry voices demanding to know what was going on.

'There's a notice on the door,' said one. '*Closed until further notice.*' The muttering grew dark and Bessie became anxious in case trouble was brewing. She glanced around for her father, but couldn't see him. Perhaps it would be better just to go home, she thought as she squeezed through the crush until she was clear.

She headed back towards Water Street. If there was no work today, she could help her mother with the washing. She knew how hard it was for her in the wintertime when it was difficult to get things dry, especially now that she had Grandma to look after as well.

Her mother was hanging clothes up on the rack when she got back in. Grandma kept taking things out from the basket set at her feet and she tried to keep a grip on them when her mother reached for them and it was taking her a while to get it all set to dry.

'Shut?' asked her mother when she saw her. She didn't sound surprised.

'Aye. Everyone's been locked out.'

'Where's thy father?'

'I don't know. It looked like trouble so I decided to come away before it began.' She took a shirt from her grandma and handed it to her mother, then moved the basket on to the table.

'I hope he's had the sense to come away as well,' said her mother as Bessie handed items to her. 'I don't want him caught up in any more rioting.' She tugged on the pulley and the rack rose out of reach, the washing hanging over the fire to dry. 'Put some more coal on,' she said to Bessie. 'I've another lot to put on to boil then I've to take yesterday's back to Miss Cross.'

'I'll take it,' offered Bessie.

The town seemed busy as she crossed the market place on her way to Church Street. As well as the hundreds of mill workers who were at a loose

26

end, it was thronged with housewives, browsing amongst the stalls, looking for a bargain.

She skirted the edges and went down to Miss Cross's shop. It was a double-fronted establishment with men's hats and gloves in one window and ladies' hats and trimmings in the other. Bessie paused to look longingly at the display of bonnets adorned with feathers and plumes and ribbons. She would love a new bonnet for Easter, but now it seemed that she would have to buy some ribbons and retrim her old one again, even though the brim was looking a bit worse for wear. Not knowing how long she would be without work, she would feel too guilty to spend all her savings in one go.

She pushed open the door and the bell jangled. Miss Cross looked up, over the top of wire-rimmed spectacles that perched on the end of her nose. She was a woman past middle age, yet she was always beautifully dressed and never had a hair out of place even though she always seemed busy. As well as selling hats and gloves, she ran the post office.

The mail coach must have just been because Bessie saw she had a stack of letters spread out in front of her on the counter.

'Take a seat,' she said, pointing to the wooden chair placed adjacent to her glass-topped display of gloves. 'I'll be with you in a moment.'

'I'm not here to buy anything,' said Bessie, unsettled by the woman's courtesy. 'I've brought your laundry.'

Miss Cross glanced at the basket Bessie was holding but still motioned her to sit down. Bessie perched on the edge of the chair, with the basket on her knee, and gazed at the pairs of kidskin gloves in an array of pastel shades that were artfully arranged for the inspection of customers. How she would have loved a pair, she thought. Especially the lavender-coloured ones that were the latest fashion. These gloves were intended to be worn by ladies at dances and supper parties and for social calls. They weren't the rough gloves worn by the working classes to protect their hands and keep them warm in winter. She could only imagine the softness and elegance of easing such things on to her own hands and having a maid to fasten them up with an ivory buttonhook, and she could only guess at what they would cost as no prices were displayed. She knew that they would be expensive. Miss Cross didn't cater for ordinary girls like her. Her customers were the Hornbys and the Feildens and the Harts – those who had made money from the mills and could afford such luxurious items.

She looked at the gloves she was wearing. They were knitted from grey wool and one needed darning where it was coming into a hole. She felt embarrassed by their shabbiness.

When Miss Cross was satisfied that the letters and packets were all sorted she stowed them into the cubbyholes ready for collection, then turned her attention to Bessie.

'Laundry?' she said.

'Yes. I'm giving my mother a lift today.' She placed the items on the counter as Miss Cross checked them off one by one in her little book and then opened her drawer and counted the money into Bessie's hand.

She slipped the coins into her purse, thanked Miss Cross and with the empty basket returned to the teeming market place. Her mother had told her exactly what she was to buy, warning her not to be drawn in by any little extras no matter how much the stall-holders tempted her with their bargains. Money would be tight until the mill was back working and they would struggle to make ends meet.

As she headed towards the stall that sold vege-tables, she saw the woman coming towards her – the woman that her mother always avoided. She wasn't sure why she did, but since Bessie was a small child her mother had always grasped her by the hand and hurried her off in a different direction if she saw this woman coming. Habit almost made Bessie do the same, but she was curious. She'd only ever seen the woman from a distance and she wondered what it was about her that her mother so disliked. As she drew closer she saw that she was a small woman with an overlarge nose. Her shawl had slipped back on her head and Bessie saw that her hair, which had probably once been a sandy colour, was faded now and greying at the temples. Her mouth had a downward slant at the corners that made her look displeased even before her eyes met Bessie's. As they drew level the woman glared at her with an expression of distaste, as if she was something nasty waiting to be stepped in. Then, with an audible sniff of disapproval, she hurried past. Bessie realised that she was trembling. The woman obviously knew who she was, but what she, or her family, were supposed to have done to deserve such treatment she couldn't imagine. Her mother was always going out of her way to help people, and her father, although he could be difficult sometimes, was well liked by his friends and acquaintances.

'What's to do, love?' asked the stall-holder as she stood staring at the carrots and potatoes, not able to remember what it was she was supposed to be getting. 'Tha looks like tha's had a bit of a shock.'

'I'm all right,' said Bessie, gathering herself and trying to concentrate on her errand. 'Weigh me five pounds of those spuds – and I don't want no bad ones in amongst them.' She tried to sound like her mother, but for some reason the chap didn't take her as seriously. He laughed as he poured them from his scales into her basket. 'They're all beautiful,' he said. 'Just like thee.' He winked and she felt herself blush even though she wanted to say something scathing in reply. She wished it was true, but she knew that her face was plain, not like Peggy's. Peggy was the pretty one.

She bought onions and a sack of oatmeal and then headed home. The weight of the basket pulled on her arm, but the encounter with the woman weighed more heavily. Her look had been filled with pure hatred and it had upset Bessie. She wanted to ask her mother who the woman was and what had happened to make her dislike them so much. But when she'd asked in the past her mother had refused to speak about it, simply saying they were a bad family and she was to have nothing to do with any of them.

Her mother was running some sheets through the mangle in the back yard and pegging them out to dry. It was cold, but fine, and they'd dry to damp enough for ironing by the end of the day.

Bessie put the shopping away and started to get some dinner ready, wondering if her father would come home or if he'd stay in the beerhouse with his Chartist friends. But as the hooters sounded for the break in the mills that were working, she heard his clogs clattering up the street and he came in, banging the door behind him.

'They're sayin' as hard times are comin' again,' her father commented as he sat down and waited for his food to be put in front of him. 'They say as mill owners are goin' to cut wages again. We'll not stand for it,' he told them. 'They'll find as workers'll not be goin' back unless they're paid fairly for their work.'

'Is that wise?' asked her mother. 'Surely some wages are better than none at all?'

'They're taking us for fools,' he said. 'And they'll not go without owt, with their big houses and fancy clothes. Why should we make their money for 'em when they can't pay us a fair wage?'

'I thought I might go for a walk,' said Bessie after her father had gone off out again and she'd helped her mother wash up. 'Unless tha needs me?' she said, hoping that her mother would say no.

'There's nowt much that needs doing,' she said. 'Go and get a breath of fresh air. It'll do thee good.'

Bessie craved the fresh air. She headed out of town and away from the pall of smoke that hung there, clinging to everything. Once the land began to rise the air was sweeter and by the time she reached Ramsgreave the skies were clear apart from a few greyish clouds. She took the familiar path towards her grandparents' cottage. A few early snowdrops were nodding their heads in the shade of the woodland. Spring was on its way and the thought cheered her. She loved the spring-time and everything that it brought – the unfurling leaves on the trees, the fresh growth in the cottage gardens, the twittering of birds as they built their nests under the eaves, and the increasing warmth of the sun. Not that she had much chance to enjoy it, but on Sunday afternoons when her work and her chores were done, she delighted in walking and walking as far as she dared, to remind herself that there was a beautiful world beyond the confines of the dirty, noisy cotton town.

Her grandparents' cottage was locked up. No one lived there now. No one wanted houses in the countryside. People clamoured for a place to live in Blackburn. All around the mills, street after street of terraced houses were being built for the workers. All alike in row upon row – two rooms upstairs and two down, and, if you were lucky, a privy at the bottom of the yard.

Bessie walked around the back of the cottage and looked at her grandad's garden. She'd helped him with it when he was alive, even though there was only so much she could do on her Sunday visits. But she'd hoed and pulled out weeds, and helped him sow some seeds and gather in the small harvest in the autumn. Then he was gone. She'd kissed him goodbye one Sunday and walked home with blackcurrants and redcurrants in her basket to make jam. She'd turned and waved just before the path dipped away and he was lost to sight. He'd waved back and gone inside. It was the last time she'd seen him. The next morning there'd been a message to say he'd got up as usual, but had suddenly dropped to the floor and when Grandma Chadwick went to help him up she'd found that he was dead.

Bessie peeped in through the window, wiping away the spiders' webs with her grubby gloves. It looked so familiar. There was the hearth, the corner where Grandma Chadwick kept her spinning wheel, the place under the window where the loom had stood to catch the best of the light. She could almost see them there, a stew cooking in a cauldron over the fire and her grandma singing softly as she worked. She'd been happy here once and she longed to feel that peace again rather than the constant worry that seemed to beset them now that they had no work except that provided by the mills.

When she turned away, she noticed how low the sun had sunk in the sky and knew that it was time to go back if she didn't want to be caught out on the moors in the dark. She took the track back towards Blackburn, knowing that she'd be in trouble if she wasn't home before her father came in.

Chapter Five

As Peggy turned the corner on to Church Street next morning, she saw John Sharples lingering outside Miss Cross's shop window. He didn't see her for a moment, but when she reached the shop and he saw her reflection in the window, he turned and smiled.

'Good morning!' he greeted her and she suspected that he'd been lingering on purpose so that he wouldn't miss her. The thought excited her.

'Good morning,' she replied.

He hesitated, then: 'It's not so cold today,' he said.

It was the first time he'd said anything beyond a greeting and Peggy stopped. It would seem rude to keep walking without answering, she thought.

'It does seem a little warmer,' she said.

'I see thee most mornings.'

'Yes. We often pass.'

'Tha's Margaret? Margaret Eastwood?'

'That's right,' she said. He must have enquired about her name and she wondered who had told him.

'I'm John Sharples,' he said.

'I know,' she replied.

'I work at Hart's – in the office.'

She nodded. 'I teach at the Girls' School.'

'Well, it's nice to meet thee, Miss Eastwood.' He raised his hat and continued on his way, and Peggy resumed walking towards Thunder Alley. He was nice, she thought. Not handsome though. He was too slight for that. He seemed all bones, like a skeleton with clothes on. And his hair, when he raised his hat, had been straight and flat and a bit sandy-looking. His eyes were nice – on the grey side of blue – but his lashes were pale and his eyebrows almost invisible. He wasn't a man who would attract the lasses with his looks, she thought, and yet she found him interesting and the idea that he'd been deliberately waiting for her was flattering.

'You look pleased about something,' observed Miss Parkinson when she reached the schoolroom. 'Though I don't know what. I hear that the Brookhouse Mill is closed. It's where your father and sister work, isn't it?'

37

'It is,' said Peggy, trying to rearrange her expression with some difficulty. 'But it's only shut whilst they fit a new boiler.'

'Still. It'll be hard for them whilst it lasts. No one likes to be idle. Did you ask your father about the scholarship?'

'I did. He's keen for me to take the exam.'

'Good. When you get it, it'll be one less mouth for him to feed,' she said. 'I'll let the inspectors know that you're a candidate.'

All through prayers and Bible story, when Peggy should have been watching the pupils to make sure they were paying attention, she found it was her own thoughts that kept straying. She wondered if John Sharples would speak to her again the next morning and if so what he would say. She supposed that they could discuss the weather again, and even though there was only so much that could be said on that subject, she found herself hoping that he might say more. Despite the warnings, she wanted to get to know him better – if only to find out what the great falling-out had been about. But she knew better than to mention to either her auntie or her mother that she'd spoken to him. Although she was sure that there was no harm in it, she knew that they would forbid her to do it again, and rather than defying them she decided that it would be simpler if they didn't know.

The next day she was up earlier than usual. It wasn't often that she was the first out of the warm bed that she shared with her little sister, but whilst the mill was closed Bessie was taking advantage of an extra hour's sleep.

It was still cold and there was a thin layer of ice on the jug of water on the small chest of drawers so she carried it downstairs and added a little boiling water from the kettle and washed her hands and face at the kitchen sink. She brushed her hair, checked that it was tidy in the little mirror that was propped up on the window-sill and then helped her mother carry the spoons and plates through to the parlour to lay the table.

Her father came down and sat next to the fire. He looked out of place when he wasn't hurrying to get ready to go to work.

'Shift thy feet!' her mother told him irritably as she reached for the boiling kettle to make the tea. 'I hope tha's not goin' to sit there all morning. I've got washing to put to dry.'

'I'll go out in a bit and see if I can get a scrap o' news about what's happenin' at yon mill,' he told her. 'But at least let me have a sup o' tea in peace before tha starts naggin' me.'

Bessie came down and poured a cup of tea for Grandma Chadwick, who was singing hymns to herself in her bed.

'I know thee!' she said to Bessie as she took the cup.

'Aye. I'm Bessie. You're my grandma,' she told her.

'I'll be off then,' said Peggy after she'd rinsed her cup in the water in the kitchen sink. She got her shawl and pulled it round her shoulders.

'That's thy Sunday bonnet,' observed her mother as she watched her fasten the ribbons. 'What's tha wearin' that for?'

'I just thought I needed to think about looking smart – seeing as I'm going for the scholarship,' Peggy told her.

'Aye. Well, don't get it spoiled,' said her mother. 'There's nowt to spare for a new one.'

Peggy let herself out of the house into the cold morning. There was a chill wind blowing down from the hills and she wished that she'd just pulled the shawl over her head as she usually did in the wintertime. It would have kept her head much warmer than the flimsy bonnet with its green ribbons and faded pink flower. She knew why she'd put the bonnet on though. She wanted to impress John Sharples. She was hoping that he would stop and speak to her again.

She set off at a quick pace; then she told herself to slow down. She didn't want to be early and miss him. When she reached Church Street there was no sign of him and her hopes plummeted. She slowed her steps to a dawdle and then paused outside the hat shop, pretending to look at the display in the window.

She heard footsteps but didn't look up, not wanting to feel disappointed if it wasn't him. The footsteps stopped beside her.

'It'll be Easter soon,' he said. 'It's early this year.'

'Yes. It's next month,' she said. She could see his reflection in the glass.

'Tha'll be wanting to trim a bonnet. There's some pretty ribbons there.'

'There are,' she said, still not looking directly at him.

'What colour takes thy fancy?' he asked.

Peggy stared at them. 'Yellow's nice for Easter,' she said. 'Or green. Although I like the pink.'

'Tha'll be wantin' 'em all!' he said and she heard the laughter in his voice. She glanced at him and he was smiling at her.

'I'd best go,' she told him. 'I mustn't be late.' Now that he had come and he had spoken to her again she was unnerved and not sure what to say.

'Don't let me keep thee,' he said. He sounded a little disappointed and so she smiled at him to try to reassure him that she was pleased he had spoken.

'Miss Parkinson doesn't like me to be late,' she explained. 'She says it sets a bad example. And I've the slates and chalks to lay out before the girls come in.'

'Aye. I've got my work too,' he said, then he touched his hat, wished her a *good morning* and moved on.

Peggy almost skipped up the street. She could feel herself smiling and she had to pause before she turned the corner into Thunder Alley to try to get control of her face. This was to be her secret and she mustn't give herself away by looking too happy.

Chapter Six

Jennet spooned the porridge into her mother's mouth. It was like feeding a baby, she thought, remembering how she'd done the same for Peggy and then Bessie. But with them there'd been hope. Hope that before long they'd be feeding themselves, growing, thriving, living their own lives. This was different. Her mother had, had her life and this old woman who sat by the fire and sang her songs and nursed her rag doll wasn't really her. She was a stranger in the frail body of what had once been. Although, just occasionally, there were glimpses of her mother. They gleamed for a moment like the flames when the fire caught hold, but they didn't last; they fizzled and faded into dull smoke, like the fire when the coal was too damp to burn.

'Come on. One more mouthful,' she coaxed. Her mother needed to eat. Jennet had been shocked at how thin she'd become and blamed herself for not going up to Ramsgreave more often to take care of her. She'd been fine until her husband died. It had been so unexpected, and Jennet believed that her father had died from grief. It had only been a couple of weeks after the chapman had told him that he couldn't buy any more cloth from him that it had happened. Her father, who'd worked at his loom all his life, since being a lad, was left with no purpose as well as no money – and although she and Titus had reassured him that they would help and see that they didn't go hungry he had fretted and worried until, one morning, old Seth, who'd been his neighbour, had come to tell them that her father was dead.

Her mother had seemed to bear it well at first. She'd seen him buried and said that she'd stay on at the cottage, but it had affected her mind – slowly at first so that Jennet didn't really notice. But on the day she'd gone to visit and found her mother in her night clothes in the garden, searching for her dead husband, she'd realised that something was very wrong. When she'd taken her inside to help her dress she'd seen how much weight she'd lost and although the pantry was well stocked, her mother had little idea of when or what she'd last eaten.

'She can't manage on her own. She needs to be looked after,' she'd told Titus that night, and to give him his due he hadn't argued but agreed that Grandma Chadwick should move in with them.

'I know thee,' said her mother, fixing her with a puzzled look.

'Aye. I'm Jennet.'

'I used to know a Jennet. She were my daughter.'

'That's nice.' It was a conversation that had been repeated many times and Jennet had realised long since that it was pointless trying to explain.

'When's Titus coming home?' her mother asked.

'He'll be here in a bit for his dinner.' It was strange that she always remembered Titus but not her, thought Jennet. She knew it was just the vagaries of the mind, but it hurt more than anything.

She took the bowl away and washed it, wondering if Titus would come in for his dinner. Although he'd gone off out every day since the mill had shut, and she was glad of it, she worried about where he was. He wasn't a drinker, but he was still too involved with the radicals for her liking. She'd thought it might stop with the Parliamentary Reform, but that hadn't changed anything and now, as well as his clubs and unions, he'd got himself mixed up with the Chartists and she worried about where it would end. The family needed his wages and Jennet thought it would be better if he kept quiet and simply did his work rather than going about stirring up trouble. But Titus would never be satisfied until he could have the vote. It was his life's ambition and she thought that if it were ever possible for him to be a Member of Parliament himself he would probably throw his hat into the ring for that as well. She'd be glad when the mill started up again and she knew that he was out of harm's way, for some of the time at least.

Jennet heard the door and thought it was Bessie. She was a good lass: she'd taken over delivering and collecting the laundry as well as going to the pump for buckets of spring water. It was a huge help and she knew that she'd regret her going back when the mill reopened. But hanging about with no proper job was no life for a young lass. Bessie had done well for herself at the mill and Jennet was proud of her. She seemed to enjoy it too, though she could never tell with Bessie. Unlike Peggy, who made her feelings very clear about everything, her younger daughter was reticent and rarely talked about herself. But perhaps it wasn't surprising that they were so different, given that they had different fathers. Jennet sometimes wondered if Bessie took after George

Anderton, because if the truth was told she'd never known him very well.

But it was Titus who came whistling in, looking pleased with himself. 'There's talk of a big petition!' he told her.

'Petition?'

'Aye. They want everyone to sign it. They're going to demand that the People's Charter is made law. They're going to march to London and ask that they're heard by Parliament!'

Jennet could see how excited he was.

'Will it make a difference?' she asked.

'It will if it's accepted. It'll give every man the vote!'

She said nothing, but she didn't think it would happen. Although Blackburn now returned its own members to Parliament, the gentry in London were still not interested in the struggles of ordinary people and Jennet doubted that a petition would change anything, no matter how many folk signed it.

'Tha's not thinking of going to London?' she asked him, wondering if that was the source of the gleam in his eye.

'Someone'll have to take it and the more that go the better. They need to see that we're a force to be reckoned with.'

'But the mill will be up and running again in a few days,' she said.

'Well, t' petition's not ready to go yet,' he said. 'Signatures have to be gathered first. Tha'll sign it, won't tha?' he asked. 'Peggy and Bessie an' all.'

'Aye, I'll sign it,' she said. She knew he'd never let the matter drop until she did. 'But tha's to think on that tha's got a job and a responsibility. I don't want thee swanning off to London. It's too far away.'

'Tha always were too meek, our Jennet,' he said. 'It's wrong to let the gentry walk all over us like they do. If takin' this petition to London makes things fairer for t' workin' man then I shall go.'

Jennet didn't ask what he expected her to live on whilst he was away. The laundry money wasn't enough to feed them and she hated taking all Bessie's wages when Peggy was earning nothing. She began to make their dinner. Perhaps it wouldn't happen, she thought. She was too tired to worry about it.

Chapter Seven

Bessie followed her father up to the mill. The new steam boiler had been started up the previous day to test it and this morning work was to resume. The hooter was already sounding across the town and daylight was creeping over the horizon. They'd been without work and wages for weeks and most were glad to stumble from their beds at the sound of the knocker-up and return to their looms and spindles.

As they approached the gates Bessie could already hear the grumbling and the words *short time* being muttered throughout the crowd. She saw her father speaking to the overlooker, arguing and pointing a finger towards the engine house with its new boiler. The man was shrugging his shoulders and shaking his head. It affected him as well. More men crowded around Titus and the discussion grew heated as they moved to block the entrance so that no one could get inside.

But some workers were keen to go in and scuffles were breaking out around the gate as those that wanted to work joined in a pushing match with those who'd decided that they weren't going to let them in. People began to argue and Bessie moved away from the gate to stand where it was relatively quiet so she could wait to see what would happen.

She felt let down by her father and his Chartist friends. Some work was better than no work at all. If they refused to work they would have no wages and she thought of her mother, struggling to earn enough shillings to feed them. And she thought about the colourful ribbons that she'd seen in Miss Cross's shop when she returned her laundry – the ones she'd hoped to buy to trim her bonnet ready for Easter once the mill began working again.

The workers around her were straining to hear what was being said. It seemed that not only was the mill to run on short time, wages were also being reduced. The Chartist refrain of *A fair day's pay for a fair day's work* began to be repeated by the gathered crowd and before long it turned to *Strike* as the few workers who had wanted to go in now had their way firmly barred by the discontented workforce.

Bessie watched her father, who had climbed up on to a box near the mill gates. He was telling the workforce that they would never accept a cut in wages. They were cheering his words and the chant of *Strike! Strike!* took hold.

He loved being the centre of attention, thought Bessie, but he would still come home for his tea and expect there to be food on the table. She would have gladly gone back to her work, even at a reduced rate, simply to take some of the worry from her mother. But her father seemed to think of nothing but Chartism and unions, and whilst he had a point Bessie thought that there was no glory in starvation. The mill owners would never back down. They were greedy and stubborn and she'd heard that in Manchester they were bringing in workers from Ireland who were glad of any employment and who didn't demand more than the mill owners were willing to pay.

After a while, the crowd began to disperse as people went back home. The mill gates remained shut and although the new steam boiler was running the looms stayed silent and still. There would be no work done today – and maybe not for many days to come as the mill owners and the workers waited to see who would back down first.

*

Jennet looked up as the door opened and Titus came in, his face as dark as a thunder cloud.

'What's to do?' she asked. 'I thought there were work today?'

'Aye. But it's not good enough!' he said. 'They're only offering reduced wages after they've spent all their money on yon fancy boiler. They say there's not enough work and we're to finish every day at four to save lighting the lamps. We'll have none of it!' he raged at her. 'If they can't offer us a fair day's work for a fair day's pay, then we'll not work at all. That'll show 'em!'

Bessie crept into the house behind him and Jennet could hear the clogs on the street outside as other folk returned to their homes.

'Tha's gone on strike?' she asked. 'Hast tha lost thy mind? What'll we live on? Tha knows as all the savings have gone and we've my mother to feed an' all.' She felt her anger growing, suspecting that Titus had been one of the men behind the decision. 'We'll get no charity now,' she told him. 'Tha knows there's no outside relief any more. The only help that folk can get is by turning themselves into the workhouse, and I'll not see my mother taken into that place!'

'It won't come to that,' Titus told her. 'They'll back down as soon as they see we're serious.'

'How canst tha be so sure? And what if we starve in the meantime?' She wanted to slap him, to knock some common sense into him. Talking of a petition was one thing, but refusing to work was something she could never accept. 'Dost tha think as thy tea appears on the table by magic?' she asked him.

'Of course not! Don't talk daft, our Jennet. Tha knows nowt about it. If we just carry on workin' they'll cut our wages again and again, and we'll be both workin' and starvin'. Summat has to change and it's time for folk to rise up and make their voices heard.' He turned and wrenched open the door.

'Now where's tha goin'?'

'Down to th' assembly room. We're getting together to plan what needs to be done next. If we can get the hands to come out at all t' mills then t' mill owners'll have to think again.'

He went out and Jennet was left staring at Bessie, who still had her shawl clutched around her head.

'Thank the Lord I've not been to the market yet,' Jennet said. 'I've a half-crown I'd been keepin' to one side and I were going to buy some mutton for a pie. Now it'll have to last us until thy father comes to his senses.'

53

Chapter Eight

John was waiting for Peggy outside the hat shop as he did every morning now. They'd both begun to arrive a little earlier so that they had time to exchange a few words with one another, but today Peggy was late. The knocker-up had been told not to come for the time being. They couldn't afford to pay him when no one had to be at the mill, so she'd overslept and found herself rushing around in a near panic in case John had gone to his work by the time she got there.

He smiled when he saw her coming.

'Good morning, Miss Eastwood.' He raised his hat.

'Good morning, Mr Sharples.'

'It's a lovely day.'

'It is.' Peggy had been in such a rush that she hadn't even noticed the weather. It was fine, she'd realised that much, but now that she considered it she saw that the sun was just visible through the smoke that hung in the air.

'It'll be a clear day up on t' tops,' he said.

She nodded. It would be nice to feel the sun warm on her back. It had been a long winter.

'It's not often the sun breaks through here.' John stared at the dirty sky. 'Not that it bothers us when we've work to do,' he added, and she thought that he was anxious to be off so he wouldn't be late. She was cross with herself for her tardiness. 'Dost tha ever walk up on t' moors on a Sunday?' he asked.

'We always used to walk to Ramsgreave to see my grandparents.'

'But not any more?'

'My grandfather died.'

'I'm right sorry to hear that.'

'My grandma lives with us now, so we don't walk that way any more. My mother likes a sit-down on a Sunday afternoon and my father's got his meetings.'

'I like a bit of a walk,' said John. 'Perhaps tha'd like to walk with me one Sunday? If tha's nowt better to do,' he added, looking a bit sheepish.

'I'd like that,' she said. 'Maybe the weather will hold and it'll be nice this Sunday.'

'Aye. Happen it will.' He was smiling again now, pleased that she hadn't turned him down.

'I usually starts out from the churchyard after dinner – about two o'clock.'

'Well, I'll look out for you,' she said. 'If I decide to come.'

With a nod of his head he hurried on his way to the ropemaker's office. She watched him for a moment before she went on her way. No one would question her if she said she was going out for a walk. The hardest part would be shaking off Bessie if she said she wanted to come, but she'd find a way. She didn't want her little sister tagging along to spoil things for her.

When Sunday came it was easier than Peggy thought. After morning service they went home for a bite of dinner and when she picked up her shawl again her mother didn't ask where she was going. As they'd eaten the potato cakes that her mother had made earlier and then heated on the griddle, Peggy had talked about how hard she was going to have to study for her exam, and how she'd asked her Uncle James to give her some extra tuition. It was enough to make them think that was where she was going, and it meant she didn't have to tell a direct lie when she fastened the ribbons of her bonnet under her chin and said that she would be back by teatime.

The clock was chiming two as she crossed the street to the churchyard. He was there, feigning an interest in some of the gravestones, and she slowed her steps as she approached, not wanting to look too keen.

He took off his hat when he saw her. 'Good afternoon!'

'Good afternoon,' she replied.

'So tha fancied a stroll?'

'I did,' she told him.

'I thought we might go up by the Big Can and take a look at Revedge.'

Peggy thought that he might offer her his arm, but he didn't, although she could see that he was reining in his usual long strides so that she wouldn't struggle to keep pace with him as they started up the hill towards the Preston road. The weather had stayed fine and was unseasonably mild for late February and as they climbed she loosened the shawl she was wearing over her best jacket.

'So tha works as a schoolmistress?' he asked.

'Yes. I haven't got my certificate yet, but I'm studying for it. I'm to take the Queen's Scholarship exam later in the year. If I pass I'll get a place at one of the schools where they train teachers.'

'So tha'll be going away?' He looked disappointed.

'Yes, but not until next year. And I need to pass the exam first.'

'I wish I'd had the chance of more schoolin',' he told her. 'I go to the Mechanics' Institute some nights to study, but it's not the same as being tutored. Better than going back to my lodgings and sitting on my own, though. They've a champion library up there.'

'So you've no family?' She knew that he had, but she wanted to hear what he had to say about them. It was partly curiosity about the falling-out that had prompted her to walk with him, as well as the desire to get to know him better.

'I have family,' he said, 'but I don't have much to do with 'em. I see my sisters sometimes, but that's about it.'

'How many sisters do you have?'

'Two ... well, three really. One went to America. The other two are both married. What about thee?' he asked.

'I have a sister, Bessie.'

'She works with thy father at Brookhouse Mill, doesn't she?'

'You seem to have made enquiries about me!'

'Folk talk,' he said as they reached the brow of the hill, near the house where Dr Barlow, who'd saved her mother's life when Bessie was born, used to live.

'And you work in the office at the ropeworks,' she said as they paused to catch their breath. She didn't want him to think he was the only one who could find out about people.

'That's right. I'm a bookkeeper. I like adding up and such, and getting the figures in order,' he said.

'And your sisters?'

'Weavers.'

'You didn't think the mill was for you then?' she asked. She knew that he could probably have earned better money in the spinning room than doing office work, at least when times were good.

'I did work there as a lad.' He paused and glanced at his gloved hand. 'I had an accident. It means my fingers aren't good for much now.'

'I'm sorry,' she said.

'I prefer the book work,' he told her. 'Shall we go on?'

They crossed the road and headed up the fields towards the reservoirs on the side of the hill. As they passed the Can, Peggy saw that quite a few people were taking advantage of the fine afternoon to draw water from it to save them having to come up during the week or join the long queue at the All Hallows pump.

'Look. There's a kingfisher!' said John, putting his hand to her arm and pointing. Peggy raised a hand to shield her eyes from the sun as she watched the flash of blue as it darted low over the water. 'In a bit the swallows'll be coming back. They nest in the old barns. I like to come up and look out for them.'

'What's that one?' asked Peggy, pointing to a bird with long legs and a red bill that was running along the edge of the water with a long twig clutched in its beak.

'It's a moorhen. They're starting to build their nests – messy things they make, mostly a pile of sticks, but the young hatch out all right – fluffy little black things that chirrup and run after their parents until they're fed.'

She was seeing another side to him. She would never have guessed at his interest in birds and she found that it pleased her. He was a caring sort of person, she thought, as he offered his hand to help her over some rough grassland. It made the question of why she'd been forbidden to have anything to do with him even more intriguing.

'Tha can see how the smoke hangs over the town even on a Sunday,' he said as they reached the top and stopped to look back down into the valley. 'It's no wonder the gentry are building their houses up here.'

Peggy looked down at the myriad chimneys and the long rows of streets. There was no beauty there, but the hills beyond were lovely.

'They say as tha can see the Welsh mountains on a clear day,' he told her. 'Not today. But tha can see Belthorn, and over yon's the Darwen moors, and if tha looks t'other way that's Pendle Hill.'

They stood a while, taking in the scene before a strong wind blustered up and Peggy pulled her shawl tighter again.

'Shall we go on?' he asked. 'Or would tha rather go back down?'

'We'll go on a little way,' she said, and they began to walk along the road. Peggy knew that her father had helped to build it, but she said nothing. It had been when he'd come back from prison, in the times that no one talked about.

They walked on until they came to Mile End, where there was a row of handloom-weavers' cottages. Most were still occupied and it made Peggy think of her grandfather. Her mother said that he would never have passed away if he'd been able to go on with his work. But it was a dying trade. Handwoven cloth was better quality, her grandfather had always said, but it took time to weave and folk wanted cheap cotton now, woven quickly in the mills.

They came to the Dog, a small inn on the road-side, and John hesitated. 'Would tha like to go in?' he asked. She stared at the building, wondering if she dared. 'We can get a sup of tea,' he told her.

'I haven't brought any money.'

'My treat,' he said.

'Do we have time? I don't want to walk back in the dark.'

'It'll be light for a while yet,' he said. 'A cup of hot tea'll set us up for the walk back down.'

She agreed and they went inside. The landlord showed them into the parlour where there was a log fire burning invitingly. Peggy went to sit near it to warm herself and a young lass came through carrying a tray loaded with cups and saucers, a teapot, and bread and butter on a plate.

Peggy took off her gloves to pour the tea and offered the plate of bread to John before she took a slice for herself. She knew she shouldn't stare, but the raised scar across the back of his hand seemed to draw her eye. She could almost make out the marks of the stitches where his fingers had been sewn back, but there seemed to be little or no use in them. She could see that he would struggle to do much with it. He noticed her gaze and dropped the hand to his knee under the table and took the bread with his left hand.

'How do you manage to hold a pen?' she blurted out. One of her tasks as a pupil-teacher was to walk around the rows of desks and ensure that the girls were all holding their pens correctly, in the right hand, but it was obvious that John would be unable to grasp anything between his thumb and the first two fingers.

'I write with my left hand,' he confessed. She was unsure what to say. Miss Parkinson would be horrified. She believed it was a defect and would not allow it in her classroom. 'I wouldn't be able to work otherwise,' he added, 'although I have to take extra care not to smudge the ink and sometimes I'm not as quick as Mr Hart would like.'

Peggy took a bite of the bread to save herself from having to reply straight away.

'What happened?' she asked at last.

'I were piecing a thread and I were careless,' he said. 'I didn't shift my hand fast enough and it got caught. My mother always told me as I were a dreamer and no good would come of it – and she were right.'

'So what did you do after that?'

'I were at home for a while until it healed up. Later I worked at the stables in Thunder Alley until I got my job at the ropeworks.'

'You did well then.'

'Aye. Someone put in a good word for me.'

He avoided her eye and Peggy suspected there was a lot he wasn't telling her. She wanted to question him more about where he'd learned to write and do arithmetic. She was sure that none of the Sunday schools would have allowed him to use his left hand. And what had happened to make his parents fall out with hers? She wondered if he knew.

When they'd had their tea, John took some coins from his pocket and paid the landlord. The sun was low when they came out and Peggy was anxious to get back down the hill.

'I'll see thee in t' mornin' then?' he said when they got back into town.

'Yes.' She thought it would be strange to greet him as usual after they'd spent the afternoon together.

'I hope tha's enjoyed thyself?'

'I have. Thank you for the tea. It was a nice treat.'

'Tha's welcome.' He smiled. 'Would tha like me to walk thee home?'

'No! No. Don't go out of your way.'

'All right then.' He sounded relieved and they parted company at the top of Northgate before Peggy hurried home. The clock was chiming five and she didn't want to be late.

Her parents and Bessie were already at the table when she got in. She took off her outdoor clothes and hung them up on a peg before sitting down. Her father had taken the chair with his back to the fire and she was left with the chilly side of the room.

'Where's tha been?' asked her mother. 'Tha's covered in mud.'

Peggy looked down to see that the hem of her skirt was splashed with filth from the puddles she'd been unable to avoid as they'd hurried home. She'd need to sponge it later.

'I've been for a walk.'

'I thought tha were goin' to Auntie Hannah's,' her mother said as she passed her a cup of tea.

'Well. It was such a nice afternoon I thought a breath of fresh air would do me more good.'

'Tha'll not pass yon exam if tha doesn't get thy head down and study for it,' her father told her. 'Gallivantin' all over t' fields'll not help thee!'

'It was only one afternoon.'

'Even so. If tha's goin' to study for a schoolteacher tha needs to work hard.'

'Where did you go?' asked Bessie. 'I would have come if I'd known you were planning a walk.'

'It was a spur-of-the-moment thing,' said Peggy. 'I met up with a friend and we walked up to the Can. That's how I got mud on my skirt.'

She took an oatcake and spread a little treacle on it even though she wasn't hungry. The serving of bread and butter at the Dog had been generous and John had urged her to eat plenty.

'Who did you meet?' asked Bessie.

'No one you know.' Peggy wished that her sister would stop asking questions.

'Aye, well, think on,' said her father. 'This exam's important and thy Uncle James has offered to give up his time to help thee, so next time I don't want to hear that tha's gone off up th' 'ill instead.'

Peggy was glad she had a mouthful of oatcake. It stopped her replying to him and then being in trouble for giving cheek. He'd been in a bad mood ever since the strike had begun to break. Folk had worried that they'd starve with no money at all and gradually most of the workers had gone back at the reduced hours and on reduced pay so that they had something to feed their families. It had been a blow to her father's pride and he'd grumbled about it constantly, but in the end he'd gone back and Bessie as well.

Chapter Nine

There was one good thing about the mill shutting down for the day at four o'clock, thought Titus as he watched the spindles come to a gradual standstill when the power from the new boiler was cut. It meant that there was time to continue to gather signatures for the petition. The late afternoon, when men should have been at their work but were idle at home instead, not knowing how best to occupy themselves, was a good time to persuade them to add their names.

He pulled on his fustian jacket, took his cap from its peg and followed the other workers, the sound of their clogs echoing on the iron staircase that led down to the street. He'd left his pages of the petition at home. He'd already got the signatures of the men he worked with and now it was time to go around the streets, knocking on doors. He might even call at some of the shops and businesses too. The need for Reform was in the interests of every man.

Back home, on Water Street, he took the pages from the sideboard drawer and smoothed them out on the table. Many of the sheets – ruled in columns of four to hold two hundred signatures each – were already filled and these Titus put carefully away, taking with him only a couple of sheets. Four hundred more signatures was his aim for the evening.

He looked up as Bessie came in.

'Do you want some help?' she asked when she saw the sheets.

'No. Give thy mother a hand,' he said as he went out.

Bessie watched as he passed the window. She'd tried, she told herself. All her life she'd tried to make him like her, but every time he rejected her, and every time it hurt. This petition was important. It needed women to sign it as well as men, and women were more likely to add their name or their mark if it was a woman who persuaded them. She knew that she could have helped him to get more signatures if only he'd allowed her to go with him.

'I'm cold,' complained Grandma Chadwick and Bessie went to throw more coal on to the fire. There wasn't much left in the bucket and when she went to the coal store to fill it she saw that there wasn't much there either. She hoped there was enough money for some more sacks and decided that when she gave her wages to her mother at the weekend she'd refuse the few shillings that her mother would offer her back. Her bonnet would do for Easter with last year's trimmings. It was more important that her grandmother didn't catch cold.

'I thought I heard thy father,' said her mother, coming in from the back yard with some laundry.

'He's gone out again,' said Bessie as she took two corners of a sheet to help her mother fold it. Her mother snapped the cotton and they folded it over and over again before coming together for her mother to grasp all the corners. She set it aside to be pressed and Bessie helped her fold the rest.

'He'll have gone getting more names,' said her mother. 'Just as long as he doesn't think he can go off to London with it.' She sounded worried, although there were times when Bessie thought her mother would be glad to be rid of him, for a while at least. They rubbed along most of the time, but there was little affection between them. They slept in the same bed, but she couldn't remember ever seeing them kiss or even hug one another. And it wasn't that her father was a womaniser.

Reform was his mistress and she knew that her mother could never fight that.

As her mother heated her irons, Bessie got the bag of oatmeal from the shelf ready to make a batch of oatcakes, then she peeled potatoes and set them to cook. There was little else on the pantry shelves except for half a bag of sugar and some tea, which they were using so sparingly now that it was scarcely better than a drink of boiled water.

After a while, Peggy came in. She took a sheet of paper from her pocket and smoothed it out on the table. It was covered in signatures.

'I got these at dinnertime, and some on my way home,' she said. 'Mr Towers on Fleming Square has changed his mind and added his name since none of the Chartists have given him any business. I've never seen his shop so quiet.'

So Peggy was allowed to help, thought Bessie as she shaped the oatcakes and laid them out on a tray for the oven.

'Don't get flour on it!' cried Peggy as she snatched up the paper and took it to the sideboard. Bessie didn't reply. She opened the oven door with a rag and pushed the tray inside.

'I'm too hot,' said Grandma Chadwick as the blast of heat reached her.

'Tha's all right,' said her mother. 'Stop fussing.' Bessie heard the irritation in her voice and saw that her mother was tired out. Although she was doing her best to help in the house, Bessie thought that Peggy could do more. Between canvassing for the petition and studying for her exam, her sister seemed to get away with doing nothing at all.

Titus made his way down Chapel Street, knocking on each door and explaining what the petition was about. Most folk had already heard about it and cut off his speech in their eagerness to sign. It wasn't a difficult task to fill the pages and it reassured him that he was doing the right thing.

As he walked back in the dark, the pages filled, he thought about what it would be like to go to London. He couldn't even imagine the city, but he knew that he wanted to see it. The journey was a long one and they would march all the way, but he was still young enough and fit enough to do it. In fact, it would please him to get away for a while. He knew that Jennet didn't want him to go because she would struggle to feed the family whilst he was away. He knew it wasn't because she would miss him. They never talked about what had happened but it remained between them like an insurmountable brick wall, especially now that Bessie was grown up and it was obvious that the lass had questions about why she was so different from her sister. He had such pride in

Peggy. She was so clever and pretty too, with shining dark hair and lustrous eyes. But Bessie's piercing blue eyes had always marked her out as different and every time he looked at her he was reminded of George Anderton, until he found that he could hardly bear to look at her at all. She wasn't a bad lass, but he could never love her. Some days he even found it hard to like her. He knew that it wasn't her fault. He knew that he should blame Jennet more, but he still loved Jennet even though he wasn't sure whether she loved him. She'd waited for him when he was in prison, but that was sixteen years ago and these days she seemed to mostly snap at him when he was at home, until he found that he preferred to be out at a meeting with his friends rather than enjoying his own fireside.

He turned into Water Street with mixed feelings. He wanted to show Jennet the papers and hear her say how well he'd done, but he knew that she probably wouldn't. Even though she'd signed the petition in her shaky, unsure hand, she wasn't really committed to it. She worried that it would only make things worse and that he would be turned out of the mill – although he wondered if that really mattered when there was only short time work and paltry wages. The mill owners said that if the current order was completed then more might come and work would increase, but Titus didn't believe a word of it. They were all being used and then cast aside. A vote for every man was the only thing that would change it.

Chapter Ten

'The fair will be here next Monday,' said John one morning when he and Peggy met as usual outside the window of the hat shop. 'Would tha like to go to it?'

Peggy loved the Easter Fair. She thought Easter was her favourite holiday. Much better than Christmas when the days were dark and cold. When the fair came, it came with the hope of spring and she always associated the holiday with warmth and sunshine even though it often poured with rain and, on occasions, snowed.

'Do you not have to go into work?' she asked. She wasn't sure if the ropemaker's would close, as the mills did even though the holiday was not an official one. The mill owners didn't like it, but there wasn't much they could do when none of the hands turned up, and she knew that over the years they'd resigned themselves to it. Not that it should worry them too much this year, she thought. All the mills were on short time now.

'Mr Hart says we can take the afternoon off. What about thee?'

'The school's open, officially, but no one will come. Miss Parkinson will probably send me home by dinnertime,' she said.

'So tha'll come?'

Peggy hesitated. It wasn't that she didn't want to go to the fair with him – she did. But she was worried about people seeing them. Going walking in the countryside on a Sunday afternoon was one thing, but at the crowded fairground they would be sure to bump into someone they knew and tongues would wag. It would be much too easy for her parents to hear that she'd been seen with John Sharples.

'What's wrong?' he asked. 'I hope tha's not ashamed to be seen with me?'

'No,' she reassured him. 'No, it isn't that. It's just that I haven't told my parents that I've been meeting you – and I'm not sure what they'll say if they find out from someone else.'

'Aye,' he said. 'I can understand that they might not be too happy about it.'

'What happened, John?' she asked him. It was a question that she'd almost asked before, but had never dared. 'What did they fall out about?'

He looked uncomfortable. 'It's a long story,' he said. 'There isn't time now.'

'But you will tell me?' she persisted.

'Aye. I suppose tha needs to know,' he said. 'Canst tha slip away and meet me later?'

'Yes, of course,' she said, not knowing how she could manage it, but determined anyway.

'Come to the Temperance Hotel on Northgate,' he said. 'I'll be there about eight o'clock.'

Her father went out to a Chartist meeting when tea was finished. They were going to tally up all the signatures and decide which delegates were to march with the petition to London. He went with a spring in his step. He was sure he'd gathered more names than anyone else and would be chosen.

Her grim-faced mother was busy settling Grandma Chadwick into bed when Peggy picked up her shawl and told Bessie that she wouldn't be long. Bessie looked curious, but didn't ask where she was going. She probably thought she was going to the Chartist meeting to hear the count as well. Peggy slipped out; then she ran down the street in case her mother came to the door to look for her.

She pulled the shawl around her head like a mill girl. She didn't want to draw any attention to herself and she hurried through the gas-lit streets to her rendezvous with John.

She'd never been in the Temperance Hotel before, but by its very name she knew that it was a respectable establishment. She pushed open the door and saw him waiting for her – a cup of dandelion and burdock on the table in front of him. He stood up when he saw her and guided her to a chair.

'I wasn't sure that tha'd come,' he said.

'I nipped out whilst my mother wasn't looking. I'd best not be too long.' He brought her a cup of the sweet herbal liquid and she took a long drink before she looked him in the eye. 'Tell me what happened,' she said.

He stared at the table for what seemed a long time and then he began to speak, quietly, so that she had to lean forward to hear him.

'When I hurt my hand, my mother took time off work to take me to the surgeon. Whilst she was away the overlooker gave her looms to thy mother, and when she went back my mam accused thine of stealin' her job.'

'Is that all?'

He shook his head. 'No. There's more. Because I couldn't work in the mill no more, I were stuck at home for a bit and I got into bad company. There were a lad, a few years older than me. He were a bad lot. He'd been in trouble before and in prison for pickpocketing. But he were persuasive, like, and asked me to go and ask some gents for the time because he had business to attend to.'

'He asked you to be his accomplice whilst he picked pockets?'

'Aye.' He looked shamed by the confession. 'But I were only a lad and I didn't know what he were up to. When he gave me a sixpence I thought it were money he'd earned. He always said as he were *doing business* and I believed him. I were a bit innocent, I suppose,' he said and took a drink.

'So, what happened?'

'I were caught by the police,' he told her. 'They locked me up in the cellar at the Old Bull. I'll never forget how dark it were down there, and cold.' Peggy could see that he'd been badly frightened although he didn't say so. 'Then in the morning I were taken before the magistrate and I got five years in prison.'

'That was harsh,' she said, thinking that he could easily have been transported for such a crime. She'd heard of people who had been and whose families never saw them again.

He kept his eyes on his drink and wouldn't even look at her. Peggy could see how ashamed he was, and how hard it was for him to tell her about his past. But she still couldn't understand why it made his parents hate hers so much. She couldn't see what it had to do with them.

'What happened to the other lad?' she asked.

'He ran off when he saw the police come for me.'

'And did they catch him?'

John shook his head. 'No. He got away with it.'

'But why did it cause a falling-out between your parents and mine?' she asked him. 'I don't understand.'

'Well, the thing is that this lad were livin' with thy parents. They'd taken him in when he came out of prison for his first offence. Thy father were fond of him, by all accounts. He'd taken him under his wing at the House of Correction.'

Peggy stared at John, not knowing what to say. She wasn't even sure that he was telling the truth. Yet, when she thought about it, she did have a memory of someone, she didn't know who, lifting her high in the air and swinging her around. The memory came back to her now and she wondered if it had been the lad John was talking about.

'But if my father knew he was guilty he would have handed him in to the police. I'm sure he would,' said Peggy. She didn't believe that her father would harbour a criminal. He was always talking about fairness and justice.

79

'I thought so too,' said John. 'Thy father spoke up for me in court and said that this lad had tricked me, but it didn't do any good. They still sentenced me. All the time I were in prison I never knew what had happened to him. I thought he were probably caught and it upset me to think that he might have been hanged. He were a nice lad, really. I liked him.'

'So how do you know he got away with it?' she asked.

'It were my sister, Mary, that told me, after I got out. She said that thy father had helped him to escape.'

Peggy stared at him, trying to make sense of it all. She could feel her anger rising at the unfairness of it.

'My parents hate yours because they let me take all the blame,' John said.

Peggy didn't know what to say. She knew that her parents hated the Sharples family although they'd never said why. She'd always presumed that they'd done her mother and father some great wrong, but if what John was telling her was true, it was her parents who had wronged them. Her father, despite his campaigning for fairness for all, had aided a criminal to escape the law and John had gone to prison instead. She found that she was shaking her head.

80

'It's all true,' John told her.

'It doesn't make any sense,' she said. She wondered if she dared ask her mother about it when she got back. Surely there must be another side to the story.

John shrugged. 'Tha wanted to know and I've told thee what happened, as straight as I can,' he said. 'Why would I tell thee a lie?'

'I don't know,' she said. If it was true, it turned everything she thought she knew about her father on its head. She couldn't believe it, but as John said, why would he lie to her? If what he'd told her was true there was more reason for him to want nothing to do with her than for her to avoid him.

'But you said that you'd fallen out with your parents,' she said. 'Why didn't you go back home when you got out of prison?'

'I did for a while, but it were difficult. I were happier in lodgings,' he said. 'And I never said I'd fallen out with 'em, just that I didn't have much to do with 'em.'

Peggy was sure there was more to it, but her head was thronged with what he'd already told her and she couldn't take any more in until she'd had a chance to think about what he'd said.

'I need to go,' she said, pushing the half-full cup away from her and gathering her shawl. She

81

needed to get away, to be on her own, to think and try to make sense of it.

'Shall I see thee safe home?'

She almost refused him, but she knew that the streets of Blackburn after dark weren't the best place for a woman to walk alone, so she nodded. 'Just to the end of the street,' she said.

They walked side by side, but Peggy kept a distance between them. It wasn't like the strolls they'd shared on a Sunday when sometimes she'd given him her hand. And they walked in silence.

When they reached the end of Water Street, she thanked him and hurried down towards her home. She paused at the front door and looked back. He was still standing on the little bridge, waiting to see her safely in. She raised her hand and he turned back towards Northgate. He looked despondent and she wondered whether things could ever go back to how they'd been between them after what he'd told her.

'Where's tha been?' demanded her mother.

Peggy almost said that she'd been with Uncle James and Auntie Hannah, but she knew she'd be found out and get into even more trouble.

'Just out for a bit of air,' she said, hanging up her shawl.

'Hast tha been meeting up with someone? I hope tha's not been drinking!' Her mother came closer to see if she could catch a whiff of beer or, worse, gin on her breath.

'Of course I've not been drinking!'

'But tha's been meetin' with someone. I hope it's not a lad,' she said.

'I'm not a child. I can have friends.'

'Aye, but tha doesn't want to be getting involved with a lad – not if tha's going to study to be a schoolteacher.'

'Maybe I won't be a teacher. Maybe I'll go in the mill, like our Bessie.'

'Don't let thy father hear thee talk like that,' her mother warned. 'Tha knows he has his heart set on thee being a teacher.'

'I don't have to do as he says!'

Bessie looked up in surprise at Peggy's raised voice. It was so unlike her to say anything against her father.

'Shush. Tha'll wake Grandma,' warned her mother. 'I don't know what's got into thee tonight, our Peggy, but I think tha'd best get off to bed before thy father comes in.'

Peggy didn't reply but lit a rushlight from the fire and went up the stairs. On the walk home she'd decided that she was going to ask her mother about the Sharples family and about the mysterious lad who'd once lived with them, but there'd been no opportunity and she was annoyed that her mother had been cross with her. It was as if she wasn't in control of her own life. Everything she did was to please her parents and now she was beginning to wonder whether they really had her best interests at heart, or if her studying to become a teacher was simply because they wanted to boast about what a clever daughter they had.

Chapter Eleven

Jennet watched her elder daughter stalk off to bed and wondered where she'd been. Peggy had never been an easy child, unlike Bessie, who'd never been a minute's trouble. Peggy had always had a stubborn streak and now Jennet was worried that she might suddenly decide against taking the scholarship after all. It would break Titus's heart. He'd been set on her doing well ever since she was a little girl with her slate and chalk.

She heard his footsteps outside and resolved to talk to him about it. Perhaps they were pushing Peggy too hard. She'd always dug in her heels if she thought she wasn't getting her own way. Or maybe they should let her try the mill. She'd soon change her mind when she'd been working at a loom for twelve hours.

Titus pushed open the door and came in with a self-satisfied smile.

'I'm goin' to London!' he proudly told her before he'd even taken his cap off. 'I'd a couple of hundred more names than anyone else when it were all tallied up.' He hung his cap on its peg. 'There were over sixteen thousand altogether. That's nearly half the population of the town. Not just mill workers, but shopkeepers and brewers and cabinetmakers – all manner of folk are calling for change. They'll not be able to ignore us this time!'

'What about thy job?' asked Jennet, wondering how she was expected to cope without his wages whilst he was gone.

'Well, we're on short time,' he said, 'and with the cut in wages it's hardly worth fretting about.'

'But tha might have no job at all by the time tha gets back.'

'It'll be different then,' he told her, settling himself into his chair by the fire and lighting his pipe. 'When yon Parliament has heard our grievances, then the mill owners will be forced to give a fair day's pay for a fair day's work. They'll not be able to treat us like slave labour any more. We deserve to be freed just as much as them black folks in America.'

Jennet poured him a cup of tea and without having to be told Bessie shifted from her chair and said that she would go to bed.

*

Bessie went up the stairs, leaving them to talk. Peggy had got into bed and had her eyes closed, but Bessie could tell that her sister wasn't asleep. She undressed and slipped in beside her without a word. She was curious to know where Peggy had been. She suspected that she was meeting a lad and the thought of it gave her a guilty thrill. If their father found out he would be furious and it would be a change to see her sister as the target of his displeasure for once.

Peggy sighed and turned over. 'What are they saying now?' she asked Bessie.

'Father's going to London with the petition and our mam's furious with him.'

'Is that all?' She sounded relieved.

'Did you think they were arguing about you?' Bessie asked. 'Guilty conscience?'

'Be quiet!' snapped her sister.

'Well, you've been somewhere you don't want them to know about. And you've come back in a rare temper.'

'I heard some talk,' said Peggy. 'About the Sharples family.'

Bessie recalled the woman on the market and was immediately curious. 'What about them?' she asked. 'Have you discovered what the falling-out was about?'

'I've been told something, but I don't know what to believe,' she said. Then, bit by bit, she repeated to Bessie most of what she'd learned from John.

'Well, that's a turn-up,' said Bessie. 'Who told you all this?'

Her sister hesitated, and didn't reply.

'Who?' asked Bessie again. 'It must be someone who knows them or you wouldn't be taking it so seriously.'

'Swear you'll not say a word?'

'Cross my heart and hope to die,' said Bessie, making the sign of the cross across her chest. 'Tell me!'

'John Sharples.'

'John Sharples! Is that who you've been slipping out to meet? Father'll kill you!'

'*If* he finds out.'

'He's bound to find out. And what if it gets serious? What will you do then?'

'Well, it can't get serious, can it?' said Peggy. 'I'm going to be a schoolmistress and schoolmistresses can't be married. But it's beside the point. The point is, can we believe what John Sharples told me about Mam and Dad? Would they really have helped a criminal to escape the law?'

'It seems unlikely,' agreed Bessie. 'Do you think he's making it up?'

'I don't know what to think,' said Peggy. 'Blow out the light,' she added as she heard their parents coming up.

They lay in silence as they waited for their parents' door to close.

'It makes no sense,' said Peggy after a while.

'I don't think you should see him any more,' said Bessie. 'I don't trust him. I don't trust any of them,' she said, remembering how Nan Sharples had glared at her when she'd passed her in the market place. 'I think he's telling you a lie.'

'He isn't. I'm sure he isn't,' protested Peggy. 'He's nice. You'd like him if you met him.'

'Well, don't say you weren't warned,' Bessie told her. 'Father lets you get away with most things, but he won't let this one pass.'

She turned over and snuggled down under the covers, holding on to them tightly as Peggy tried to yank them away from her.

'I'm beginning to think there's a lot we don't know,' said Peggy. 'They think I was too young to remember, but there was someone who used to be here. Someone with blue eyes. I remember him.'

Bessie didn't reply, but her sister's words struck her like a knife. Blue eyes. She had blue eyes. The only person in the family to have them and she'd always felt like the odd one out. What if this criminal was really her father? It seemed a

ridiculous thought and she wanted to say something, just to get reassurance from Peggy that it
couldn't possibly be true. Her father was her
father. Of course he was. But blue eyes, she
thought, as she lay awake long after Peggy had
gone to sleep. It would explain why her father
seemed to hate her.

No, she thought, it was a silly thing to think.
Her mother would never have slept with a criminal – unless he'd forced himself on her. Thoughts
tumbled around in her imagination as she exam-
ined them for an answer that might make sense.
None of them did and although she knew that
she could have got the reassurance she needed
by asking her mother directly she doubted that
she would dare. It was a delicate subject to raise
and, besides, she would have to repeat what
Peggy had told her, and she couldn't betray her
sister. At some point she must have drifted off to
sleep because it was morning when she woke,
with knots in her stomach and no answers to any
of her questions.

Chapter Twelve

The mill engines powered down mid-afternoon and Bessie fastened off some loose threads before following the other workers to the door. The next day would be Easter Sunday and on Monday it would be the fair. No one would turn up for work so the mill would be closed all day.

'Meet me here on Monday morning. We'll go together,' said Ruth as she tossed her shawl around her. Bessie nodded in agreement. She knew she probably wouldn't see her friend the next day. Her family didn't go to the parish church. They were Methodists.

Rather than going straight home she made her way up to the centre of the town. It was busy with the market in full swing and she made a few purchases for her mother before going towards Church Street and looking longingly at the ribbons in Miss Cross's window. Even though she was back at work, money was still tight and she was reluctant to waste any of the wage packet in her pocket. She knew her mother would be glad of it all. Her bonnet would have to do, she thought as she reluctantly turned away from the display. There were more important things to worry about than new ribbons.

As she approached the crossroads, the bugle sounded and the coach from Liverpool rounded the corner at speed, making people leap out of its way. It drew to a halt outside the Old Bull hotel, the horses steaming and panting with exertion.

A few weary passengers clambered down from the outside seats and the door was pulled open for the businessmen to step down, donning their top hats as they reached the ground. Then came a young lad who made Bessie look again. She knew that it was rude to stare, but she'd never seen anyone quite like him. His skin was dark, like polished rosewood, and before he put on his hat she saw that his hair grew in curls around his head. He was followed by another, older man, who stood and looked around for quite a while, until the younger one touched his arm to draw him away from the coach. Bessie lingered as their bags were taken down and she watched as they headed towards the hotel door. She wondered who they were. They didn't look like the usual rag, tag and bobtail of characters who descended on the town for the fair to show off their tricks or sell their wares. They were both well dressed and looked as if they weren't short of a bob or two.

'They sound like they might be travelling doctors,' suggested her mother when Bessie told her what she'd seen. 'They used to be quite common when I was a child. Thy grandma there would bring us into town to see them sometimes. They'd take a room at the Old Bull and see the gentry privately, but when it was market day they came out and put up a makeshift stall with bottles filled with all sorts of pills and potions. They used to be so passionate about their cures. Every one of 'em would say that all the others were hawkers and pretenders, but that they were genuine and could even cure the folks that were deemed incurable. Thy grandma used to buy one of their brown bottles for a farthing. She swore it were the making of her, though it were probably nowt but coloured water.'

'Maybe we should get her one – if they're still selling them,' suggested Bessie. 'It might do her good.'

'Nay. Don't waste thy money,' said her mother. 'I don't think there's owt to be done for her now.'

Bessie looked at her grandmother and wished that she could be made better, that she could be turned back into the person she used to be. Perhaps she'd buy a bottle anyway if her mother let her keep a shilling for the fair. Surely it wouldn't do any harm.

The church bells rang out across the town next morning. There was a feeling of excitement in the air as Bessie walked to the morning service with Peggy and her mother. Her father didn't go to the church, not even on Easter Sunday, and although Bessie knew his absence was a source of worry to her mother, it meant that she could leave him to look after Grandma Chadwick for an hour or two so she could go without fretting.

They were all wearing their best bonnets and Bessie hoped that no one would notice the trimmings on hers weren't new. It was always something of a competition to see whose was the best, although the mill lasses could never compete with the better-off who had their new bonnets sent up from London, ready trimmed in the latest fashions.

They arrived early so that they could watch the gentry come in. Mrs Hornby wore a bonnet lined with pale pink satin and matching ribbons, with pink, white and lilac flowers on the outside of the brim. Bessie thought it was exquisite. Then came Mrs Feilden and her daughters. Their bonnets were just as glorious, with coloured ribbons tied in bows and brims overflowing with springtime flowers. The short time working at the mills hadn't meant they had forgone their Easter finery and whilst Bessie adored the bonnets she felt the unfairness of it too.

She glanced about for the man she'd seen getting down from the coach and the dark-skinned lad, but there was no sign of them. They must not be churchgoers. She did see John Sharples, though, and she noticed him glance towards her sister. It concerned her. The tale he'd spun to Peggy couldn't possibly be true, she thought. He was trouble, like the rest of the Sharples family, and she wished that her sister would stay away from him. Peggy always did exactly as she pleased and usually got away with it, but this time she was playing with fire and Bessie was worried that it wouldn't end well. Not that she would ever tell on her. Apart from the fact that she'd made a promise, she suspected that their father wouldn't believe her anyway, and her mother had enough worries without her adding to them.

As the congregation milled about in the church-yard, exchanging greetings and admiring one another's bonnets, Peggy found that John was standing beside her. She looked around to see where her mother was, terrified that she would notice, but she was busy talking to Mrs Whittaker, the vicar's wife.

'Will tha walk out with me later?' he asked. She hadn't seen him since the evening at the Temperance Hotel. She'd got up extra early every morning to avoid him. 'I'll not leave thy side until tha says aye,' he warned as she glanced towards her mother again.

'All right,' she agreed. 'I'll meet you back here after dinner.'

Satisfied, he moved away from her and she turned to see that her sister had witnessed the exchange. Peggy had begun to regret confiding in Bessie. Her sister was close to their mother and she was worried that Bessie would tell on her despite her promise.

'I'll never forgive you if you say anything!' Peggy warned her.

As soon as dinner was finished Peggy jumped up from the table and said she was going out. Bessie glared at her. It meant that she would have to do all the washing up. And her mother frowned. She'd managed to get a piece of mutton to cook with some roasted potatoes and Peggy knew that she'd been hoping for more appreciation than a daughter who gobbled it down as fast as she could because she'd rather be elsewhere.

As Peggy walked to meet John she saw that the fair had arrived. There were tents on a patch of ground adjacent to the church and some swarthy-looking men were sticking up posters to announce the acts at the open-air theatre. The main attraction was to be Monsieur Plège and his tightrope walking, as well as an exhibition of laughing gas, followed by a dog show.

'Dogs!' said Peggy when she reached John. 'I'd like to see them doing tricks.'

'So tha'll come with me?' he asked.

She hesitated, but only for a moment. 'Yes,' she agreed. There would be crowds of people, she reasoned. People came from all over for the fair. Perhaps no one would notice them if they were careful.

They took their usual walk up to the Can. It was busy today with lots of the better-off people walking up and down on the Preston road to show off their new Easter bonnets. Peggy was conscious that hers was slightly shabby. Like Bessie, she'd been unable to retrim it this year.

'I got a little something for thee,' said John as they sat on a wall, looking down over the town. He reached into an inside pocket and took out a small package wrapped in brown paper. Curious, Peggy took it and laid it on her knee to unwrap it. Inside were several lengths of ribbon in yellow and pink – the ones she'd admired in Miss Cross's shop. 'I'm sorry they're too late for thee to put on thy bonnet for church this morning,' he said. 'I wanted to give 'em to thee earlier but I've not seen thee all week.'

Peggy fingered the silky lengths. 'They're beautiful,' she said. 'Thank you. I'll put them on my bonnet tonight, ready for tomorrow,' she promised.

'Then tha'll look a treat,' he told her with a shy smile.

Peggy wondered if he was expecting her to kiss him, but he just sat looking at her, slightly ill at ease. It was obvious he wasn't used to giving presents and she wondered how much they'd cost him. With the ribbons and the tea he'd bought for her she was becoming quite indebted to him and it made her feel a little guilty. She liked him well enough but it was a relationship that could never go anywhere. Her father would never agree to it and, besides, she'd be going away next year. Still, she decided not to spoil the moment, or the day, and rather than kiss him she patted his hand.

'It's very generous of you,' she said.

Bessie had scrubbed all the pans and washed all the pots and been down to the spring to replenish the buckets of water even though it was Easter

Sunday. She'd helped her mother with Grandma Chadwick and made a cup of tea for her father.

'Dost tha know what our Peggy's up to?' asked her mother when they eventually sat down.

'No.'

'She's not told thee owt?'

Bessie shook her head.

'She's meetin' someone,' said her mother. 'I'd just like to know who.'

'I thought she was going to Auntie Hannah's.'

'Aye, so did I. But when I mentioned how hard she was working thy auntie said they'd not seen much of her lately.'

'Tha'd better speak up if tha knows summat,' said her father.

'She doesn't tell me anything,' replied Bessie, flushed with guilt about telling a lie.

'I just hope she's not meeting a lad,' said her mother. 'It'll make things too complicated if she's to go away to school.'

'She'll not even pass t' scholarship if she doesn't set 'er mind to it.' Her father's face was grim. Bessie knew that he would feel badly let down if Peggy didn't get her teacher's certificate.

Her sister arrived back just as they were sitting down to tea. She looked flushed and excited and proceeded to describe all the ladies she'd seen and the bonnets they'd been wearing. Then she went on to tell them about the posters for the fair, advertising the open-air theatre, the tightrope walker and the dog show. By the time she'd finished, their parents had forgotten all about asking her who she'd been with. Their mother went off to the evening service at St John's. It was to be lit by gas lamps for the first time and she was keen to see it. Their father went out too, probably to meet with his union friends at the beerhouse, and Bessie was left alone with her sister and Grandma Chadwick, who was fast asleep.

Bessie watched as Peggy took her bonnet off and put it on the table. She took the sharp needle-work scissors from the drawer and began to cut away the old ribbons.

'Are you not going to wear that again tomorrow?' asked Bessie as she watched her sister work with her head bent over the task and her tongue between her lips in concentration.

'I've got some new ribbons,' she said, folding back the paper on her package to show Bessie, who gazed at them enviously. They were the ones she'd seen in Miss Cross's window.

'Where did you get the money from?'

'They were a gift.'

'From John Sharples?'

Peggy looked up and smiled. 'I think he likes me,' she said.

'They were asking me earlier if I knew who you were meeting.'

'You didn't say anything?' For a moment Peggy looked alarmed.

'No. I promised I wouldn't. But I don't like telling a lie.'

Peggy shrugged. 'Then I'm sorry I told you anything.'

'They'll be furious when they find out.'

'They're not going to find out.'

'You can't be certain.'

Peggy pulled a face. 'If they say anything I've a few awkward questions to ask them,' she said. 'I wonder what they'll say when I ask them about harbouring criminals!'

'You're asking for trouble,' Bessie warned her. 'How do you know that anything John Sharples says is true?'

Peggy considered for a moment as she began to sew the new ribbons on to the bonnet. 'I believe him,' she said. 'Why would he lie?'

'I don't know.' Bessie wondered if her sister would share any of the ribbon with her, but it didn't seem to occur to Peggy, who fastened the bright colours into bows and stitched until she was satisfied. 'Are you meeting him again tomorrow?' Bessie asked.

'Why? Did you want me to take you to the fair?'

'No. I'm old enough to go alone, in case you hadn't noticed,' she said. 'And anyway, I'm meeting Ruth.'

'Well, there's no problem then,' replied Peggy, and quickly gathered up her bonnet and ribbons as she heard their mother coming.

Chapter Thirteen

There were crowds of people making their way towards Blakeley Moor on Easter Monday morning, not just from Blackburn, but from the surrounding towns and villages too. Peggy, in her newly trimmed bonnet, tucked her hand under John's arm to prevent them being swept apart by the mass of excited fair-goers.

As they walked through Fleming Square she saw that the pot fair had arrived too. There were stalls and booths selling all sorts of earthenware and porcelain that had come from China. Not only was it stacked on the stalls but it was piled up on the ground for people to view and touch. Some was bound to be broken and more stolen, she thought as she saw a woman glance about before slipping a cup and saucer into her basket.

As they walked on, the shouts and patter of the pottery sellers were replaced by music from the main fairground where gongs and drums and trumpets were vying in a discordant chorus for attention. There were stalls selling gingerbread, brandy snaps, toffee, pies and hot black puddings, with ginger beer to drink for those, like John, who had signed the pledge and endless quantities of beer and ale for those who hadn't.

They passed swingboats and roundabouts and chairs that went up and down. Peggy would have loved to try them all out, but John was keen to get to the very centre of the fair where Monsieur Plège was to give his first performance at twelve noon. As they approached the arena, Peggy saw the tightrope slung high in the air between two poles.

'They say as he'll dance across there pushing another chap in a wheelbarrow,' John told her.

He took out some money and paid one of the dwarfs at the entrance so they could climb up to the makeshift seats that would give them a good view. Others crowded in behind them and when there were no seats left, the dwarf pulled a rickety gate across the entrance and, with a flourish of trumpets, the show began. First a horse rider galloped into the ring to a lively tune played by the band. He leaped to his feet in the saddle and circled around, juggling two, three, four and then more balls than Peggy could count as they flew around his head, under his legs and even behind his back where he caught them without even being able to see them. The crowd applauded. The rider made his bow and then came the main attraction: Monsieur Plège. He came out with a long pole and climbed up a flimsy ladder to the high tight-rope, walking across it whilst balancing precariously. The crowd gasped every time he seemed about to fall, but Peggy realised he had been teasing them when he tossed the pole to the ground and ran back across the rope as if he were flying through the air. The crowd laughed and applauded as he danced to and fro, juggling balls as he went, then tossing coins in the air and catching them in a cup he held in his mouth.

'He's amazing!' she said to John as Monsieur Plège came back down the ladder and took his final bow. 'I'd never have believed it was possible if I hadn't seen it with my own eyes.'

Then came a little skewbald pony that could do simple sums. 'He should have a job in our office!' said John. Then another horse that could dance and finally the dogs that Peggy had been waiting for, who sat and stayed and fetched on command, then jumped through hoops. There were acrobats, a muscle man, a giant who could reach up and touch the high rope, an escapologist who broke out of chains, and finally Monsieur Plège again.

It ended with a parade of all the performers and animals and Peggy clapped and clapped until her palms hurt. Then they climbed down from their seats and wandered around the rest of the fair. John bought her toffee and ginger beer and they rode on the roundabout with the painted horses. She hurried him past the boxing ring, not wanting to see men drawing blood from one another's faces. She tried to persuade him to have a go on the shooting gallery, forgetting in the excitement about his useless hand and then feeling bad when she remembered. So she pulled him towards the swingboats and they sailed up and down, up and down, until her stomach hurt and she thought that she'd never been so happy in her whole life.

As the light began to fade, the crowd thinned as folk made their way home and Peggy realised that she had missed both her dinner and her tea.

'I'd best get back,' she told John, 'before they begin to worry about me.'

'I'll walk with thee.'

'Just to the end of Water Street,' she reminded him.

He leaned in and kissed her on the cheek when they reached the bridge. 'I'll see thee in the morning?' he asked.

'Yes! Thank you for a lovely day!' she said before she skipped down the street. She was so happy and she thought that she'd never enjoyed a day so much. John was so nice, and kind, and generous. She wondered if she was in danger of falling in love with him and she found that she didn't care if she was.

She pushed open the door and went in, untying the ribbons on her bonnet. Her father and mother and Bessie were sitting at the table. Their plates were empty except for crumbs. Grandma Chadwick was sleeping in the chair by the fire. Peggy was about to apologise for being late for her tea, but her father's face quelled the words.

'Where's tha been?' he demanded.

All Peggy's excitement drained. Her father was rarely angry with her, and even when he was she could easily charm him out of it. But this was different. She'd never seen him so furious.

'At the fair.'

'Who with?'

'A friend ...'

'Tha's been seen with John Sharples.' Her father almost spat the words as if the very name left a bad taste in his mouth.

She looked at Bessie. Her sister shook her head to say she hadn't said anything.

'Who told you that?' she asked her father, straightening the new ribbons on her bonnet and wondering if she could brazen it out with a denial.

'It were Mrs Bailey from up the street,' said her mother. 'We were walking home and a group were standing chatting on the corner by the bridge. She called out to us. *How long's thy Peggy been walking out with that Sharples lad?'*

Peggy wasn't sure how to reply. She didn't want to tell a lie.

'Is it true?' asked her father.

'I ... I often see him on my way to school,' she said. 'We sometimes exchange a few words.'

'Mrs Bailey seemed to think tha's been on the fair with him,' said her mother.

Peggy twisted the ribbons between her fingers. 'It was nothing serious. He asked if I'd like to go and I said yes.'

'Tha knows we have nowt to do with that family!' shouted her father, making Grandma Chadwick jump awake and look around in alarm.

'But he's nice,' protested Peggy.

'That's beside the point. Tha's to have nothing more to do with him. Dost tha understand?'

She didn't reply.

'Dost tha understand?' he repeated.

'But why? Why can't I have anything to do with him?' she asked. She was angry too. She was nearly eighteen, not a child any more. And if what John had told her was true, her parents were more at fault than any of the Sharples family.

'Because I say so!'

'That's no answer.'

'Peggy! Don't speak to thy father like that!'

'But I want to know! I want to know why I've to have nothing to do with him.'

'Because tha's set to study for a schoolteacher, that's why!' said her father.

'So you'd rather see me an old maid than see me happy?'

'Get upstairs!'

'No! I want to know why you think the Sharples family are so bad! I want to hear your side of it!'

'Peggy!' Her mother stood up and grasped her by the arm. 'Peggy, go upstairs! Tha's upsetting thy grandma.'

'No!' She shook her mother's hand off. 'I want to know what you have to say. I want you to tell me why you helped a criminal escape and let John take the blame!'

There was a stunned silence in the parlour. Her mother sat back down as if her legs couldn't hold her. Her father stared at her and Bessie's gaze flicked between them all in horror and disbelief. They weren't a family given to fighting and she looked shocked and afraid.

She saw her father glance at her mother. 'What's he told thee?' he asked Peggy.

'He said that he was arrested when there was another lad picking pockets and he got all the blame, and that the other lad lived with us and that you helped him get away.'

'That's nonsense.' Her father looked uncomfortable. 'He's spinnin' thee a tale. Typical Sharples. They're all trouble.' But he avoided her eye and Peggy didn't believe him.

'Is it true?' she asked her mother.

She was shaking her head. 'It was a long time ago.'

'So it is true?'

'It's complicated,' said her mother. 'But we don't want tha seeing that Sharples lad. Tha's to have nowt more to do with him.'

Peggy, sensing that she had the upper hand, flounced out of the parlour without a word.

'What about thy tea?' her mother called after her.

'I've had my tea, thank you,' she replied, and went up the stairs to her room, slammed the door behind her, flung herself on to the bed and sobbed. The day was ruined. She'd been so happy and now they'd ruined it. She hated them. They were telling her lies and she'd never forgive them. And she wouldn't stop seeing John either. They had no right to forbid it. Not after what they'd done.

Bessie cleared the table and washed up the pots. She could hear her sister crying upstairs and she hoped Peggy didn't think she'd said anything. She'd never breathed a word and she never would. But she sensed there was more to it than her parents simply disapproving of John Sharples. They kept giving one another looks, although they were sitting in tight-lipped silence, and she had the impression that there were things they wanted to say that they weren't going to say in front of her.

Unable to bear the atmosphere in the parlour and knowing that she wouldn't be allowed to go back out in the dark, Bessie reluctantly went up to the bedroom. She doubted that she'd be any more welcome up there, but other than going to sit out on the privy she had no option.

'Go away,' muttered Peggy when she heard her come in. 'I want to be on my own.'

'Maybe so,' she said, 'but I'm not sitting down there. It's like being next to a powder keg that's about to explode. I've never seen them so angry and upset.'

'That's not my fault.'

'It is, our Peggy! You knew what would happen when they found out. And they were bound to find out when you were walking out with him for all the world to see. I saw you at the fair, and so did Ruth. She commented on it too. It was bound to make folk talk.'

Her sister sniffed and reached for a rag to blow her nose. 'They've spoiled everything,' she said. 'I hate them.'

'But you knew it could never be. Why did you agree to go to the fair with him? You must have known there'd be trouble.'

'But they wouldn't answer when I asked them about that criminal, would they?' said Peggy, sitting up. Her eyes were red and puffy and she kept wiping them on the heel of her hand. 'They denied it, but they're hiding something. What did they say after I came up?' she asked.

'Nothing,' Bessie told her. 'They're just sitting there, seething. I couldn't stand it any longer.'

'See. They're hiding something,' said Peggy. 'They know they're in the wrong. I hate them,' she said again. 'I don't have to do anything they say.'

'You're not going to carry on seeing him?' Bessie couldn't believe that Peggy would defy their father.

'How can they stop me?'

Bessie considered it. 'They could shut you in here. Or in the privy.'

'Don't be stupid. They'll not do that. And he's going off to London with his charter anyway.'

'Maybe he'll take you with him.'

'He'd never take me away from my studies,' Peggy replied, 'even if I wanted to go.'

Chapter Fourteen

'Perhaps tha shouldn't go to London after all,' said Jennet to Titus when they eventually got to bed. She could tell how upset he was and she was angry with Peggy for behaving so badly. If it had been Bessie it would have been easier. He would still have been angry but he wouldn't have felt so let down. Peggy had always been the one who could do no wrong and he was finding it very hard to accept that she had not only betrayed him, but had lied to him too, and seemed to feel no remorse for what she'd done. It was as though she was a changed person and Jennet worried about exactly what John Sharples had told her to turn her against them like this.

'I'm not sure I can stop her seeing him if I'm here on my own,' she said. 'I'm that busy with my work. I can't be watching her all the time.

And tha knows what she's like. She takes after thee, she's that headstrong.'

'I'll not let t' Chartists down. I've promised as I'll go so I shall.'

'But what'll we do about Peggy? Should we tell her the truth? I know we always vowed we'd say nowt about it, but she's heard a version from him and she seems to believe it.'

'It's a rum do when a child believes ill of its parents on the word of a stranger,' he grumbled.

'She's young. She's starry-eyed over this lad and if we don't tell her the truth it might make things worse,' said Jennet, worried that she might lose her daughter to the Sharples family.

'I thought she were all set on taking this scholarship. Dost tha think she's been with this lad when we thought she were studying?'

'It's possible.'

'I'll kill 'im if he's laid a finger on her. I'll kill 'im even if he hasn't. He knows he's stirring up trouble. It's probably the only reason he's asked her to walk out with 'im – so he and his family can get their own back on us.' Titus thumped the bolster in his frustration. 'I can't let 'em down when I've been chosen to go,' he repeated.

Jennet blew out the rushlight and they lay side by side in the darkness, a sliver of moonlight striping the floor through a gap in the curtains.

It seemed that Titus was determined to march with the charter and even this trouble with Peggy wasn't going to stop him. She wondered if she ought to tell her daughter the truth. The problem was that once the truth began to unravel the whole thing might have to be told and that would affect Bessie as well. They'd agreed years ago that they would never tell her that Titus wasn't her real father, but how could she explain to Peggy the reason she'd agreed to help Sam Proctor escape without revealing everything?

When Peggy came down dressed for school the next morning, Jennet wondered if Titus would refuse to let her go, but when she got up to put on her shawl he reached for his cap.

'Mill's shut again today,' he said. 'I'll walk up to Thunder Alley with thee.'

Peggy hesitated and Jennet wondered if she was about to refuse to go, but the thought of spending the day with him watching over her at every hour seemed to bother her daughter more.

'If you like,' she said and went out, making him break into a trot to catch her up as they passed the window.

'And what's tha planning on doing all day?' Jennet asked Bessie, more sharply than she intended. It wasn't fair to let her younger daughter take any blame, but she suspected that Bessie had known something and kept it to herself.

'Ruth and I thought we'd take a last look at the fair.'

'No. Tha can run a few errands for me if tha's no work.'

Bessie didn't protest and her acquiescence made Jennet feel guilty. She was a good lass – never a minute's trouble – and it was unfair to blame her for what had happened.

Once she'd packed up the parcels of laundry to be delivered, she took a small key from her pocket and unlocked the drawer in the sideboard where she kept her money. She took out a shilling and put it in Bessie's hand. 'Go to Lamb's on Darwen Street and buy two new collars for thy father,' she said. 'I'll not have him going to London looking like a tramp.'

Bessie let herself out and, after delivering the laundry, she walked round by Blakeley Moor. The fair was mostly packed up. The stalls had been taken down and some of the men were dismantling the rides and lifting the pieces on to the backs of carts. In a few days' time it would all be put up somewhere else, for other folk to enjoy.

There was no sign of Ruth. She must have given up waiting for her and Bessie was sorry to have let her friend down. She turned away from the moor and walked back into town. As she passed the stonemason's yard she saw the man again, the one with the dark skin. He was standing waiting as the older man spoke to the mason. It seemed that they weren't part of the circus, or travelling doctors, and Bessie was curious about what had brought them to Blackburn.

Suddenly aware of being watched, the dark-skinned man looked right at her. He was only young, probably not much more than her own age, and he smiled with a flash of straight white teeth. Flustered, Bessie looked away. She hoped that she hadn't hurt his feelings, but he must be used to being the subject of interest, she thought. Like the dwarfs and the giant who had come with the circus, he was bound to attract attention when he looked so different.

She bought the shirt collars from Lamb's and then wandered back, past Miss Cross's shop where she was changing the display in her window. No one wanted Easter bonnets now and she was putting out delicate straw hats for the coming summer. Bessie gave her a half-smile, but the woman pretended that she hadn't seen her, so Bessie walked on, not wanting to go home just yet.

When Miss Parkinson dismissed the class of girls for their dinner, Peggy lingered in the schoolroom, wiping the slates and putting more coal on the fire. She'd been busy all morning and it had been a relief because it meant she hadn't had time to dwell on the humiliating encounter between her father and John Sharples.

John had been waiting for her as usual. When she'd seen him she'd wondered how he would react when he saw her walking towards him with her father at her side. He'd started towards them, trying to keep his eyes averted, but when he reached them, her father planted himself firmly in the way. John had raised his hat with a wary look.

'Good morning, Mr Eastwood … Miss Eastwood.'

'Tha doesn't need to think tha can get away with it!' her father had told him. 'Tha knows how things stand between thy family and mine and I want thee to stay away from my daughter!'

John had glanced at her and she'd shaken her head to try to convey that she was helpless in the matter and that it wasn't her choice.

'Dost tha understand?' demanded her father.

'Aye. Aye, I understand,' he'd muttered, looking anxious. He'd met her eyes again, but her father had hurried her along, leaving John standing alone in the street.

Peggy wondered if she dared walk down to Hart's office and try to speak to him, to explain, but she had no idea if he was given a dinnertime and, if he was, whether he came out or stayed inside. She could write a note to leave for him that explained matters, she thought, but she knew that she was expected next door for her dinner and that her father might well check with her auntie and uncle to make sure she'd been.

She got her shawl and went to the schoolhouse. It was noisy as usual with her young cousins released from the schoolroom for an hour. Auntie Hannah told them to go and play outside for five minutes until their dinner was ready.

'What's the matter with thee?' she asked Peggy when they'd gone. 'Tha looks like tha's lost a pound and found sixpence. Tha's not worrying about taking the scholarship exam?'

'No,' said Peggy, 'because I'm not going to take it.'

'What?' Her auntie turned from the oven, almost dropping the dish of pie she held between two thick cloths. 'I thought thy father were keen for thee to go?' She set the dish on the table and fetched a big spoon to serve it. 'Shall I ask Uncle James to talk to him?'

'No. It's not that,' said Peggy. 'I don't want to go.'

'But why not? It's such an opportunity. Tha'd be a fool to let it pass, our Peggy. It'll give thee a better life than tha could ever have if tha stopped here.'

'I don't want to be a schoolmistress,' she said, knowing that she sounded like a petulant child.

'What on earth's brought this on?' asked her auntie.

'John Sharples,' said her uncle as he came through the door. 'Your father tells me you were seen with him at the fair.'

'Mary's little brother?' asked her auntie.

'Not so little these days,' replied her uncle. 'Titus is in a right state about it.'

Her auntie gave her a hard look. 'Whatever is tha thinking of, our Peggy? It's bad enough being seen with a lad, but why him?'

'There's nothing wrong with him,' she said. 'It isn't his fault if his family fell out with my mam and dad. And from what he's told me they're not entirely blameless.'

Her auntie exchanged a glance with her uncle. 'What's he told thee?' she asked.

Peggy hesitated for a moment, but then blurted it out. 'He said as my mam and dad were housing a lad who was a pickpocket and that they helped him get away from the law so John took the blame and went to prison.'

Her auntie sat down at the table, the pie forgotten. 'Hast tha said owt to them about it?' she asked.

'I mentioned it. My dad said it wasn't true. Mam said it was a long time ago.' She looked at her auntie and then her uncle. She could tell by their faces that they knew something too. 'But it is true, isn't it?' she asked.

Her auntie was shaking her head. She picked up the spoon again and began to put the dinner out on the plates.

'You know something about it, don't you?' persisted Peggy.

'It's not for me to say,' replied her auntie. 'Talk to thy mother about it. James, call the childer in, and make sure they wash their hands.'

Peggy could see that the subject was firmly closed. It was so frustrating and the way that none of them would talk about what had happened made her certain that there was some truth in what she'd been told.

Chapter Fifteen

Titus was up early on the Sunday morning to join the deputation going to London. Jennet had washed and starched his best shirt and he was wearing one of the new collars. His trousers and his fustian jacket were a bit shabby, but she'd brushed them as best she could and made sure that any holes were mended. She'd darned his socks, put a change of underwear and a clean shirt into his pack, and wrapped up some oatcakes and cheese for him to eat along the way. She'd made sure he had money to pay for food and lodgings if he needed them. It was an expense, but she would just have to make more economies, she thought as she straightened his necktie and laid a hand on his freshly shaven cheek.

'Tha looks a treat,' she told him. 'Very handsome!'

He settled his cap on his head. 'I don't know when I'll be back,' he said.

'I'll manage. I've managed before,' she reminded him, and then wished she hadn't. Last time he'd come back to her she'd presented him with another mouth to feed that wasn't even his. Still, there was no chance of that happening this time.

'Keep an eye on our Peggy.'

'I will,' she promised. She knew that he'd warned John Sharples off and Peggy's whereabouts had been accounted for every hour of every day since the fair. She was allowed nowhere except to school, church and Hannah's house. Jennet felt a bit sorry for her. She remembered what it was like to be young and in love, and she wondered whether Titus remembered too. He used to come calling for her on Sunday afternoons and they would walk out together all across the countryside to Langho, Whalley and even as far as the castle at Clitheroe. Then he would fetch her home and stand awkwardly on the step until her mother called him in and asked if he'd like to stay for his tea. The difference was that her parents had approved of him. He'd been a hard-working weaver from a local family. His father had died and he had tenancy of a cottage at Pleck Gate. He had, in fact, been what her mother referred to as a *bit of a catch*. And Jennet had counted the days to those Sunday afternoons.

She'd linger by the window after she'd eaten her dinner, watching for him coming and hoping that she wouldn't be disappointed. Then, when she saw his familiar figure coming down the path by the stream her heart would begin to thud and she'd be unable to keep the smile from her face. By the time he got to the door, she'd be waiting with her boots and shawl already on. And he'd come – sun, rain and storm; he'd come without fail to court her until he plucked up the courage to ask her father if they could be married.

They'd been good days, thought Jennet, watching him now as he took up his pack and opened the door.

'I'll see thee later,' he said and she nodded and stood at the door to watch him walk to the end of the street. She supposed that she still did love him in a way, but it seemed more like a duty now rather than the heady intoxication that she recalled.

'Has he gone?' asked Peggy, coming into the parlour. She stayed upstairs a lot of the time, avoiding him. Jennet couldn't blame her for being angry. She hoped that with Titus out of the house, she might get the chance to talk things through with Peggy, telling her enough to make her understand without revealing too much. She wanted her to be happy, but she didn't want her daughter to think badly of her.

'Aye, he's gone,' she said. 'But don't think that gives thee an excuse to be seeing John Sharples again.'

Peggy slumped down in her father's chair and began to poke the fire. Her father never allowed her to do it when he was there.

'Don't get ashes all over the hearth. I've swept up once already,' said Jennet.

'What happened, Mam?' she asked. 'What happened to make you hate the Sharples family so much?'

Jennet sighed and sat down in the chair opposite her daughter. 'It's a long story,' she said.

'Well, I've nothing else to do, so I've time to hear it.'

Peggy sat back in the chair and waited, and Jennet knew she would never be content until she learned more about the feud.

'It began when John hurt his hand and his mother took time off work. The overlooker gave me her looms and she weren't best pleased when she came back and was told she'd have to work in the carding room instead.'

'Well, you can hardly blame her.'

'Aye, I know. But I hadn't much choice in the matter. I worked where I were told. It was either that or no work at all – and I needed the work because it were when thy father were at Preston.'

'In prison?'

'Aye, but only because he got caught up in some loom breaking. He didn't break owt himself.'

Peggy nodded. She knew some of this already although it was rarely spoken of.

'John said there was more to it.'

'Aye. That Sharples lot made trouble for us at every opportunity. Nan were always bad-mouthing us to other folk and trying to turn them against us. She got a job weaving at another mill, but even that didn't stop her. She'd got her knife in and she kept twisting it.'

'And what about the lad who was a pick-pocket?' asked Peggy.

'He turned up at the door one day,' said Jennet. 'He'd been with thy father in the prison and thy father had taken a bit of a shine to him and written down the address. We were still living on Paradise Lane then and the Sharples family were next door. He were a bad lot. He told us he had work and we let him lodge for a bit, but it turned out he were picking pockets and he'd persuaded young John to be his lookout.'

'Then when John got arrested you helped the lad to get away and John took all the blame,' Peggy finished for her.

Jennet didn't know what to reply. 'Thy father were fond of him,' she said at last. 'He'd always wanted a son and t' doctor told me I'd never have no more babies after Bessie were born. Sam had already served one sentence and thy father wouldn't see him hang ...'

'So you helped him get away.'

'Thy father spoke up for John at his trial.'

'But he still went to prison, even though he'd done nothing wrong.'

'Well, he weren't entirely blameless. He had been helping Sam.'

'He says he didn't know what that lad was doing.'

'So he said,' replied Jennet. She could see that her daughter was judging her and she felt ashamed. She couldn't explain the full story to her – that she'd only agreed to help get Sam away because she felt so guilty that she couldn't give Titus the son he craved. If she hadn't gone with George Anderton and got herself pregnant with Bessie then she might never have had the traumatic delivery that left her barren. She might have given Titus a son to replace the little lad she'd lost so many years ago.

'How can you blame them for being angry?' asked Peggy.

'You don't know what it was like,' Jennet told her. 'They made our lives a misery. They shouted insults every time they saw us on the street. They spread stories about us. They banged on the walls and shouted at us at all hours of the day and night, making all sorts of threats. We couldn't even go to the privy in peace. I was afraid to be there on my own when thy father were at work. In the end we had to move out to get away from them.'

Peggy was silent for a while as she took it all in. 'But it wasn't John who made the trouble,' she said at last. 'He wasn't even there and he doesn't live with them now. If he hated you why would he be so kind to me?'

'I don't know, Peggy,' Jennet said. 'I really don't know. But I'm worried that he's just using thee to get back at us. He might seem nice enough, but there are other lads. And if tha's going to be a schoolteacher, tha's better not falling into that sort of temptation anyway. And I know tha does want to teach,' she told her. 'Tha's never wanted owt else since tha sat on that hearthrug there and tried to teach our Bessie her letters. Don't throw it all away over a lad, Peggy. Tha can better thyself. Don't throw it away,' she repeated. 'I'll be that sad to see thee go, but I want to see thee do well and not have to spend thy life washing other folk's dirty laundry like me.'

Chapter Sixteen

It was 26 April 1842, the anniversary of Lizzie Anderton's death. It was a date that Jennet never forgot. Every year since George had gone away to America, she'd kept her promise to him to remember his wife, and although there was no headstone that marked her grave in the churchyard at St Alban's, Jennet always laid a posy on the spot where Lizzie lay.

Once she'd put the laundry to soak she asked her neighbour, Molly Chambers, to listen out for Grandma Chadwick, then she set out to gather some wild flowers.

The sun was warm on her back although the biting wind from the north chilled her as she walked head on into it, towards Ramsgreave and the cottage where she'd been brought up. It looked sad and forlorn now that her mother had moved out, and Jennet couldn't stop herself peering in through a grimy window, even though it grieved her to be locked out of it now that the rent was no longer being paid. She could see the range where her mother had always had something good cooking in a pot for them – fresh vegetables from their own plot and sometimes a rabbit snared in a trap. They'd grown most of their own food, kept hens and occasionally reared a pig for winter bacon. There'd always been enough and their lives had been good, governed by their needs and the seasons of the year. She looked at the spot that caught the best of the daylight from the long window where her father had had his loom, and she remembered the rhythmic thud of the frame as he'd woven the cloth. Or, if the weather had been fine, he would leave the women spinning and go to tend his vege-tables, and then work long into the night to get a piece finished if he'd spent too long outside.

She turned sadly from the window and went around the back to the vegetable patch that had been her father's pride and joy. It was mostly overgrown with a tangle of weeds, the natural brambles that grew there taking hold once more, although one bed looked like it had been weeded and she wondered who might have done it. All their neighbours were long gone – either to the graveyard or the mills – and she'd thought that she was the only one who still came here.

Her father had always loved flowers. His favourites had been the early snowdrops with their nodding white bells and the yellow primroses that grew along the banks of the stream, but they were all faded now and so she began to search along the woodland floor for the first of the bluebells. She would take some for Lizzie's grave, some would go in a jar on the sideboard to remind her mother of home, and before she went back to Blackburn she would leave some in the churchyard at Pleck Gate for her little lad.

Afterwards she walked back towards St Alban's. There, she made her way to Lizzie's resting place and stopped in her tracks in complete bewilderment. There was a headstone. It looked new. It hadn't been sullied by the filthy air and at first Jennet thought she'd misremembered the place. Perhaps, like her mother, she was growing forgetful. As she approached it she saw that it had been engraved with a name and a date, although she couldn't be sure that the name was Lizzie's. Surely the grave hadn't been reused so soon, she thought as she laid down the flowers and knelt to trace with her finger the lines and curves of what was written there.

A shadow fell across her and she jumped, aware that someone had come up behind her and that she hadn't heard them. She got to her feet as quickly as she could, stiff from her long walk, and stared into the once familiar blue eyes.

'Jennet,' he said. 'Tha kept thy promise.'

For a moment she was unsure that it was really him. He looked older, but that was not surprising as it was sixteen years since she'd last seen him. He looked prosperous too. He looked like gentry, she thought, as she took in his suit with its floral jacquard waistcoat, the gleaming chain of a pocket watch, his silk necktie and the tall hat which he held in his hand. His hair was still thick, but it had greyed – like her own, she thought ruefully as she pushed a wisp of it back under her bonnet and wished that she hadn't come out in her working clothes. What must he think of her?

'George?' she said quietly. 'Is it really thee? Tha's grown a moustache,' she said and then cursed herself for voicing her thought out loud.

'Aye, it's me,' he said. 'Tha doesn't need to look like tha's seen a ghost or summat.'

'But I thought tha went to America?'

'Aye. I did go to America, and I've done all right for myself. I've made a bit o' money. But it's plagued me for years thinking of my Lizzie with no stone to mark her burial, and so I made up my mind to come back and set things right.'

'So it were thee as put this up?' she asked. 'What does it say?'

'It says: *In loving memory of Elizabeth Anderton, wife of George Anderton. Born 11 September 1789. Died 26 April 1826. Her ways are ways of pleasantness, and all her paths are peace. Proverbs 3:17.*'

'That's nice,' said Jennet. 'She would have liked that.'

'Aye, she would.' He stared at the memorial and Jennet could see the tears brimming in his eyes as he remembered his wife, even after all these years. 'I brought flowers too,' he said, and she noticed the bouquet of lilacs and irises that he'd been holding behind his back. It looked expensive, bought from a flower seller rather than picked, and it put her feeble offering of wilting wildflowers to shame. He seemed uncomfortable about laying it down and propped it to the side of the stone. Jennet bent to move hers aside and placed his centrally on the grave.

'That's better,' she said, brushing away some loose petals, glad that she was wearing gloves and he couldn't see how rough and reddened her hands had become from constantly being in the soap and water. 'They look nice,' she said. 'Lizzie would have loved them. She always liked a few flowers.'

He nodded and wiped his face. 'It brings it all back, being here,' he said. 'I'm sorry.'

'There's no need to tell me tha's sorry,' said Jennet. 'I know that tha loved her and missing folk doesn't get any easier. It's like a cut that's scabbed over. Tha thinks it's healed but then summat comes along and knocks it and it starts bleedin' all over again.'

He nodded. 'What about thee?' he said. 'Tha looks well.'

'Aye, I'm all right,' she told him.

'Titus?'

'Aye. He's just the same. He's gone off on t' march to London with the People's Charter.'

'I've heard about it,' said George. 'It's a worthwhile thing. I hope they get Parliament to take notice.'

'Aye. I'll just be glad if he gets back without fallin' into some sort o' trouble.'

George nodded. Like her, he seemed to be remembering when Titus was last in trouble and what had happened that night at the inn in Lancaster.

'I hope tha's been happy,' he told her.

'I've been happy enough.'

'And little Peggy?'

'Not so little now. She's plannin' on being a schoolteacher.'

'She were always a clever little lass,' he said. 'Did any others come along?'

Jennet hesitated. She could feel her cheeks flushed red and knew that this was her opportunity to tell him the truth, but she baulked at it. 'I've another daughter. We baptised her Elizabeth, but we call her Bessie.'

'That's nice,' he said.

'Is tha planning on stayin' long?' she asked. She knew it sounded rude, and although she was glad to see him and know that he'd done all right, she worried about what would happen if Titus came home and saw him. He'd always vowed he'd kill him if he set eyes on him again.

'I thought we'd stay a while and take a look at some of the old places.'

'So tha's brought a wife with thee?' She could hear the disappointment in her voice and she cursed herself for it. There was no reason for her to be jealous. She'd made her choice all those years ago.

'No! I never married again. I came with a friend – a young lad. We're stoppin' at the Old Bull,' he told her. 'Let me treat thee and the lasses to dinner there. On Sunday?'

Jennet wasn't sure what to say. Although she longed to talk to him more and hear all about his life in America, she was unsure about him meeting Bessie – and as well as that she wasn't sure she had clothes smart enough to go into a fancy dining room.

'Please say aye, Jennet,' he said. 'I'd like to talk with thee more, but this isn't the place,' he added with a glance at the headstone.

'Aye, all right,' she said. She could see that he wasn't going to take no for an answer, and it would be better to do it now, she thought, whilst Titus was away.

Jennet pressed her frock and brushed her jacket until Peggy warned her she was making it thread-bare. She polished up her boots and found some little lace gloves at the bottom of her drawer. She rubbed lanolin into her hands to soften them and even washed her hair on the Saturday night, combing it out as it dried in front of the fire.

'Who is this George Anderton that you're taking such pains to impress?' asked Peggy.

'He used to be a neighbour.'

'And now he has money to take us all out to dinner at a fancy hotel?' she asked.

'He's done well for himself in America,' Jennet told her, glad it wasn't Bessie asking the questions. Both her daughters had been surprised at the sudden invitation, but Peggy was the one who seemed convinced that there was more to it than she was telling them. 'Besides, he wants to thank me for tending his wife's grave.'

She saw her daughters exchange glances, but no more was said except for Jennet telling them that they needed to look their best if they were going to the Old Bull.

'Right. Are we ready?' Jennet asked at last the next morning after she'd fussed over every item that they were to wear. She frowned as she watched Peggy put on her bonnet with the new ribbons. She suspected they'd come from John Sharples, but she wasn't going to tell her to take it off. What would be the point? Besides, it was Bessie she was more concerned about, she thought, as she adjusted her younger daughter's hat and brushed some fluff from her shoulders. 'Come on then,' she said, taking a deep breath. Anyone would have thought they were marching into battle, not going out for their dinner.

Although she was familiar with the outside of the Old Bull, Jennet had never been inside before. It was where the gentry and the well-to-do people went. It wasn't for the likes of them. Even so, she held her head high as she climbed the steps, defying anyone to say that she wasn't good enough to enter.

The hotel was old. The Old Bull had been built many years before as a coaching inn and, unlike the modern houses that were being put up now and the mills with their plain brick walls, it was constructed from oak frames filled with wattle and daub, reminding her of the old barns in the surrounding countryside. A large gable end hung out over Church Street and the entrance from Darwen Street led into a galleried courtyard where some of the stagecoaches pulled in to disgorge their passengers.

She hesitated in the doorway, suddenly unsure, but a familiar voice called out to her.

'Jennet! I'm so glad tha's come!'

He came across to them and grasped her hand, drawing her into the lobby. She thought for a moment he was about to kiss her cheek, but he seemed to think better of it as he glanced behind her at her daughters.

'Peggy!' he said, offering her his hand. 'I bet tha doesn't remember me!' Jennet's daughter shook his hand briefly. 'And this must be Elizabeth.'

Jennet watched in alarm and anticipation as he looked at Bessie. The similarity between them was striking – not just the colour of their eyes, but the shape of their jawlines. Jennet was certain that George would guess the truth – and not only George but Bessie too.

'Tha's got two fine daughters,' he observed. 'They're a credit to thee.'

They were shown into the dining parlour where the mullioned windows that looked out on to the street were so thick that the people outside appeared distorted. It gave some privacy, thought Jennet as they were led to a table that was laid with a white linen cloth and set with silver cutlery and sparkling glassware. Chairs were pulled out for them and Peggy sat down beside her with Bessie and George opposite.

A waiter came and poured spring water into the glasses. Then a plate was set in front of each of them and dishes were placed on the table so they could choose what they would like to eat. There were pots of salmon, roasted fish, ham, eggs, cold meat, potatoes, bread and butter, cabbage and peas, as well as oatcakes, fruits and cheeses. Jennet stared at it all spread before them. She didn't think she'd ever seen such a variety of food on one table.

'Help yourselves,' encouraged George. 'Take as much as tha likes,' he urged Jennet.

She hesitantly took a slice of ham and a fried egg before passing the serving spoons to Peggy who helped herself enthusiastically to almost every dish. Jennet nudged her under the table and tried to frown at her without George noticing, but she supposed she couldn't blame the lass. She knew what it was like to go without.

But George didn't seem concerned. He watched Peggy indulgently.

'It's not often we have the chance to dine out,' said Jennet, trying to excuse her.

'We never dine out!' said Peggy. 'I've never even been in here before.'

'Then I'm glad to make amends,' George told her. 'She were always clemmed when she were a baby,' he said, turning to Jennet.

'Aye, and she'd have gone even hungrier if it hadn't been for thee,' she told him. 'I'll not forget thy kindness then, or thy kindness now.'

'It's the least I can do to show my thanks to thee for minding Lizzie's grave,' he said as he watched Bessie help herself and then began to fill his own plate.

'Was Lizzie your wife?' asked Peggy.

'Aye. We lived next door to thee on Paradise Lane. She thought the world of thee when tha were a little 'un, but she died before I went to America.'

'I don't suppose tha remembers,' said Jennet. 'Lizzie helped me nurse thee when tha were sick with the scarlatina. And George were good to us when thy father were away. He used to bring food when we had none. He'd sit thee on his knee and sing to thee sometimes an' all.'

'I remember thee,' George told Peggy. 'Tha were a pretty little thing. Tha's still pretty now. I bet there's plenty of lads asking thee to walk out with them.'

'Peggy's busy with her studies,' said Jennet. 'She's no time for walking out. She'll be going to one of the teacher-training schools next year if she passes her scholarship exam.'

'Is that so? And what about Elizabeth?' he said, turning to her other daughter. 'What dost tha do?' he asked her.

Jennet's heart was in her mouth and although she'd put food on her plate she found that she could eat none of it. He was gazing straight at Bessie. Surely he would see it. Surely he would guess.

'I work in the mill,' Bessie told him.

'She's a four-loom weaver,' added Jennet.

He nodded. 'Then tha's done well,' he said. 'Dost tha like it?'

'It's well enough,' she said, sounding unenthusiastic, 'when there's work. But t' mill's shut again at the moment.'

'Aye. I heard that trade's not so good,' he said.

'What about thee?' Jennet asked him, desperate to deflect his attention away from Bessie. 'Did tha find work in t' mills in America?'

'No.' He shook his head. 'It's like I told thee. There's land to be had cheap over there. When I arrived in New York I saw some pamphlets advertising parcels of land in Wisconsin. It were another long journey, on horseback and by boat, but it was what I wanted – space, clean air, and a place to call my own. I wanted to be my own master again, like my father were afore me. I'd never have had that if I'd stopped here. I cleared some forest and started to farm. I always wanted to farm.'

'And is that how tha made money?' she asked. She'd had no idea that farming could generate as much wealth as he appeared to have.

'I made money mostly from farm machinery,' he told her. 'There's a lot of wheat grown over there and planting and harvesting by hand were time-consuming and uneconomic. It didn't take much thinking to come up with better ways and it not only made my yield much higher, other folk paid to use my inventions.'

'Tha always were clever with machines,' said Jennet, remembering the money he was paid for his work on the looms – some of which he'd given her to help her manage. She felt consumed with guilt as she remembered that it had gone to Sam Proctor.

'What's America like?' asked Bessie. She was gazing at him with an expression that had awe in it. Jennet didn't know whether to be proud or worried. Bessie was usually so quiet in company and shy with people she didn't know.

'It's not like England,' George told her. 'It's a huge country, with dense forests and vast lakes. It's beautiful,' he said, 'although it can be dangerous. The natives aren't always friendly and there are wild animals like wolves and bears. But the land is rich. Not just for farming. There are lead mines which are bringing in money, and there's talk of other rich pickings under the ground an' all.'

'Did it take tha long to get there?' Jennet asked him, thinking back to the morning he'd left her.

'Aye. We were weeks at sea after we left Liverpool. Every day when I got up and went on deck and gazed at that endless water, I thought that I'd never see land again. But then, one day, there were such shoutin' and excitement and New York had been spotted on the horizon. I were that glad to see it, I can tell thee!'

'What's your farm like?' asked Bessie.

'It's not as big as some, but I'm planning to expand it,' he said. 'The hardest work is clearing the forest to make fields. Once that's done, the crops grow well. I have a cabin. It's all built from tree trunks – not bricks like the houses here. And the wood is burned for heat and cooking. It's plentiful so I can be as warm and cosy as I like without havin' to fret about affordin' coal. And the trees that are cut down are all well used.

What's not used for building and fencing is floated down the river for other folks to buy.'

Jennet watched him as he talked. He was still a handsome man, she thought, and it was obvious that her younger daughter liked him, even if Peggy looked unimpressed and kept giving him stony looks. Did she remember him? wondered Jennet. Did she resent him for trying to take the place of her father? She doubted it. But it was obvious that something was troubling her. Perhaps it was a good job she hadn't agreed to go with him all those years ago. It would have been hard bringing up a daughter who resented her stepfather and Peggy could be difficult enough as it was without having more reason to be obstinate.

George seemed charmed by Bessie, she thought as she watched them. He was telling her all about his voyage upriver and how they'd been attacked by the natives and she was listening in fascination. Jennet had rarely seen her so interested in anything and it occurred to her that Bessie might well have been happier if they had gone. Still, she thought, she'd made her choice and nothing could change it now. When she'd watched him walk away from her on Paradise Lane that morning, she'd never thought that she would see him again. She recalled how she'd gone home and sobbed at their parting. And he'd stayed in her thoughts over the years because Bessie had been a constant reminder of him. She watched as he smiled at their daughter. How could he not guess? And how long would it be before someone commented on the likeness? She almost wished that he hadn't come back, but she had to admit to herself that when she'd seen him at Lizzie's grave she'd been filled with a joy that she hadn't felt for a long time.

Bessie had wondered if the dark-skinned man would join them, but it wasn't until they were leaving that she caught sight of him in the corner of the lobby. George must have noticed her looking because he beckoned him over.

'Come and say hello,' he told him. 'This is Joshua,' he said. 'He travelled with me. Joshua, these are the friends I told you about. Mrs Eastwood, and her daughters Miss Margaret and Miss Elizabeth.'

'I'm pleased to meet you,' said Bessie, offering him her hand to shake.

'I'm pleased to make your acquaintance, miss,' he said.

Bessie saw Peggy offer a hand too, although she seemed unable to wrench her gaze from the man's face.

'I appreciate tha giving us all our dinner,' her mother was saying to George. 'It was very generous.'

'It were my pleasure. It's been such a joy to find that tha's still here. I thought tha might have moved on or summat.' George was holding her mother's hand firmly in his and Bessie realised that there was something between them. Her mother was looking at him in a way she'd never seen her look at anyone before. It was as though she thought a lot of him, which seemed odd because although she often talked about their friends and extended family, especially now that Grandma Chadwick was living with them, she'd never heard her say a word about a George Anderton.

'It's him!' hissed Peggy in her ear as they went out on to the street.

'Who?' She glanced around, bewildered by what her sister meant.

'Him! That George Anderton. He's the one they helped get away. The criminal. The pickpocket.'

'Don't talk daft!' She pulled away from Peggy, who was clutching at her arm. 'He can't be.'

'I'm telling you he is.' She hurried Bessie down Church Street, ahead of their mother. 'I remember him,' she told her. 'I remember him being in our house.'

'He might well have been if he was a neighbour.'

Peggy was shaking her head. 'There's more to it,' she said. 'Did you not notice the way they kept looking at each other? It was obvious they're keeping something secret.'

Bessie glanced back at her mother, who was following at a distance. She seemed lost in thought.

'They're old friends,' she said. 'It must be strange to meet someone again after all that time.'

'You can never see what's right under your nose!' Peggy told her. 'He's no good. I'm sure of it!'

Bessie didn't answer, but she knew that this time her sister was wrong. George Anderton was no criminal. She was certain. Perhaps if Peggy had taken the opportunity to actually talk to him and hear what he had to say instead of giving him sour looks all through the meal she would have realised that. Bessie thought to herself that she liked him. He was an interesting man and she'd enjoyed the way he'd told her about America. And she'd liked Joshua too.

'How can he be the pickpocket?' Bessie asked her sister as they strolled through the empty market place. 'John Sharples told you he was only a lad, and George Anderton is as old as our mother at least.'

'Well, I'm going to ask John,' said Peggy. 'He'll know.'

'I think he was just a neighbour.'

'But did you not see the way he held our mam's hand? Did you not see how they looked at one another? There's summat between them that they're not telling. I'm sure of it.'

Bessie agreed that her sister was probably right. 'Maybe they were sweethearts before she met Father.'

'How could that be? Mam and Dad lived at Pleck Gate and were married there.'

'You don't suppose ...' Bessie hesitated to voice the thought that had occurred to her. It was unthinkable.

'What?' asked Peggy.

'It doesn't matter,' she said. She wasn't going to accuse her own mother of carrying on with another man whilst her father had been away. It couldn't possibly be true. They'd just been good friends. That was all. 'I think he helped her out when Father was away. That's all. She's just grateful to him.'

'Still, it's odd that she's never mentioned him before.'

'She had no reason. She's probably never even thought about him,' said Bessie.

'Well, I'm going to find John and ask him,' said Peggy. Bessie didn't try to dissuade her. At least her sister might be satisfied when John told her that George Anderton was not the pickpocket who had got him into trouble.

Chapter Seventeen

Jennet worked her way through the pile of ironing without giving much thought to the task. Her mind was full of George Anderton. Seeing him again and sharing a meal with him was a treat that she'd never expected. Whenever she'd thought about him over the years, she'd hoped that he had found a good woman to be his wife and to care for him. She'd even wondered if he might have more children and she'd imagined him with his own babies on his knee, singing to them the way that he used to sing to Peggy. It surprised her that he hadn't wed again. It flattered her too as she wondered whether it was because of her.

She dismissed the idea. She was being silly. Perhaps she was growing like her mother, indulging in fantasies. The real reason he'd remained unmarried was probably because there were no women in that wild and beautiful country that he'd described to them. It would have been hard if she'd gone with him, she thought. She would have had to ride on horseback and paddle a canoe. She would have had to help him build a house from nothing more than cut logs and there would have been no shops, no markets, no doctor to consult if any of them had fallen ill. If her life here had been hard, then making a life in America would have been harder. Yet he seemed well. He looked prosperous and she couldn't help but imagine herself as the wife of a man who wore a top hat and a pocket watch on a silver chain.

She folded the last of the laundry and set her irons to cool. She was being ridiculous, she told herself – worse than Peggy. She was a woman with two grown-up daughters, a husband and an elderly mother to care for. The time for daydreams was long past. She'd made her choice and it was pointless to wonder what life would have been like if she'd taken a different decision.

She made some tea and helped Grandma Chadwick to drink it with a slice of bread and butter. There was no rush to get her back into her bed tonight. Bessie would help her when she came in.

She hoped that the lasses wouldn't be late home. She'd seen that they'd been full of questions about

George and she knew they'd gone out to talk about him. They'd be back soon, demanding to know more about him and she would have to think carefully about what she told them.

When the door opened, only Bessie came in.

'Where's our Peggy got to?' she asked.

'She had an errand,' Bessie told her.

'I hope it doesn't concern John Sharples.' Jennet had no idea how she could stop Peggy seeing him if she chose to, other than to lock her up in the bedroom.

Bessie said nothing. If she suspected, she was keeping it to herself. Jennet poured tea and set it on the table for her daughter.

'Will you see him again?' asked Bessie.

Jennet didn't need to ask who she meant. 'I doubt it. He'll be on his way soon – back to America.'

'He was nice. I liked him.'

'I'm glad,' said Jennet. It was true. She would have hated to see Bessie glaring at George the way Peggy had.

'Peggy didn't like him. She thinks he might be the pickpocket.'

'What?' Jennet couldn't believe what she was hearing.

'She's gone to ask John Sharples if he recognises him,' admitted Bessie.

153

'Well then, she'll soon find out that she's wrong – and I'll have a word to say to her about the way she behaved at dinnertime. It was very rude to keep looking at George like that. He kept her from being hungry when she were a baby. She ought to have been thanking him.'

'So he's not the pickpocket?'

'Of course not!'

'But there was a lad who was stealing.'

Jennet held her cup up to her face whilst she wondered what to say. It was the first time Bessie had raised the subject with her, even though Peggy had probably discussed what she'd been told with her.

'There were a lad who thy father befriended,' she said. 'He turned up here one day after he'd got out of prison. He had nowhere else to go. So we took him in for a while. I thought he had work when he brought home food and gave me money. I'd no idea he were thievin' until the constable came looking for him.'

'And is it true you helped him escape?'

Jennet sighed and set the cup down. 'The truth is that thy father were fond of him. If he'd been taken they would have hanged him – or so thy father said. He were a nice lad. I couldn't see that happen.'

'But John Sharples went to prison because of it.'

'John would have gone to prison anyway. Whether Sam were arrested or got away made no difference.'

Bessie said no more about it and Jennet was relieved. It was hard to keep secrets now that her daughters had grown up and become curious, especially since George had come back. But if she stayed calm and said as little as possible it would all blow over in a week or two. He would go back to America. Peggy would go off to her teacher-training school, and when the mills opened again, Bessie would be too busy with her work to ask any more awkward questions.

Peggy hurried down King Street, past the hotel, to the building that housed the assembly rooms. Upstairs was the Mechanics' Institute and it was here that she thought she might find John on a Sunday evening.

Sure enough, he was sitting at a table near the fire with a book spread open in front of him. As she approached, she saw that it was about birds and filled with exquisite illustrations. She stood looking at the pictures for a moment until he saw her.

'Peggy! What's to do?' he asked, looking alarmed to find her standing beside him.

'I need to speak to you,' she said.

'I don't think there's much to speak about. Thy father made things very clear,' he said as he glanced around.

'Don't worry. He's not here. He's gone to London with the petition,' Peggy told him. 'Have you got a moment? I need to ask you something.'

'Aye. Not here though,' he said. 'Let's go to the Temperance Hotel.'

They walked up to Northgate. It was crowded with people and no one paid them any attention. The bar of the Temperance Hotel was busy and she sat and waited whilst John queued to buy their drinks. He brought the cups across and put them down on the small table.

'Dost tha want owt to eat?' he asked.

'No.' Peggy picked up the dandelion and burdock and took a drink. 'Thank you,' she added. 'I'm not hungry. I had a fancy dinner at the Old Bull, courtesy of a friend of my mother's. He's the one I wanted to ask you about. I think he might be the pickpocket – the one my father helped get away.'

John stared at her. 'Really? At the Old Bull? What's he called?'

'He calls himself George Anderton.'

John shook his head. 'No, that's not him. This lad were called Sam.'

'But he might be using a false name. I need you to come and look at him, to see if you recognise him.'

'What's he look like?'

'Tall, dark hair, blue eyes ...'

John was shaking his head again. 'That's not him,' he said. 'Sam were skinny and fair-haired.'

'How old was he? Older than you?'

'Aye, but only by a year or two. I don't think he would dare to show his face around here again, much less have money to be spending in the Old Bull.' He drained his cup in one go. 'Thirsty work, studyin',' he told her, wiping his mouth on the back of his hand. It was clear he had no interest in going to find George Anderton and Peggy began to wonder if Bessie was right when she said that George and their mother were simply old friends.

'I'm sorry about the way my father spoke to you,' she said to John. 'One of our neighbours saw us together at the fair and couldn't resist telling them. They were furious.'

'Aye. I can imagine. But I suppose it were inevitable that it would get out. It's hard to keep owt a secret in this town.'

'Well, we don't need to worry so much about being seen together now,' said Peggy. 'Now that people know.'

He stared at her for a moment. He seemed hesitant.

'I don't think it would be a good idea for us to carry on meeting,' he said.

'Why not?'

'Well, tha heard what thy father said.'

'You're not afraid of him, are you?' she asked. 'Anyway, like I said, he's not here.'

'Even so, I don't want to make trouble for thee. Maybe it's best left. I do like thee,' he added. 'But tha'll be goin' away soon, after the exam.'

'That's not until December. And anyway, I might not pass it.'

'Don't lose the chance to better thyself over a friendship wi' me,' he told her. 'Set thy mind to thy studies.'

Peggy found herself growing annoyed with him. She'd thought that he would beg her to see him again, in defiance of her father, and she was finding it hard to reconcile what she was hearing with the conversation that she'd expected to have. She'd imagined that he would profess his undying love for her and tell her that they would be together no matter what. She'd never thought he would creep away like a scolded dog after a few harsh words. Maybe he didn't like her that much after all. Maybe he had just asked her to walk out with him to make her father angry and now that he'd achieved that he'd lost interest.

'I'd best go,' he said.

'Shall we walk up to Revedge again next Sunday?' She could hear the pleading tone in her voice and she hated herself for it. If he didn't want to see her again the last thing she should do was beg.

'Not next week.'

'Then when?'

'I'm sorry, Peggy,' he said, standing up. 'I think it's for the best if we don't.' He put on his cap. 'Dost tha want me to walk thee back?'

'No!' She was angry now. She wanted to pick up her cup and throw the contents at him. Why was he being so stubborn? Her father was all bluff – all talk – he'd do nothing to hurt him. And he wasn't even here. 'You don't need to go out of your way on my account,' she said. She got up, knocking over her stool, but didn't pause to set it right. She pushed through the crowd until she reached the door and got out on to Northgate, fighting back her tears. She wouldn't let him see her cry, she thought as she turned for home and walked quickly. All the way she listened out, hoping that he might follow her, hoping that he might catch her up and tell her that he was sorry. But when she reached the bridge and glanced back there was no sign of him and she leaned against the stone wall and sobbed until she managed to compose herself enough to go into the house.

Chapter Eighteen

A couple of weeks later, Jennet was in the wash-house, putting a pile of shirts to soak in lye, when she heard knocking on her front door. She felt the nerves in her stomach tighten. Friends would call and come in. A knock on the door rarely brought good news.

She hurried through the parlour, glancing at her mother who was asleep by the fire, and opened the door to find George on her doorstep. For a moment she couldn't speak and was only aware of her sleeves, pushed up beyond her elbows, her work-reddened hands and her hair escaping in greying strands from under her cap.

'George,' she said. 'Come in.' He stepped over her scrubbed doorstep and stood in the parlour. 'I was doing some washing. I must look a mess.'

'Tha looks fine to me,' he told her.

'Sit down. I'll make us some tea.' She was awkward with him, not knowing what to say or how to behave. It wasn't like it had been before he went away, but that wasn't unexpected. They were almost strangers now and, besides, she was worried about what had brought him. 'My mam's living with us now,' she explained. 'She weren't managing on her own after my father died.'

'I'm right sorry to hear that.' He glanced at the sleeping woman. 'I wanted to talk to thee,' he explained as she spooned tea into the pot. She remained with her back to him, rearranging the kettle on the hob, wondering what he was going to say. 'I got to thinking these last few days,' he went on, 'and it made me wonder.'

'What about?' she asked, trying to sound normal.

'Come and sit thee down, Jennet.'

She pulled out a chair and sat opposite him, with the table between them.

'Thy younger lass, Bessie ...' He hesitated and then looked directly at her. His eyes were exactly the same colour as her daughter's. 'She's not like Titus,' he observed.

'What's tha tryin' to say?' She could hear her voice trembling. She was certain now that he'd guessed.

'Was she born after Titus came back?'

'Aye. Titus were here when she were born. I nearly lost her,' confided Jennet. 'It were a difficult birth. They sent for a surgeon and he cut me open to get her out.'

'I'm sorry to hear that. But she looks a healthy lass. And thee? It must have been hard?'

'Aye. It were,' she admitted. 'I couldn't have any more after her. Titus were disappointed. He wanted a lad.'

'I'd have been more than happy with a lass.' He paused as if searching for the right words. 'So Titus is her father?' he asked at last. He sounded disappointed. 'I thought, I wondered ... after that night?'

'She's thy daughter,' Jennet whispered, staring at the pattern on the tablecloth and noting that there was a tea stain.

George remained silent. When she looked up he seemed to be struggling to compose himself. She could see the tears brimming in his blue eyes.

'Why didn't tha tell me?' he asked.

'I didn't know until after tha'd gone,' explained Jennet. 'And I had no idea where tha were.'

'All those years,' he said sadly. 'And I had no idea I had a daughter.'

'I'm so sorry,' she said, surprised to see how moved he was by the revelation.

'Does Titus know?' he asked. Jennet nodded. 'What did he say when he found out?'

'He weren't best pleased. He still blames thee for taking him to that meeting. He thinks he'd never have gone to prison if it hadn't been for thee – and then when he found out about Bessie ... Perhaps it's a good thing he's gone to London,' she added. Then a sudden thought struck her. 'Tha mustn't breathe a word,' she warned George. 'Not to Bessie, or to anyone. She thinks Titus is her father. We decided there were nowt to be gained by saying otherwise. In fact, it would be best if tha goes soon, afore he comes back, and afore folk start to talk.'

'Who's that?' asked Grandma Chadwick, wakening from her doze. 'I know him,' she said after staring at George for a moment.

'No tha doesn't,' Jennet told her.

'I do. It's yon George Anderton come back. Does he know he's thy Bessie's father?'

'Don't talk daft, Mam,' Jennet told her, relieved that at least she'd told George first.

'Tha thinks I'm a silly old woman, but I know what I know,' she said and Jennet wished that she hadn't picked now to have one of her more lucid moments. She rarely remembered what had happened the same day, but her memories of the past were as sharp as ever.

'I can't just walk away, not now that I know,' said George. 'I've got money. I can do something for her.'

'Tha's done enough already,' replied Jennet.

'That ten pounds were next to nowt,' he said. 'But I hope it helped thee manage for a while.'

Jennet said nothing. She didn't tell him they'd given it to Sam to help him escape.

'I've done all right,' he went on, 'and I'll not see my lass living in poverty.'

'What were tha thinking of doin' for her?' asked Jennet.

'I'm not sure. But I want her to have a better life than workin' twelve hours a day in yon mill. What would she like to do? If she had money? I could set her up in a shop or summat.'

'I don't know,' admitted Jennet. She couldn't remember Bessie ever expressing a desire for anything. She'd left school, gone to work, brought home her wages. She never complained.

'Maybe tha could ask her?' he suggested.

'Aye.' Jennet wondered how she would raise the subject. And how she would keep her mother quiet. What would she do if Grandma Chadwick blurted out what she knew about George in front of Peggy and Bessie?

'And I'd like to see her again,' he said.

Jennet shook her head. 'I don't know ...' she began, but the decision was made for her when the door opened and Bessie came in.

'Hello!' she said when she saw George sitting at the table.

He stood up and Jennet thought for a moment that he was going to kiss his daughter, but he stood, twisting his hat in his hands and staring at her.

'George were just leaving,' said Jennet firmly and moved around the table to usher him towards the front door.

'Will tha join me for dinner again at the Old Bull? Maybe tomorrow?' he asked.

'I've a lot of work,' said Jennet.

'But Bessie hasn't. Will tha come?' he asked her directly.

'Yes. I'd like that,' she said, before Jennet could stop her.

'Until tomorrow dinnertime then,' he said as he stepped out of the house and put on his hat.

For a moment Bessie said nothing; they listened to him whistling as he walked down the street.

'What did he want?' she asked. Jennet could see how curious Bessie was. She knew that there was more to it than him just being a former neighbour.

'He ... just wanted a word about summat.'

'What's going on, Mam?' asked Bessie.

'Nowt for thee to worry about. But it's best that tha doesn't go to meet him again tomorrow.'

'Why not?'

'It's complicated, and sometimes things are best just left as they are. There's nowt to be gained by digging up the past.'

Jennet went out to carry on with the washing but Bessie followed her and stood watching as she took the shirts from the lye tub and plunged them into the rinsing water.

'Was there something between you and him, when my father was in prison?' she asked.

Jennet didn't reply straight away. Bessie was coming too close to guessing the truth and it frightened her.

'He were good to us. He helped us out. He asked me to go to America with him,' she admitted. 'But I told him no. I waited for thy father to come home. I couldn't leave him to come back and find an empty house.'

'Was this before I was born?'

'Aye,' she said, wishing that Bessie would stop questioning her. They'd never talked about exactly when Titus had been in the prison or for how long because it would be too easy for Bessie to add up the dates and realise that she couldn't possibly be his child.

'So why did he ask me to dinner again? Why not Peggy?' asked Bessie, still talking about George.

'Peggy can't miss school. I think he were only being polite when he asked thee. It's best if tha doesn't go.'

Bessie went back into the house and Jennet heard her going up the stairs. She began to put the shirts into the copper to boil, hoping that she'd said enough to satisfy her daughter.

Chapter Nineteen

'I told you there was something going on,' said Peggy later when Bessie told her what she'd learned. 'Even if he isn't the pickpocket, there's something our mam's not telling us. I think they were sweethearts and they're still sweet on one another now.'

'Don't talk daft,' said Bessie. 'They're too old.'

'You need to go and meet him again,' Peggy told her, 'to see what else you can find out about him.'

'But haven't we found out everything?'

'There may be more,' said Peggy. 'Why has he come back now, when Father's away?'

'He said it was to buy a gravestone.'

'No,' insisted Peggy. 'You wouldn't travel half-way around the world just to buy a gravestone.'

'You don't think our mam's planning to run off with him, do you?' Bessie asked. The thought of being left alone with her father if both her mother and her sister went away was not one she relished.

'Go and find out,' Peggy told her.

'Tha can't go,' Jennet told Bessie the next day when she saw her daughter come down in her best frock and bonnet, ready to meet George. 'It's not seemly for thee to be dining out with a man tha doesn't know.'

'But I've already dined out with him once,' she said, 'and I'd like to see him again. I like him. Besides, you could come too.'

Jennet didn't know what to say. Peggy would have shouted and pleaded and made a scene, but Bessie remained calm, standing by the door and pointing out the truth.

'How can I? I've all these shirts to finish and take back by the end of the day, and Molly next door's gone to see her sister so I've no one to mind thy grandma.'

Bessie reached out for the door handle. 'Why are you so set against me seeing him?' she asked, wondering if Peggy was right when she said there were more secrets to be uncovered.

'Folk will talk.'

'What about? All we'll do is eat dinner in a public dining room. What's wrong with that?'

Her mother didn't reply, so Bessie opened the door. She stepped out on to the street and began to walk. Her mother didn't follow her and although Bessie felt guilty at defying her she wanted to meet George again and hear more about his adventures in America. She hoped that Joshua would be there too. She'd like to find out more about him as well.

She walked to the Old Bull and up the steps to the entrance. As soon as George saw her come in, he greeted her with a wide smile. Bessie glanced around for Joshua, but there was no sign of him. It seemed it would just be the two of them and she felt disappointed.

They were shown to a table in the corner of the dining room and George held the chair for her to sit down. She felt like a lady.

'My mother couldn't come,' said Bessie as the food was laid out. 'She's got work and no one to sit with my grandma.'

'Well, I'm glad to see thee,' George told her. 'I'd like to get to know thee.'

Bessie wasn't sure how to reply and for a moment she wondered if she should have come. She wasn't a total innocent. She'd seen how the overlookers behaved around the young lasses at the mill and she hoped that George didn't have similar designs on her. Perhaps she should have heeded her mother and not come alone. But he seemed to be a perfect gentleman, making sure she had exactly what she wanted to eat and drink and asking her about herself.

'Did tha never want to do owt other than mill work?' he asked her as they ate. 'Hast tha got any ambitions?'

'Ambitions?'

'Aye. Things tha wants to do.'

'I don't know. I've never thought much about it.' He must have had ambitions, she thought as she looked at him. His ambitions had led him across an ocean to a wild and unknown country where he'd made enough money to come back looking like gentry. He had a look of quality – Joshua too. She longed to ask where Joshua was, but didn't dare. She didn't want to seem too forward.

'Is there owt that tha really, really wants to do?' George asked her.

Bessie thought about it for a moment. At one time she'd fancied being a schoolteacher, like Peggy, but now she didn't think she'd enjoy it.

'I'd like to do something where I don't have to be beholden to the mill owners,' she told him. 'And it would be nice to have work I could rely on. The mill's been on short time or shut for weeks now.'

'Happen a shop then?' he suggested. 'What about a hat shop? Or a glove shop?'

'Aye. Gloves are nice. I saw some beautiful gloves in Miss Cross's shop a while back. Kidskin in the most delicate lavender colour with a row of little mother-of-pearl buttons to fasten them up.'

'Did tha buy them?'

Bessie shook her head. 'I've no money for such luxuries,' she told him. 'I give my wages to my mother to feed us. When there's no call for cloth, there's no work – and no wages.'

'Aye. It were the same story before I went to America,' he said. 'I asked thy mother to come with me ...' He stopped and looked awkward. 'I shouldn't have told thee that. It were a long time ago.'

'I already knew. She told me,' said Bessie. 'Were you and my mam sweethearts?'

'Aye, summat like that. But she preferred Titus so I went alone. Have more to eat,' he said, obviously trying to change the subject. 'Don't let it go to waste.'

He talked for a while about his farm until Bessie thought that she ought to get back before her mother started to worry.

'I'll see thee safe home,' he said.

'There's no need.'

'It'll give me a chance to see thy mother again,' he said.

They came out of the Old Bull into the busy market place.

'Where's this glove shop?' he asked.

'Just down Church Street.'

'Come along then.' He took her hand and tucked it inside his elbow so she had no choice but to walk with him. 'Ah, this one,' he said when they reached the window. 'This town has changed a lot since I was last here. Come on!'

The bell jangled as he pushed open the door and held it for her to go in. Miss Cross was behind her counter, and she rushed out to greet them when she saw George.

'Do come in. How may I help you today?'

'We'd like to see the ladies' gloves, please.'

Bessie saw Miss Cross look at her. She wasn't sure if she recognised her, but if she did she said nothing. She waved to the chair by the counter. 'Do sit down. I'll fetch some out. Did you have anything in particular in mind?'

'Aye,' said George. 'Kidskin, lavender, with little buttons.'

Miss Cross placed the gloves on the counter in front of Bessie. They were exquisite.

'Those the ones?' asked George.

'Yes. But—'

'Wrap 'em up for the lady,' he instructed Miss Cross.

'Does madam require a buttonhook as well?'

'Aye. Of course she does. The best tha has.'

'But they're too much,' protested Bessie.

'Nowt's too much for thee,' he said as he pressed the package into her hands.

Chapter Twenty

Titus's feet hurt and his legs ached as they trudged on. The journey to London hadn't seemed half as arduous, but the long walk home seemed to weigh him down at every step. He supposed it was because the march with the petition had been filled with hope and expectation. They'd walked day after day for two weeks, meeting up with other Chartists along the way, until the procession that reached London stretched further from beginning to end than the eye could see. When they'd arrived they'd made their way to a central hall where the sheets of signatures from all across the country were stitched together into a gigantic roll and carefully placed in an elaborate wooden casket that was carried through the streets on the shoulders of local building workers.

Then they'd set out early on the bright May morning to walk to Westminster.

'There's fifty thousand of us!' a man had told Titus as they waited for the people ahead to move off. 'And seven different bands!' Titus had felt proud to be a part of it.

Ahead of them had been men and women with flags blowing in the breeze and they'd been escorted by men on horseback through the streets where people stood, babes in arms and children waving homemade flags of their own, cheering them on their way. They'd marched through Fleet Street, the Strand, past Charing Cross and Horse Guards Parade to Parliament House. All the way, the windows of the buildings had been crowded with curious onlookers.

But it had come to nothing. When they'd arrived at Westminster, the petition had been carried up to the doors like a battering ram. Then the great mass of signatures – more than three million and three hundred thousand they'd said – had been lifted down and rolled out across the floor of the lobby. The men who had carried it were ushered inside to the gallery where they'd listened to the debate. Finally, a bell had rung and all the strangers had come out and the doors had been bolted for the vote.

'Rejected – by two hundred and eighty-seven votes to forty-nine,' someone had told them. A groan of disbelief and disappointment had spread through the crowd.

Now, all they could do was walk home with the bad news. The working man had been refused his rights yet again.

As Titus walked he began to think about John Sharples. How dare he take up with Peggy like that? The Sharples family were all trouble and he was determined that his daughter shouldn't get mixed up with one of them. He wished that the exam for the Queen's Scholarship was sooner. It wasn't that he wanted Peggy to leave home. He would miss her when she was gone, but he knew that she could be stubborn when she set her mind to something and it was a long time from now until December. Still, he'd warned the lad off and he hoped that was enough.

At last the scenery became familiar and they saw landmarks that they recognised. The Pennines in the distance, the swell of Winter Hill, and at last the road into Blackburn.

Titus walked wearily over the bridge and down Water Street. He opened the door and called out: 'I'm back!'

Jennet came in from the yard, her sleeves rolled up and her apron damp. He was so glad to see her. He'd missed her all the time he'd been away and he longed to gather her into his arms and kiss her, but those days were long past, he thought.

He wasn't sure how she'd react if he tried and he was too tired for an argument.

'Sit thee down. I'll make a cup of tea.'

'That'd be more than welcome. I'm fair jiggered,' he said as he watched Jennet move her mother from his chair back to her bed.

'Is it bedtime? It's not bedtime,' she grumbled.

'Let Titus have his chair, Mam. He's just walked all the way from London. How did it go?' Jennet asked him.

'Not well. Thousands of us took yon petition to Parliament, but they turned it down.'

'I'm sorry,' said Jennet. 'I hoped it might do some good – make things better. What'll happen now?'

'I don't rightly know,' he said, 'but there were a lot of unrest on the way back. Folk feel hard done by, and where lawful protest doesn't work, there's always those who'll take t' law into their own hands.'

'How dost tha mean?' she asked.

'There's talk of a general strike, of everyone refusing to work until there's a change of heart from the gentry.' He took the cup of tea she handed to him, stirring in the sugar. 'Ah, that's better,' he said when he'd taken a sip. 'None of these inns seem to know how to make a proper cup o' tea.' He put the cup down and eased his boots from his sore feet. They smelled bad and he could see Jennet wrinkling her nose.

'There's some hot water left over from the washing,' she said. 'I'll fetch thee a bowl and tha can soak 'em for a bit.'

'Aye. That'd be nice. Where's Bessie?' he asked. 'Is she at t' mill?'

'No, there's no work. She's gone out to meet a friend.'

'How's our Peggy? I hope she's stayed away from that Sharples lad.'

'She seems to have come to her senses. She's been studying for her exam,' Jennet told him.

'I'm glad to hear it,' he said. It was one worry less, he thought as he plunged his tired feet into the warm water and sighed with content.

He was just nodding off to sleep, his snores in unison with those of Grandma Chadwick's, when the door opened and made him jump. He pulled his feet from the water. It had gone cold.

Bessie came in, dressed in her Sunday best and followed by a man. He was tall and Titus didn't recognise him at first until Jennet said his name.

'George!'

For a moment they all stared at one another in silence. Not one of them knowing what to say.

'Tha's got a nerve, showing thy face around here again,' growled Titus.

Jennet laid a hand on his arm to restrain him.

'I'm sorry,' said George. 'I didn't know he was back.'

'Just go!' said Jennet.

'I'll see thee again,' he told Bessie, stepping back into the street. They all watched him pass the window. Titus thought that if his feet hadn't been wet and bare he would have gone after him and knocked him to the ground.

'What's he doin' back, sniffin' around?' demanded Titus as he took the towel Jennet handed him to dry his feet. 'I thought he'd gone to America.'

'He's only back for a visit,' said Jennet. 'He came to put a headstone on Lizzie's grave.'

'And where's tha been, all dressed up?' he asked Bessie.

'He took me out to dinner at the Old Bull.'

'What's tha got there?'

He saw Bessie's hands tighten around the package she held. 'It's a gift,' she said.

'What? From him? What's he bought thee?'

'Titus!' He looked at Jennet. She was shaking her head at him, warning him not to say more.

'They're just some gloves,' said Bessie. 'I'll put them away.'

'Titus,' said Jennet again as Bessie went upstairs. 'Say nowt,' she whispered. 'She has no idea.'

'And what about him?' he asked, taking the clean socks she was holding out to him.

'I told him,' admitted Jennet. 'But he'd guessed anyway.'

'And why does she think he's takin' her out to a hotel for her dinner and buying her fancy presents?' Titus was surprised at the jealousy that beset him. He'd always told himself that he felt nothing for the lass. She was no relation to him and he merely tolerated her. But the thought of George Anderton showering her with the things that he could never afford made him hate the man even more.

'I told her that George and I had been close once. I told her he'd asked me to go with him to America. I had to tell her summat,' said Jennet. 'But I never breathed a word to her about the other. I made George swear to keep it secret an' all. Tha mustn't say owt.'

'I won't,' promised Titus as he sat down to put on the socks. 'But she's bound to ask questions.'

Chapter Twenty-One

Bessie sat on the bed and carefully unwrapped the package. The gloves were as soft and as beautiful as she'd hoped. She eased them on and did up the buttons before holding out her hands in front of her to admire them. She'd never had anything as nice or expensive.

George was so generous. No wonder her mother found him attractive. Bessie thought that he was much nicer than her father and wondered why her mother hadn't jumped at the chance of going with him to America. It sounded such a fascinating country – better than this filthy town.

Reluctantly, she took the gloves off, wrapped them carefully in the paper and put them in her drawer. She didn't want Peggy to see them because she felt guilty that her sister had received nothing.

George had asked if she would have dinner with him again and she'd agreed. He'd also said that he would take her and Peggy to the exhibition of phreno-magnetism that was to take place at the Theatre Royal on Saturday night, and later that evening, after her father had gone out, she mentioned it to her mother.

'I don't know,' she said.

'He's invited Peggy as well,' said Bessie.

'I'd like to go,' said Peggy, looking up from the book she was reading. Bessie was surprised that she'd agreed. 'It's scientific,' Peggy told them. 'I've heard about phrenology, so I'd like to see it demonstrated.'

'Will you come?' Bessie asked her mother.

She shook her head.

'But you don't mind if we go?'

'I suppose not,' she said, although she sounded doubtful and Bessie wondered why. It was her mother who had introduced them to George in the first place so it seemed strange that she didn't want them to see him again.

On the Saturday, Bessie put on her little jacket, tied the ribbons of her bonnet under her chin and eased on the kidskin gloves.

'Where did those come from?' asked Peggy, staring at them enviously.

'George bought them for me.'

'Why?'

'I don't know. I just mentioned them and he walked me down to Miss Cross's and bought them.'

'I bet she thought you were his fancy woman!'

'Peggy!' Bessie felt herself blushing with shame at the thought. 'George just wants to be kind. That's why he's taking us to this demonstration. I'm sure he'll buy something for you as well. A parting gift before he leaves.'

'So when's he going?'

'I don't know,' admitted Bessie, 'but our mam thinks he won't stay much longer. It's all a bit awkward now that Father's come home. It's obvious they don't like one another.'

'I heard Dad grumbling about him,' said Peggy. 'He says he's a rogue. I think he's right. There's something fishy about George Anderton even if he isn't the pickpocket.'

'You're willing to let him take you out though.'

'Only because I want to learn more about phrenology. There may be a question about it in my exam.'

Bessie doubted it, but she didn't argue. She didn't want the evening to be spoiled.

Peggy wore her best frock and the bonnet that she'd trimmed for Easter. Bessie knew that she hated the ribbons now that she'd fallen out with John, but her sister was determined not to be outdone.

'Well, ye both look a treat!' said their mother when they came downstairs. 'Don't they look a treat, Titus?'

'Aye,' he said, glancing up from his paper. 'Don't be late,' he warned them.

They met up with George on the steps of the Old Bull and Bessie was pleased to see that Joshua was coming with them, even though he walked a few steps behind as they made their way towards Penny Street. Bessie was sorry. She would have liked to talk to him and find out more about him. When she was having dinner with George she asked him if there were more like Joshua in America.

'Black folk?' he said. 'Aye. There are. Most of 'em were slaves, and tha'd think they were slaves still the way the white folk treat 'em.'

'Was Joshua a slave?' she asked.

George frowned. 'Joshua's a free man,' he said in a tone that made it clear there was nothing more to discuss.

Bessie and Peggy linked arms on either side of George to walk down to the theatre. The streets were busy and they lifted their skirts to cross Penny Street where the waste from the Butcher's Court dwellings was oozing down the centre of the road. There was a bad smell and Peggy pulled a face.

They had to queue to get into the theatre. There was a huge crowd and they were jostled as they made their way to the reserved rows near the front.

Introducing the Great Wizard, Professor Samuel, said the programme that George bought for them, which also promised *startling observations and discoveries in science.*

As they waited for the curtains to part and the great man to come on, Bessie noticed that there was a lot of interest in Joshua. His face remained impassive but she was sure he must be aware of the curious stares and unguarded comments that were being made about his appearance. She could hear people discussing the shape of his head and wondering if he was to be part of the show. She wished that they could have more manners although she remembered with guilt that she had also stared at him when she'd first seen him.

The show commenced and the wizard appeared on the stage in a flash of powder. The bang made everyone jump and one or two ladies screamed. He wore a dark blue coat, spangled with stars and crescent moons, and a tall hat. He arranged himself in the chair that was placed beside a small table, flipping aside the tails of his coat and taking off the hat before leaning forward and addressing them in an intimate tone.

'Ladies and gentlemen,' he said. 'Tonight you are about to witness wonders that have never been seen before on these shores. I will show you not only the art of phrenology, when I will feel the head of any volunteer who dares to come forward and have their personality revealed, but I will also demonstrate the new science of phreno-magnetism, which gives me the ability to manipulate a person's mind and compel them to do whatever I bid!'

There was a gasp and a murmuring of voices.

'If you are afraid to witness this miracle, then I bid you to leave now, before it is too late!' said the wizard.

Bessie felt Peggy nudge her arm.

'You should tell George Anderton to go up and have his head felt,' Peggy said. 'Then we'd know for sure if he's trustworthy or not.'

'Shh!' Bessie tried to give her a look, but it was gloomy in the theatre and she knew that her sister didn't care if she was overheard anyway.

'Does anyone dare approach?' asked the wizard. For a minute or so, no one stirred, but then a man from the second row stood up. 'Come! Come!' called the wizard as the volunteer was helped up on to the stage. 'Come to the chair.'

The man sat down and the wizard proceeded to carefully feel the man's head with his fingertips.

'You are intelligent,' he told him, 'and shrewd, although perhaps a little too quick to anger.'

The man seemed pleased enough with the analysis and shook the wizard by the hand before he came down. He was followed by several other people, all keen to be told what their personalities were. They all seemed satisfied that the wizard was correct, but Bessie supposed it was because he only praised their intellect and said nothing bad. She wondered if he would have told the truth if a criminal had gone up.

'Now!' said the wizard, 'we come to the main part of the demonstration – the science of phreno-magnetism. Can I have a volunteer?'

Bessie grasped Peggy's hand so that she couldn't draw any attention to either George or Joshua, but a volunteer was already on his way to the stage. He was a youngish man, probably in his early twenties, she thought. He paused, as if reluctant, before the wizard waved him forward.

'Thank you. Welcome. Come and sit down in the chair,' said the wizard. 'What is your name?' he asked the man.

'My name is Jack, sir.'

'And do you live in this town?'

'I do, sir.'

'What is your trade?'

'I'm a spinner, sir.'

'Good. Now Jack, I don't want you to be afraid. You must relax and I will attempt to show these esteemed people here tonight the science of phreno-magnetism.'

The wizard now began to make a series of complicated hand movements around Jack's head. After a few minutes he paused and then pressed a finger to the man's skull.

'I call into action the organ of veneration!'

Immediately, Jack fell to his knees and raised his hands as if in prayer. People gasped and there was some applause, which the wizard quieted with a shake of his hand.

'Next,' he said as he pressed on two other places on the man's head, 'the sites of acquisitiveness and secretiveness.'

Jack rose and stared about him, then noticed a small snuffbox which the wizard had left on the table. He picked it up and slipped it into his pocket. There was a cry from the audience.

'Now, repentance!'

The wizard pressed on Jack's head again and after a moment of hesitation, Jack withdrew the snuffbox from his pocket and replaced it on the table. The audience sighed and Bessie heard a few words of approval from those around her.

'Now, aversion.' Jack glared at the wizard and would have stalked off across the stage if he hadn't moved his hands and called 'Benevolence!' At the command the man turned, produced a coin from his pocket and gave it to the wizard. Then Jack was made to sing, to whistle, to recite some verse, to speak in French and Italian, and finally suck on an orange that was in his pocket. The audience were held spellbound.

Then the wizard announced that he would enable Jack to see through the back of his head and a gentleman was called up from the front row to act as a witness. The wizard stood behind Jack. He took out his pocket watch and held it up for the audience to see with a finger to his lips to warn them to remain silent.

'What have I here?' he asked Jack.

'A pocket watch, sir!'

The audience applauded.

Then the wizard made a show of altering the hands on his timepiece. 'And what time does it say on this watch?' he asked.

'Five and twenty minutes to eight o'clock, sir.'

The wizard showed the watch to the witness, who nodded in amazement, and the audience applauded as both men were thanked and left the stage.

'What did tha make of that?' George asked them afterwards when he'd taken them back to the Old Bull for some supper before they went home.

'It could have been trickery,' said Bessie.

'So tha thinks t' other chap were in on it?'

'It's possible, isn't it?' she asked, hoping that George didn't think she was being foolish.

'Not only possible, but probable,' he agreed. 'How many folk walk a round with an orange in their pocket?'

'But he had a lovely singing voice,' said Peggy. 'And you don't know that it was a trick. Phreno-magnetism is a science and you shouldn't laugh at science.'

'Aye, science is important,' agreed George. 'But there's trickery as well, and tha shouldn't confuse the two. I've seen many a man tricked out of his money with card games and such, so I always remain a bit sceptical about these scientific demonstrations. It were good entertainment though.'

'That's him! Isn't it?' asked Peggy as a fair-haired man made his way into the dining room, attracting much attention as he passed each table, smiling and shaking hands. He had taken off the spangled coat and hat, but his smart trousers and coloured waistcoat were unmistakably those of the wizard.

'Aye, I think it is,' said George.

'Will he speak to us?' Bessie could hear the awe and excitement in her sister's voice and Peggy almost squeaked as the wizard came across to their table.

'Good evening! I'm Professor Samuel. Were you at the demonstration?' he asked.

'Aye, we were,' said George.

'I hope you found it interesting.'

'It were good entertainment,' answered George although he ignored the wizard's outstretched hand.

Bessie saw that the wizard was younger than he appeared on the stage. He was good-looking too and his smile was easy. He looked down at Peggy who was staring up at him in awe.

'Perhaps the ladies would like to have their heads felt when they've finished their supper? I have a room here at the hotel to see my more discerning clients in privacy.'

'I'm very interested in science!' Peggy told him.

'No,' said George firmly. 'It's late and it's time I escorted the ladies home.'

'Perhaps tomorrow?'

George frowned. 'I think not,' he said, and the wizard moved away to speak to some other diners.

'It wouldn't have done any harm to let him read our heads,' grumbled Peggy later when they'd got home and gone to bed.

'I suspect George thought he was a fraudster,' said Bessie.

'Nonsense,' muttered Peggy. 'He's just too stupid to understand science.'

Chapter Twenty-Two

The following Monday, Peggy reached for her shawl as soon as Miss Parkinson dismissed the girls for their dinner. She hurried down Thunder Alley, towards the market place. She hesitated at the entrance to the Old Bull, but then climbed the steps and spoke to the landlord.

'I'm here to ask about a consultation with the phrenologist,' she told him.

As she waited, she saw a door open and Professor Samuel came out with a lady in a large hat. She was thanking him and he kissed her hand.

He saw Peggy and smiled. 'Good afternoon! We spoke the other day, didn't we? You were having dinner with another lady, your sister? And your father?'

'He's not my father! He had no right to speak for me like that. I'd like to have a consultation with you – if it's possible. You did offer a reading ...'

'I did. I would very much like to read your head. I can see that you are a very astute lady,' he replied with a smile.

'I'm studying to be a schoolteacher.'

'Are you? That's very commendable. Would you like a reading now?'

Peggy hesitated. She knew there would be a charge and she wasn't sure if the coins in her purse would be enough.

'How much is it?' she asked.

He smiled again. 'I think that for a schoolteacher there would be no charge,' he told her. 'Come. Come in.'

The professor held the door to his room open and Peggy went in. An easy chair had been arranged at the centre of the room. There were flowers in a vase on the table and the blinds were drawn to shut out most of the daylight.

'May I take your shawl and bonnet?' He held out his hand as she took them off and handed them to him. He hung them carefully on a coat-stand. 'Please, sit down. What's your name?'

'Margaret,' she said as she glanced at the chair with its plump cushion. She guessed that it was stuffed with feathers and would be soft and comfortable to sink into, but she found that she

196

was reluctant now that she was alone with him. If her parents found out she would be in trouble.

'There's nothing to be afraid of,' he reassured her. 'All I will do is touch your head. It won't be painful at all.'

She seated herself in the chair and waited as he stood behind her. After a moment she felt his fingers on her scalp. They were gentle but firm as they probed the contours of her head, and her feelings of alarm subsided as she found it quite soothing.

'Ah, yes. The area related to verbal memory is very prominent,' he said, 'although the area of calculation is less so. You may find it harder to teach mathematics and arithmetic than reading and writing,' he said.

'That's true,' agreed Peggy. 'I'm not so fond of numbers as I am of words.'

'The site of causality is large,' he said as he moved his fingers to the front of her head, above her right eye. 'You are good at understanding the reasons behind events. That is an admirable skill,' he told Peggy as she wondered if it were true. Was she good at seeing the causes and effects of things that happened? She was sure now that John Sharples had only befriended her to get back at her parents. She was sorry that she had ever trusted him, let alone allowed herself to grow fond of him. If anyone was a trickster, then surely he was.

The phrenologist now moved his fingers towards the top of her head. 'Ah,' he said, 'here is conscientiousness, and hope, adjacent to it. You have a love of truth and duty, and an optimism about future events.'

'Is ... is there anything bad?' she asked.

'Not that I can feel. The qualities you have all seem to be good ones. Undesirable traits such as combativeness and destructiveness are not apparent.'

He came to face her and Peggy looked up at him. Even though the room was gloomy she saw that his eyes were blue. So many people seemed to have blue eyes, she thought. It was confusing. They couldn't all be criminals. She was sure now that it was the shape and contours of the skull that reflected a person's personality. Their eye colour was unimportant. Pickpockets must have very irregularly shaped heads, she thought, suddenly thinking of John Sharples.

The professor smiled down at her. 'It has been a pleasure,' he told her. 'It isn't often that I have a consultation with someone of such admirable traits. I'm sure you will make an excellent schoolteacher. In fact, I know that you will excel at anything you turn your hand to.'

Peggy felt her cheeks blush at his praise. 'Thank you,' she said. 'You are very kind.' Then she recalled that her dinner hour must be almost over. 'I must go,' she told him, although she found that she was now so comfortable in his chair that she was reluctant to leave.

'So soon?' he asked.

'I must go back to my work.'

'Where do you teach?'

'At the Girls' School, on Thunder Alley. Do you know it?'

'Yes. I know where it is.'

'Then you're not a stranger to Blackburn?' she asked him.

'I've been here before,' he said as he settled the shawl around her, letting his hands rest on her shoulders for a moment. She could feel his breath on her face. 'It was many years ago.'

'And how long do you mean to stay?' she asked.

'For a while. I have many people who wish to consult me.' He seemed to collect himself. 'My other patients will be waiting,' he said, 'but perhaps we could meet again? You say you are interested in science. Maybe I could instruct you further in phrenology? There have been many recent developments, as you saw in my demonstration.'

'I would like that,' said Peggy.

'Could I offer you supper? Perhaps on Friday evening? At six o'clock?'

'Yes,' agreed Peggy. She wasn't sure what excuse she could make to slip out of the house, but she would think of something. This man interested her and she wanted to learn more about the science he'd studied. It was essential, she told herself as she ran back to Thunder Alley. There was sure to be a question about such an important subject in her exam.

She saw that the girls had returned to the classroom when she opened the door. Her mood plummeted. She knew she was in trouble even before she saw Miss Parkinson's face.

'I am very sorry,' she said, throwing her shawl on to its hook and hurrying to give out the knitting needles and wool to the group of girls she was supposed to be supervising. Miss Parkinson said nothing, but after the pupils had been dismissed at the end of the afternoon, she called Peggy to the front of the room.

'I am disappointed, Margaret,' she told her. 'Up until now I thought that you were an admirable girl who worked hard and was always punctual. But lately you have been remiss, and now you are late back from the dinner hour, throwing the whole of the afternoon into disarray. Even your aunt and uncle didn't know where you were and they were very concerned.'

'I am sorry,' said Peggy. 'I had an errand to run.'

'An errand?' repeated Miss Parkinson as she puffed herself up in disapproval. 'Errands are not to be undertaken in school time. You have responsibilities here, Margaret. You are only allowed to leave the premises to eat your dinner and study with your uncle. You are not allowed to go off on errands.' She made the word sound as if it was only one step away from delinquency.

'It won't happen again,' said Peggy.

'I should think not.' Miss Parkinson paused to allow her words to sink in. 'If you miss any more of your work then I will be forced to think very carefully about my decision to recommend you for the Queen's Scholarship,' she told her. 'I cannot recommend a girl who is tardy and not to be relied upon.'

Peggy looked down at the dusty floor. She was sorry that she'd let the teacher down by losing track of the time. She wondered whether to try to excuse herself by explaining that she had used the time to begin a study of phrenology, but she was unsure if Miss Parkinson would approve. It would be hard to explain that there had been nothing wrong in spending her dinner hour alone in a room with a man she barely knew. She was in enough bother as it was, without making things worse.

'You can sweep and tidy the room and then you had better see your aunt before you go home,' said Miss Parkinson, softening slightly. 'She was worried.'

'Yes, Miss Parkinson.'

Peggy fetched the broom from the cupboard and brushed the floor, taking care to leave it spotless. As she worked she wondered what to tell Auntie Hannah. It would have to be something to satisfy her enough to prevent her saying something to her mother.

'I met an old friend who's just come back to town,' she told her when she called at the schoolhouse next door. 'I lost track of the time. I'm so sorry.' Peggy wondered whether she would ever have to stop apologising.

'Well, be sure to tell me in future,' warned her auntie. 'We didn't know where tha'd gone – and we were worried.'

'I know. I'm sorry,' she said again and, as her auntie was busy with the children, she managed to slip away without needing to say any more.

Chapter Twenty-Three

'They're asking us to go back full-time, but to take another pay cut,' grumbled Titus when he came back from a meeting with the mill owner.

'Surely it's better than short time?' said Jennet.

He shook his head. 'Why should we work more hours for hardly any more money?' he asked. 'Wages are less than they were twenty years ago,' he complained, 'and the price of food and rent keeps going up. Masters have to learn to pay us a fair wage if they want us to work. If not, folks are going to refuse. There's talk of bringing all the workers out on strike to support us.'

Jennet continued to fold washing. She knew that he was repeating the views of the Chartists. Their disappointment at the petition being rejected by Parliament had made them even more radical in their fight for justice. But Jennet knew that justice would come at a high price if there was a strike. The little bit she'd saved when he and Bessie were in work was almost all gone and soon there wouldn't be enough to keep putting food on the table.

'I think it would be better to go back,' she said. 'I'd be happier if our Bessie was working. Having nowt to do is allowing her too much time to be meeting up with George Anderton and I can't help but wonder how long it will be before he says summat, or she guesses.' Although she would be sorry to see him go, Jennet wished that George would return to America. What was done, was done. It was too far in the past to change anything.

'I would like to go back to work,' Bessie told her when she came in. 'But Father and the other men have said no, so I can't defy them.'

'Tha's a good lass,' said Jennet. 'I think thy father's mistaken in this. I don't think yon mill owners will back down.'

'George says it's different in America.'

'George?' she repeated. 'That's a bit forward, our Bessie. I think tha should be referring to him as Mr Anderton and showing a bit of respect!'

'He asked me to call him George.'

'Did he indeed?' She needed to have a word with him, thought Jennet. Things were going to run out of control if she didn't convince him to end this friendship with her daughter.

'He's been very kind to me,' said Bessie.

'Well, don't set too much store by it,' said Jennet. 'He'll be off home soon.'

'I'm not so sure,' said Bessie. She sat down at the table and watched Jennet as she ironed shirts.

'What makes tha say that?' Jennet was wary and kept her eyes firmly fixed on her work. She hadn't damaged a single item since the awful incident when she'd burned Mrs Pickering's blouse when Peggy was ill, and she didn't want something like that to happen ever again.

'I think there's something he wants to ask me.'

'What makes tha say that?'

'Well, he doesn't bother with our Peggy. It's only ever me.' She paused and Jennet glanced at her. 'Mam,' she said, reaching out a hand to stop Jennet working. 'I'm worried about what he wants.'

Jennet put the iron down on the hearth and turned to face her daughter. How long could she keep this secret, she wondered. How long would it be before she was forced to confess the whole sorry story to her daughter? She cursed George Anderton for turning up again. There would have been no problem if he'd just stayed in America.

'I've heard about men ...' Bessie was fiddling with the edge of the tablecloth. She looked uncomfortable but Jennet gave her time to have her say. 'I've heard that some older men like younger lasses,' she said. 'And he's a widower. I think he might be looking to get wed again because he keeps telling me about America and how nice it is there. I'm worried he might be planning on proposing to me,' she confessed.

'No!' Jennet couldn't help herself. She heard the horror in her voice and wished she hadn't said it like that. 'No,' she repeated, trying to sound reassuring this time. 'He's not going to ask thee to marry him. Tha need have no worries about that.'

'How can you be so certain?' asked Bessie. 'If that isn't what he wants, then what?'

'How dost tha know he wants owt? He's just being nice.'

'No, it's more than that,' said Bessie. 'Sometimes I catch him looking at me in an odd sort of way, and it makes me wonder what he's thinking.' She looked up at Jennet. 'Is there something you haven't told me?' she asked.

'Like what?' asked Jennet, folding the shirts ready to take back to Richmond Terrace.

'I don't know. Mam?' Jennet saw the pleading look on her daughter's face. 'If you're so sure he's not going to ask me to marry him, then there's a reason. You and him – you're keeping a secret.

Aren't you?' she asked when Jennet didn't reply immediately.

Jennet put the laundry aside and sat down at the table with Bessie, wondering what to tell her. 'When thy father were taken to prison, George was good to me,' she began. 'He helped me out with fetching water and brought a bit of extra food for me and Peggy whenever he could. I didn't know how I could get to Lancaster to hear the trials at the Assizes, but George had been paid a bit o' money for some work he'd done on a machine at t' mill, and he got us a couple of seats on the coach. I were that grateful to him, I can tell thee. I didn't want Titus to face it alone. There were talk of folk being sent off to Australia, or worse.' She paused, but Bessie said nothing, waiting for her to continue. 'He asked me to go to America with him, and when I thought Titus were going to be transported, I were tempted. I knew it would be hard to manage alone with a child. But when Titus were sent to prison, there were no question of leaving. George went on his own.'

'I know all this already,' said Bessie, 'but there's something else. There's something else you're not telling me.'

Jennet met her daughter's blue eyes and wondered if she'd guessed. 'Aye, there's more,' she said, ashamed at having to confess it. 'When we were in Lancaster, George got us a room, at an inn down by the quay. It were busy because of the Assizes and he could only get the one room. Well ... one thing led to another ...'

Bessie didn't understand at first; then Jennet saw the realisation on her face.

'You had a brush with him?'

Jennet felt her cheeks glowing and it wasn't just the heat from the fire. She felt ashamed and she hated the way that Bessie was staring at her, as if she couldn't believe she'd done such a thing.

'Aye,' she said after a moment. 'I was upset. He comforted me. One thing led to another. It shouldn't have happened,' she added, 'but we all make mistakes sometimes.'

'But what's it to do with me?'

Jennet didn't answer. She gave her daughter time to fathom it out for herself.

'Is he my father?' Bessie asked after a moment.

Jennet nodded. 'Aye,' she said.

Bessie just stared at her, looking confused, although Jennet could see that her mind was whirling as so many things began to make sense to her. 'But ...' she began and Jennet realised that Bessie had so many questions she didn't know where to start. 'Why didn't you tell me?' she managed to ask at last.

'Tha were never supposed to know. We decided that it were best if nowt were said, and nothing would have been said if George hadn't come back.'

'Does he know?'

Jennet nodded. 'He knows now. He didn't before he went. I didn't even know I were expectin' until after he'd gone.'

'Well, it explains it,' said Bessie.

'How dost tha mean?'

'Father – Titus, I mean. It explains why he always favours our Peggy and as often as not treats me like he hates me.'

'He doesn't hate thee!' protested Jennet. 'Where's tha goin'?' she asked as Bessie stood up.

'Out. I need time to think,' her daughter told her.

'Don't go doin' owt foolish,' she pleaded, wondering where Bessie was thinking of going. Bessie didn't reply. Her face was anguished as she reached for her shawl. Jennet tried to hug her, but Bessie pushed her away and hurried out of the house. Jennet watched her pass the window. She was crying, and it made Jennet cry too. She cried because she couldn't go back and alter what had happened and she dearly wished that she could because it had caused so much trouble – not just for her, but for Titus and the lasses too. They all deserved better, and she knew that she'd failed them.

Chapter Twenty-Four

Bessie walked and walked with no clear idea of where she was going. She walked until the ground beneath her feet began to rise, until the smoke of the mill chimneys began to diminish and until she realised that she was heading up the track to her grandparents' house at Ramsgreave. She'd always gone to find her grandad when she was upset about something and she wished that she could talk to him now. She wondered if he'd known. She wondered how many other people knew.

It explained her eyes, she thought. People always commented on her blue eyes. When she pictured George she remembered that his eyes were the same. It must be true then, she thought – he was her father. At least he wasn't going to ask her to marry him. She wouldn't have liked that. He was nice, but he was much too old to be

211

a husband. Besides, it was Joshua who interested her. She wished that she knew more about him. He was often around, in the background, when she met George, but he rarely spoke to her.

She reached the cottage. It was peaceful and she sat down on the old wooden bench that her grandfather had made. She'd often sat there beside him when he was alive and she tried to conjure up his presence, but she'd found that as time passed his face became less clear, as if he were slipping further and further away from her.

'What shall I do, Grandad?' she asked him. A robin flew close to her and perched on a branch of the apple tree, singing. Bessie hoped that it was a sign, although the answer to her question wasn't clear.

She sat for a long time, not wanting to go home, but at last she left reluctantly and began to walk back. No wonder George had taken such an interest in her, she thought. Not only had he bought her gifts, he'd kept asking her what she wanted to do with her life. He'd talked about her having a shop, but she'd dismissed it as impossible. Now she wondered if he intended to give her money. He was obviously wealthy and could afford it. She wasn't sure that she wanted to take his money, though. It didn't seem right when she barely knew him. And once he went back to

America she'd probably never see him again. She needed to talk to him about it, she thought, and picked up her pace.

It was late when she arrived back in Blackburn, even though there was still full daylight in the early summer sky. She knew she should go straight home. She knew that her mother would be worrying about her, but this couldn't wait. She needed to see George, her father, and tell him that she knew everything.

She hurried up the steps to the door of the Old Bull. The landlord recognised her.

'Are you looking for Mr Anderton?' he asked.

'Is he here?'

'I'll go and see. Sit down a moment,' he said and Bessie rested on one of the plush chairs that were set about the lobby.

A few minutes later she saw Joshua coming towards her.

'Good evening, Miss Eastwood.'

'Good evening, Joshua. I was looking for Mr Anderton.'

'He's gone out, miss. I don't know how long he'll be.'

'Oh.' Bessie was disappointed. All the way back from Ramsgreave she'd been rehearsing in her head what she was going to say, and now it would have to wait.

'Was it important, miss?' Joshua looked concerned and Bessie realised that she must look a fright with her hair unbrushed and her skirt covered in mud. She usually took trouble to look smart before she set foot in the Old Bull.

'No. Well, yes, it was,' she confessed. 'But it can wait until tomorrow.'

'Can I get you something, miss? You look tired.' Bessie was forced to smile at his tactful description. 'I'll order some tea,' he said.

Before she had a chance to protest he'd gone to find the landlord and she waited until he came back. It would be unforgivably bad manners to slip out without telling him. Besides, even though she was so upset, she knew that she'd been given a rare opportunity to talk to Joshua alone.

He came back and pointed to the chair on the other side of the low table. 'May I?'

'Of course,' she said and watched as he flipped aside the tails of his long jacket and sat down, crossing one leg over the other. His leather boots shone in the light of the lamps and she could see that his shirt and collar were immaculately clean. He dressed like gentry yet acted with servitude and she couldn't quite weigh him up.

'Have you known Mr Anderton long?' she asked him as they waited for the tea to come.

'One, maybe two years now,' he said. 'He's been good to me.'

'What do you do?' she asked. 'Back in America?'

'I work as an overlooker for Mr Anderton, on the farm. I'm a free man now,' he told her. 'Same as everyone in Wisconsin.'

'A free man,' repeated Bessie. George had said the same thing about Joshua, but she wasn't sure what it meant. She wondered if he'd been in prison, but didn't like to ask.

'Yes, miss. Everyone is a free man in Wisconsin, no matter what they say.'

Bessie nodded and the tea arrived. The teapot and hot water jug were placed on the table between them, with china cups and saucers, a jug of milk and a plate of bread and butter. Bessie suddenly realised how hungry she was. She reached for a slice and ate it quickly as she watched the maid pour the tea for them.

'Have you not always been a free man?' she asked Joshua, hoping that she wasn't prying too much.

'No, miss. I was born a slave.'

'A slave!' His words shocked her.

'Yes, miss. My mother was owned by a planta-tion man down in Mississippi. We were field slaves. We worked in the cotton fields, planting and gathering the cotton.'

Bessie stared at him. She could hardly believe what he was telling her. 'It must have been hard work,' she said, thinking of the huge bundles of raw cotton that were brought to the mills on the backs of carts. She knew that they came over the sea from America, but she'd never given much thought to who picked it.

'Yes, miss. We toiled from sunup to sundown. We had to pick a set amount of cotton each day. My mother found it hard.' He looked away from her and Bessie could see that he was upset. She reached out and put a hand on his arm.

'Where is she now?' she asked.

'She died, miss,' he said. 'They worked her to death, threatening her with the whip. It was too much for her. She died,' he repeated and pulled a handkerchief from his pocket to discreetly wipe his face.

Bessie was horrified. 'How old was she?'

'I don't rightly know, miss.'

'And what about your father?'

Joshua's expression darkened. He looked angry and resentful. 'Master fathered me,' he told her. 'Mother didn't have no say in that either.' She saw his fists clench and his shoulders stiffen. She was unsure what to say and wondered if she'd been wrong to question him about his family.

'How did you become a free man?' she asked.

He hesitated for a moment as he fought down his emotions. 'I ran away, miss. I'm a runaway,' he whispered as he glanced around, seeming to worry that he might be overheard. 'I ran away north and managed to reach Wisconsin, a free state. Mr Anderton found me, half-starved and nearly naked, trying to steal fruit from his apple orchard. I expected a beating, but he took me into his own kitchen and fed me. I'd never known kindness like it before ... I've said too much,' he told her after a moment. 'Mr Anderton warned me to say nothing. He said folk didn't want to hear about it. All this ...' he went on, looking around at the diners and travellers who were walking past and giving them suspicious looks. 'All this comes at a price.' He was angry now and Bessie felt awkward.

'I shouldn't have asked. I'm sorry,' she apologised.

'I'm glad you did, miss. I'm glad you know what I am.'

It explained why he was always so reserved, so polite and almost reverential towards George, she thought, but she could see what a terrible burden he carried.

'You'll not say anything, miss?' He looked worried now.

'Of course not.'

'Please don't tell Mr Anderton I told you.'

'Not if you don't want me to.' She picked up her cup and drank down the tea. 'I'd better go,' she said. 'Will you tell Mr Anderton that I'll call on him tomorrow?'

'I will, miss. Shall I see you home?'

'No, there's no need,' she said, pulling her shawl around her. 'Thank you for the tea,' she added, hoping that she wouldn't be in trouble when she got back.

Chapter Twenty-Five

'She knows,' Jennet told Titus when he came in. 'Bessie. She knows that George is her father.'

'Did he tell her?'

'No.' Jennet shook her head. 'It were me,' she said and explained what had happened.

'How did she take it?' he asked.

'She were upset. She went off. She's not come back yet.' Jennet glanced towards the window and saw that it was growing dark. 'I hope she's all right,' she said, her mind filled with the images of a hundred and one calamities that might have befallen her daughter. She just wished that Bessie would come home. 'I tried to explain that we kept it secret for her own good, but she wasn't in a mood to listen. I never thought George would come back. Maybe I'd have been honest with her if I'd ever thought he would.'

'Well, perhaps it's for the best that it's out in the open,' said Titus as he warmed his feet at the fireside. 'He might do summat for her. He seems to have plenty o' brass.'

'Aye,' said Jennet, thinking that Titus would be glad to be relieved of any responsibility for the lass.

She looked towards the window again as she heard footsteps, but they went past, down the street. 'I just wish she'd come home,' she said.

'She'll be back soon enough,' said Titus, filling his pipe with a twist of tobacco.

'Hast tha seen thy sister?' asked Jennet as soon as Peggy came in.

'Aye. She was coming out of the Old Bull. I think she's been with George Anderton again. I'll swear she's sweet on him!' Peggy laughed.

'She's no such thing!' snapped Jennet and Peggy looked taken aback.

'I was only saying,' she grumbled and went upstairs to put her bonnet away.

Peggy lingered in the bedroom. She could hear her parents talking in the back kitchen and she heard Bessie's name. She stood with the door slightly open, trying to catch what they were saying, but they were using fierce whispers and she wondered what her sister had done.

She was just trying to decide whether to go down or wait for her mother to call her when she heard her sister come in. Their mother's voice softened as she fussed over her and after a few minutes Bessie came up the stairs. Her skirt was dirty, her hair was untidy and she looked as if she had a lot on her mind.

'Where have you been?' asked Peggy, knowing that her sister could never have got into that state at the Old Bull.

'I walked up to Ramsgreave to look at the cottage.'

Peggy didn't ask why she'd been in the Old Bull afterwards, but it was plain that something was wrong. 'I think you're in trouble. They've been talking about you,' she said.

'What did they say?' asked Bessie.

'I don't know. I couldn't hear. But they were asking if I'd seen you when I came in. What's happened?' she asked as her sister sat down on the bed. 'Tell me,' insisted Peggy. 'Something's wrong. I can see that.'

Bessie looked up and Peggy saw that tears were welling in her eyes. 'He's not my father,' she said.

'What? Who?'

'Him.' Bessie jerked her thumb towards the staircase. 'Your father. He's not my father.'

'What do you mean not your father?'

'It's George Anderton,' she said. 'George Anderton's my father.'

Peggy stared at her. She wasn't sure what to say.

'Are you sure?' she asked after a moment. Bessie nodded and wiped her cheek with her hand. 'How do you know?'

'Mam told me.'

Peggy listened in disbelief as her sister related the story of what had taken place in Lancaster all those years ago.

'I never would have believed it of our mam,' she said when Bessie had finished. 'Just think – we could have been Americans if she'd gone with him! And he's rich. We'd have been like gentry,' she said, imagining an existence where she had a carriage and a maid and went out to supper parties.

'I doubt it,' said Bessie. 'He might have money now, but he's had to work hard for it.'

'What are you going to do?' asked Peggy. 'He might offer to take you back to America with him. Will you go?'

'I don't know.' Bessie sounded bewildered. 'I feel like I don't know anything any more. Besides, I haven't had a chance to talk to him yet. I went to the Old Bull but he wasn't there.'

*

The next morning, after Peggy had gone to school and Titus had gone off to one of his meetings, Bessie came downstairs, dressed as befitted a visit to the Old Bull and wearing her lavender gloves. She was still surprised that the landlord had let her in the day before, in her working clothes and shawl. She must have looked such a mess, sitting with Joshua and drinking tea in her dirty skirts and mud-covered boots.

'I'm going out for a bit,' she said to her mother. They hadn't spoken properly since the revelations of the day before. When she'd come in last night, she'd said that she was going straight to bed and even though all she'd eaten was bread and butter she'd refused the offer of food and a hot drink because she couldn't face sitting at the table whilst her mother quizzed her about where she'd been.

'Is tha meeting him?' asked her mother. She didn't need to say who.

'If he's there. I looked for him last night, but he'd gone out,' she said. She hated the sad look on her mother's face. She wanted to make things right between them, but she wasn't ready to forgive her yet for keeping the truth from her.

Her mother nodded. 'Don't be late back,' she said. 'I were that worried about thee last night ...'

She didn't need to say that she'd thought Bessie had done something foolish. It was clear from her face.

'I'm sorry,' Bessie apologised. 'I didn't mean to worry you. I just needed some time to take it all in.'

Her mother nodded again and, taking it as permission to go, Bessie closed the door gently behind her and set off. She felt nervous. It was stupid, she told herself. It wasn't as if she was meeting him for the first time, but now it was different. Now she knew that he was her father.

When she reached the Old Bull, he was sitting in the lobby, reading a newspaper. She had the impression that he was waiting for her.

He stood up and folded the paper when he saw her.

'Bessie,' he greeted her. 'Joshua said tha were here last night, lookin' for me?' He seemed anxious.

'I know,' she blurted out. 'Mam told me everything.'

He reached out and grasped her hand, folding his other hand over the top of it. 'I'm glad,' he said, looking directly at her. 'I was longing to tell thee but thy mother had made me swear I wouldn't. Tha's not upset about it, is tha?' he asked, looking concerned.

'It was a shock,' she said, 'but then it was a relief, because I'd always had this feeling that something wasn't quite right.'

He nodded. 'Coffee?' he asked as he drew her towards a chair. 'Or chocolate?'

'Chocolate,' she said. 'Please.'

He ordered it and they were both awkward as they sat and waited for it to come. Before, they'd talked easily, but now it seemed that they were both overcome with shyness.

'I had no idea,' he said. 'I hope tha knows that. I had no idea until I came back. And then, the first time I saw thee, I felt as if I already knew thee. It were strange and I couldn't fathom it at first, but then it dawned on me – although it took longer than it should have done. Tha looks just like my mother,' he said. 'She were right pretty, just like thee.'

Bessie was glad that the chocolate came just then. She was disconcerted by the way he was staring at her. She busied herself with the little pots, pouring some for him and handing him a cup.

'When Joshua said that tha'd come in lookin' for me I wondered if tha'd found out the truth,' he said. 'I'm sorry I wasn't here. I had some business over Preston way and wasn't back until late. I wondered about callin' round, but I didn't want to upset Titus again.' He took a sip of his chocolate. 'Has he been good to thee?' he asked.

'My father? Titus?' she added, correcting herself.

George waited for her answer.

'I've never gone without,' she told him, 'but it was obvious to me, even when I was little, that he favoured Peggy. I suppose I can't blame him. It's not every man that would have agreed to bring up another man's child.' She thought of the workhouse with a shiver of horror. At least she hadn't been sent there.

'I wish I could make it up to thee,' said George. 'I wish things could have been different.'

'Do you think my mother would have gone with you – if she'd known?' asked Bessie.

He shook his head. 'Tha'd have to ask her that question. But I wish she had. I'd have been a good father to thee, and Peggy an' all.'

'I know you would.'

'I will make it up to thee,' he said. 'What can I do? Anything. I have money. Dost tha want a glove shop?'

'I don't know,' she said. 'It's all been so sudden. I'm not sure what to think.'

'I'll not see thee goin' back to workin' twelve hours a day in yon mill, that's for sure,' he told her. 'Not a daughter of mine. Tha's not to set foot in that place again.'

'I can't go back whilst there's this talk of a general strike anyway.'

'Tha must be short of money.'

Bessie watched as he unfolded a five-pound note. 'No,' she said. 'I can't take that. What would I do with it? It's too much!'

'Happen so, but tha must have summat for thy purse,' he said, digging into his pocket for change and taking out some shillings and florins and half a crown which he tipped into her palm. 'And don't go givin' it all to thy mother,' he warned her. 'It's for thee.'

Bessie put the coins in her purse and tied it tightly with the strings. She'd never seen so much money in her life and she was terrified of losing it.

'I'll not go back to America until I've seen thee settled,' he told her. 'I need to know tha's all right before I sail. If it isn't a glove shop tha wants, then what? Maybe a tea shop?'

'I'm not sure that I want a shop,' she said, over-whelmed by his generosity.

'Then have a think about what tha does want,' he told her. 'Whatever it is, I'll see thee right.'

She nodded. The idea of making choices was new to her. She'd always done as she was told and now she'd no clear idea of what she could ask for. The idea of working for herself appealed to her, but she had mixed feelings about not going back to the mill. She wondered what her friend Ruth would say. She would miss working beside her and seeing her every day.

Bessie glanced up to see Joshua at the other side of the lobby. George beckoned him to come over.

'Excuse me for interrupting,' said Joshua. 'The gentlemen from Preston have arrived.'

'Aye, I'll come,' said George. He looked apologetic. 'I'm sorry to leave thee so soon,' he told Bessie, 'but I've business to attend to. Joshua will see thee home.'

Bessie stood up. George leaned towards her and kissed her cheek. 'I'm right glad there's no secrets any more,' he said. 'Think on what I said, won't thee?'

'I will,' she promised before he strode off to meet two men who greeted him with warm handshakes.

'Railwaymen,' said Joshua.

'Railway?'

'Aye, miss. They were the gents Mr Anderton was seeing last night. He wants to invest in their railroad. They're planning to link Preston to Blackburn with a new line. Let me see you home, miss,' he said.

228

She nodded and took the arm that he offered as they reached the street.

'Let's walk through the market,' she said, wanting to spend a little more time with him.

They strolled through the stalls and before long Bessie became aware of the attention they were attracting.

'Does it bother you?' she asked. 'The way people stare?'

'I suppose they ain't seen nothing like me before,' he said. 'It makes 'em curious.'

'Do people stare at you in America?'

He shook his head. 'In America it's like you don't exist unless your skin is white. I think I'd rather be stared at than made to feel worthless.'

They walked on until they came to the bridge at the end of Water Street.

'This is where I live,' said Bessie. 'Would you like to come in?'

'No, miss.' He shook his head emphatically. 'No disrespect, miss, but Mr Anderton might be needing me.'

'Of course. Thank you for walking with me.'

'It was a pleasure!' He gave her his widest smile and tipped his hat before walking back the way they'd come. Bessie saw a couple of women nudge each other and watch him go by, their mouths agape. He touched his hat to them and they moved on, pulling their shawls more tightly around themselves. Bessie felt a little sorry for him, but she felt an odd pride in him as well. Pride that he'd felt able to confide in her about his past. Pride that she hoped he might think of her as a friend.

Chapter Twenty-Six

The good thing about all the fuss over Bessie was that Peggy was able to slip out of the house on the Friday evening without anyone noticing. She walked up to the Old Bull and went in. It was becoming quite a habit, she thought.

The landlord seemed to recognise her.

'Miss Eastwood,' she reminded him. 'I'm here to meet Professor Samuel, the phrenologist.'

'Of course. I was told to expect you. Please, come this way.'

Peggy followed him into the dining room where the wizard was waiting. He stood up when he saw her and greeted her warmly.

'Shall we serve the food now, Mr Samuel?' asked the landlord.

'Yes, please do.' He settled Peggy on to a chair and smiled at her warmly. 'I'm so pleased you came.'

'Did you think I might not?'

'I wasn't sure,' he admitted. 'Tell me about yourself,' he said when he'd seated himself. 'You rushed off so quickly the other afternoon that I had no opportunity to learn anything about you.'

'You know that I'm a schoolteacher – well, an assistant at the moment, and that I'm determined to better myself.'

He nodded. 'I know that,' he said, leaning forward in his chair. 'But what about your family? Is your father a very important man?'

Peggy shook out the linen napkin and spread it across the skirt of her Sunday-best frock. 'He's not important at all,' she said. 'He's just an ordinary working man.'

'I don't believe that!' said the wizard. 'I'm sure he must be an extraordinary man to have a daughter like you. What work does he do?'

'He's a cotton spinner. Although he's not working at the moment. The mill owner wants the workers to go back for less money – but they won't.'

'I've heard about the trouble,' he said. 'Not so much from the workers, but from the wives of the mill owners who've been to see me. They're troubled,' he told her. 'They tell me that their husbands are struggling to sell what's woven and can't afford to pay any more.'

'My father says that's nonsense,' said Peggy. 'He says it's greed and a determination to keep the working man in his place. He went to London with the People's Charter.'

'So he's a Chartist? I knew that there would be something special about him. I'd like to read his head.'

'He wouldn't come,' said Peggy.

'That's a shame. Tell me about your mother.'

'She's a laundress.'

'And have you any more brothers and sisters, apart from the one I met?'

'No, there's just me and Bessie.'

'So, you do come from an ordinary family,' he concluded. 'I thought that you must be the daughter of one of the gentry who have the big houses on King Street. But ...' He lowered his voice and beckoned her to lean towards him. 'Their heads do not always reveal the qualities that yours does. Of course, I hesitate to tell them, but some have distinctly poor shapes to their skulls.'

'How long have you been a phrenologist?' Peggy asked him.

'Oh, quite a while now. I've made it my subject of study. I like to educate people about the science and, as you saw, my demonstrations are very popular.'

He paused whilst the dishes of food were laid on the table in front of them.

'Do help yourself. Would you like wine?'

'Yes, please.' Peggy didn't like to admit that she'd never tasted wine and had no idea whether she liked it or not. The strongest drink she'd ever had was tea. But she knew that if she was to move in better circles she needed to acquaint herself with the habits of the upper classes.

She watched as the dark red liquid was poured into one of the crystal glasses. When she tasted it, she thought it was rather sour and it seemed to spread like fire through her body, down to the tips of her fingers and toes.

'It's very good,' she said, setting the glass down, wondering if she dared to drink it all. 'Now,' she said, feeling emboldened. 'What about you? Tell me about your family. Where do you come from?' Her questions came in a rush with no pause for answers.

He laughed. 'I'm not very interesting,' he said. 'My father was a doctor – a surgeon. He wanted me to become a doctor too, and I studied for a while, but then I discovered the science of phrenology. It fascinates me.'

'What about your mother?'

'Ah.' He looked saddened. 'She died when I was only young. I barely remember her.'

'I'm sorry,' said Peggy.

'Please, don't apologise. I was brought up by a nurse whom I loved very much.'

'And do you have brothers and sisters?'

'Alas, no. I am an only child.'

'You said you'd been to Blackburn before,' she said. 'When was that?'

'It was a long time ago,' he told her.

'Then you must have come with your father,' she said, remembering the story her mother told about the doctors who would set up their wares in the market place and how Grandma Chadwick swore by their brown bottles.

'I must have done,' he agreed. 'I don't remember clearly.'

But he'd known where Thunder Alley was, thought Peggy as she ate her food. She wondered if he was being entirely truthful with her, but she could see no reason for him to lie – and it was a name that might have stuck in the mind of a small boy.

'I saw an advertisement for the coach to the seaside,' he said, pointing to the flyers that had been left at the hotel. 'I'd like to go. It's a long time since I saw the sea. Would you like to come with me?'

'To the seaside?' asked Peggy. 'Isn't it a long way?'

'About thirty miles,' he said. 'But it doesn't take that long to get there. Look.' He stood up to retrieve one of the flyers to show it to her. 'The coach leaves the Eagle and Child on Darwen Street at half past six on Sunday mornings and goes to Lytham. It comes back from the Ship Inn at four in the afternoon. That would give us plenty of time to see the sea, and even go bathing if you wanted to. Seawater is very beneficial to health.'

'Bathing? In the water?' Peggy asked him.

He laughed and then reached across the table to pat her hand. 'I'm sorry,' he said. 'It was rude of me to laugh, but your face was a picture. Surely you've heard of sea bathing?'

'Yes, of course. I've seen the posters,' she said. 'But it wasn't something I ever thought I'd do.'

'Well, this is your chance. Please say that you'll come.'

Peggy was unsure. 'I have no costume.'

'We'll get you one. Now, no more excuses,' he told her. 'I shall book the tickets.'

Peggy told her mother that she was going out for the day with a friend and on the Sunday morning she got up very early and left the house without waking anyone.

Professor Samuel was waiting for her outside the Eagle and Child. He was wearing the colourful waistcoat that he'd had on for his demonstrations and was holding two parcels under his arm.

'This is for you,' he said, holding one out to her. 'It's a bathing costume.'

Peggy loosened the string and peeped inside the brown paper. 'How do you know it will fit me?' she asked.

'It'll fit,' he said. 'Come on, the coach is here.'

Mr Frankland, the owner of the coach, reined in his two horses and climbed down to assist his passengers aboard. Peggy found herself in a forward-facing seat, squeezed in between Professor Samuel and a woman she didn't know. She felt awkward about the close proximity and tried not to make too much contact with either of them, but the professor let his legs sprawl and she had no option but to knock knees with him at every bump in the road.

After a while she began to relax. The sun warmed them as they bowled along in the open air, Mr Frankland shouting encouragement to the horses, and the other ladies excitedly discussing just how the bathing machines worked. They stopped off at Preston for some breakfast and the professor bought bacon with bread and butter and a pot of tea. Then they were off again and before long the horses began to prick their ears and trot more eagerly and the woman beside Peggy said that she could smell the salt in the air.

When they reached the coast, Peggy saw the sea and thought it was even better than she had imagined. She'd thought it was going to be a bit like the Can, but this water seemed to go on for ever and ever. She could see sailing ships on the horizon and she found it hard to believe that anyone sailed out into that nothingness and eventually arrived in another country far, far away.

The coach pulled up outside the Ship Inn and after eating a light dinner, Professor Samuel walked her down to the shore. It was lined with what looked like wooden sheds on wheels.

'Those are the bathing machines,' he told her. 'The ladies here – and the gentlemen down there.'

The water was rolling up the sand in waves. It wasn't like the river that trickled along outside the house on Water Street. 'Is it safe?' she asked, remembering her mother's dire warnings about water giving off all sorts of bad miasmas.

'It's perfectly safe,' he reassured her. 'I would come and hold your hand if I were allowed, but sadly gentlemen are not allowed anywhere near the ladies' bathing area. Here.' He pressed a coin into her hand. 'Give this sixpence to the woman over there and she'll show you to a bathing machine. I'll meet you back here at three o'clock.

No later,' he warned her. 'We don't want to miss the coach and be stranded here all night.'

Hesitantly Peggy walked towards the bathing machines.

'Number four,' the woman instructed her as she pocketed the sixpence.

Peggy opened the door of the hut and went in. There was a narrow bench down one side, a small window, high up, to let in some light, and a row of hooks for her clothes. She held on tightly as the horse was hitched to the front and she was drawn down the beach into the sea. It felt strange to begin to take her clothes off anywhere except in her own bedroom, or occasionally in front of the fire for a bath if her father was out for the evening. She wriggled out of her best frock and put it carefully on a hook. Then off came her bodice, her petticoats, her stockings and her bloomers until she stood, naked, shivering with the chill and the excitement of it all. She unwrapped her parcel and saw a bright blue costume, with bloomers that reached to her ankles when she pulled them on. There was also a cap to cover her hair. When she was ready, she opened the door to see that the waves were rushing up over the bottom of the steps and she could hear other women shouting and screaming as they plunged into the water.

Peggy stepped down, allowing the seawater to wash over her feet. It was freezing and she was cautious as she ventured further down until she was immersed up to her knees.

'Come on,' a plump woman called to her. 'Don't stand there dithering. Tha needs to get right into t' water if it's to do thee good.'

'Watch out for her!' said the woman who had travelled in the coach with them from Blackburn. 'She's a dipper. She'll push you right under if you don't watch her!'

Peggy took a deep breath and stepped away from the bathing machine. The cold made her gasp even though the sun was warm on her face. The waves pulled her this way and that and she struggled to stay on her feet. She wished that Professor Samuel had been allowed to bathe alongside her so that she could have held on to his arm. But, as she became accustomed to the cold and the movement, she found that she was beginning to enjoy herself. The water felt good against her skin and she splashed at it with her arms as she walked along, pressing against the current.

'Don't go too far out!' someone shouted. As she turned to see who was calling to her, her foot slipped on a rock and a moment later her vision was filled with blackness and bubbles and she couldn't breathe. She fought against the water, but it seemed an eternity before she managed to escape it and, coughing and gasping, come up into the sunlight.

'Well, tha's had thy dip now,' laughed the plump woman as she got hold of her by the arm and hauled her back into shallower water by the bathing machine. 'Stay here,' she instructed. 'I don't want thee drownin' on my watch.'

Peggy sat down on the steps to get her breath back. Everything was dripping – her cap, her hair, her nose. She was well and truly soaked. Suddenly she felt the urge to laugh. She kicked water high into the air with her bare feet, pulled off the cap to wring out her wet hair and felt an elation that took her completely by surprise. She didn't know what her parents would say if they found out, and she didn't care. She felt wonderful and she was so grateful to the professor for persuading her to come.

'Time's up!' the woman who'd taken her money told her after a while. Peggy was sorry. Once she'd got used to the sea she'd found that she loved it and had even tried to swim. But she'd been no good at it and had gone under again, her ears and nose filling with water. After that she'd contented herself with paddling and splashing.

Now she climbed back up the steps, weighed down by the water that had soaked into her bathing costume. The fabric clung to her skin and she had to wriggle about to get it off before she could reach for the towel and begin to get herself dry. She was still slightly clammy as she pulled on her petticoats. Everything seemed to stick to her skin and she could smell the saltiness of the seawater on her arms as she lifted her frock over her head. She squeezed and plaited her hair before trying to blot up any excess water with the towel. Most of the other women had managed to keep their hair dry, but hers hung down her back and made the bodice of her frock cling to her skin with dampness. She hoped it would be dry before she got home. She'd enjoyed herself so much that she didn't want the day to be spoiled by having to make excuses to her mother.

She heard the horse being hitched to the machine and held on tight as she was drawn back up the beach where she stepped out on to the shingle. She handed the wet towel to the woman who'd taken her money and wrung the bathing costume out as best she could, unsure what she would do with it.

Once she'd moved away from the ladies' machines, she saw Professor Samuel waiting for her. His face was flushed and his hair was standing up in damp spikes, making him look far more boyish than she could have imagined. He greeted her with a grin.

'Did you enjoy it?' he asked.

'I did! My hair's wet through though.'

'Did you go right under?'

'Not intentionally,' she told him. 'I slipped.'

He laughed. 'Well, you've truly been for a dip then. Come on,' he said, glancing at his pocket watch. 'We've time for a pot of tea before the coach comes for us.'

They went back to the Ship Inn and managed to find seats amongst the crush of excited bathers. Professor Samuel ordered tea and it came with copious amounts of bread and butter, which Peggy ate hungrily. The sea air had given her quite an appetite.

She momentarily thought of John Sharples and the Sunday teas he'd bought for them at Revedge. There was no comparison with this, she thought as the bathers began to make their way to their coaches and carriages to go home. This was living, she thought as she drained her teacup. It was the most fun she'd ever had in her life.

Chapter Twenty-Seven

'May I see you again?' asked Professor Samuel as he helped Peggy down from the coach outside the Eagle and Child. The sun had set and it was beginning to grow dark, and she was surprised by how tired she felt. She'd almost fallen asleep leaning on his shoulder as they travelled back.

'Yes, of course,' she told him.

'Have you ever been on a train?' he asked.

'The steam locomotives?'

'Yes. They come as far as Preston now and there are some day excursions on Sundays.'

'Where do they go?' she asked.

'There's a train at half past six that goes to Fleetwood. From there we could take a short trip on a steamboat to see the ruins of Furness Abbey. Would you like that?'

Peggy nodded enthusiastically. 'It sounds wonderful!' she told him. She'd never thought she would ever have a chance to ride on a train, let alone sail on a boat. She could hardly wait for next Sunday to come.

'May I walk you home?' he asked.

She hesitated, but only for a moment. 'Just as far as the bridge,' she said, hoping that her mother wouldn't be out on the doorstep. She didn't want any of her family to see her walking with Professor Samuel. She wasn't sure why, but after the trouble with John Sharples she thought it was probably better to keep quiet about him. And it wasn't as if anything could come of it. He'd be on his way soon and she would be going to do her teacher training, but whilst he was here and she was free, she saw no reason not to enjoy herself and make the most of his generosity.

She tucked her arm into his elbow as they walked. The damp bathing suit, clutched inside its disintegrating brown paper wrappings, had made a wet patch on her frock and she was wondering how to get it into the house without her mother seeing it. She was tempted to toss it into the river, but didn't want to part with it. Even if she never bathed in the sea again she wanted to be able to hold it to her nose and breathe in the salty smell.

'You don't need to come any further,' she said as they reached the top of Water Street.

'I hope you enjoyed yourself?' he asked.

'I did!'

'Then I will see you again next week.' He took her hand and kissed it. His lips felt warm and slightly moist. Then he smiled and walked away towards the Old Bull.

Peggy watched for a moment; then she turned down the street towards her own house. There was a gap in the curtains and she could see that only Grandma Chadwick was in the parlour. Her mother must be down the yard. She opened the front door and hurried through to the stairs and up to her bedroom with the wet parcel. She pushed it into a drawer, to be dealt with later, and then went back down.

'Tha looks like tha's been wet through,' observed her mother when she found her at the kitchen sink, drying herself after washing away the scent of the sea. 'Has it rained?'

'It poured down earlier. I got caught in it.'

'I hope tha's not been with that John Sharples again?'

'Of course not,' she said as she went into the parlour and picked up a book to avoid having to answer any more questions.

Bessie met George most days. She knew her mother was worried about it, but she wanted to get to know him better. They needed to make up for all the years when neither of them had known the other existed. And he might decide to go back to America soon. The thought saddened her. The prospect of being parted from him, perhaps for ever, was too cruel when she had only just found him.

He was waiting for her in the dining room at the Old Bull. He stood and kissed her cheek and asked her how she was before pulling out a chair for her to sit down.

'Do you mind if Joshua joins us?' he asked.

'No, of course not.'

'We went over to Preston yesterday to look at the railroad,' George told her as the food was put on the table. 'Joshua was impressed by it.' He smiled across the table as Joshua helped himself to the pie and peas. 'There was an advertisement for a day excursion on Sunday,' he told Bessie. 'The train goes to Fleetwood, which is at the seaside. There's sea-bathing machines there, and boats as well. There's a steamer that takes folks over to the peninsula where there are some ruins of an old abbey.'

'Really?' said Bessie. She'd never been much further than Blackburn and it sounded amazing. 'Can you really go all that way in a day?'

'It's an early start,' said George. 'But I'll take thee if tha'd like to go.'

'Can Peggy come too?' she asked. Even though she would have preferred not to ask her sister, Bessie doubted her mother would agree if Peggy wasn't included in the invitation.

'Aye.' George smiled at her indulgently. 'Peggy can come an' all if tha'd like her to.'

They all looked up at the sudden shouting in the market place outside. George frowned. 'There's trouble brewing,' he observed. 'It does no good for men to be without work. Don't go walking around the town alone,' he warned her. 'I've a meeting with some of these railroad investors this afternoon, but I'll see thee safe back home when we've had our dinner.'

'It's too nice a day to be inside,' said Bessie, recoiling from the prospect of having to spend the rest of her day helping her mother to peg out wet washing.

'What would tha like to do?' asked George.

'I'd like to get out of town altogether,' she told him. 'I'd like to go for a walk up to Ramsgreave. It's where my grandparents lived.'

'Aye. So I recall,' he said. 'It's bonny up there and I would have offered to walk with thee if I didn't have this meeting.' He looked across the table at Joshua. 'Maybe Josh would walk with thee,' he said.

Bessie glanced across the table. 'I don't want to be a burden,' she said, although she was hoping that he would brush her concerns aside and agree to go with her. 'I can go alone.'

'No.' George was firm. 'There's trouble afoot and I'd be happier if I knew tha were being looked after.'

'I'd like to come, miss,' said Joshua. 'I'm keen to see more of the countryside, to walk in it. I've spent too much time riding in carriages. I feel the need to stretch my legs.'

'Then that's settled,' declared George.

As Bessie and Joshua were preparing to leave the Old Bull for their walk, a working man ran into the lobby asking for the landlord.

'Tha needs to tell thy friend the magistrate to send for t' militia,' he told him. 'I've heard 'em talkin'. They're meanin' to go round every factory and shut them down so's all the workers have to come out.'

'Go. Quickly,' George told them. Bessie took Joshua's arm and they hurried across the market place and down Darwen Street. There were groups of men gathering, some with stones in their hands and the sound of glass shattering rang out. Joshua looked worried.

'Perhaps we should go back inside?'

'I think we're better out of it,' Bessie told him. 'It's not far,' she said as they dodged the gathering crowds until they reached the edges of the town and began to climb the track that led to Ramsgreave.

Titus had been in the Dog and Duck on Northgate waiting for the other members of the local Chartist group to come in when he'd become aware of the whispered conversation between a group of men near the fireplace.

'These new steam boilers all have plugs in 'em,' one was saying. 'So all we need to do is pull 'em out and it'll stop production. There's no need to persuade all the workers to strike, though like as not they'll join us when they sees what we're up to.'

'And if they don't agree to turn out, we'll persuade 'em,' said another to the agreement of his companions.

Titus had glanced across at them and recognised the older man, who seemed to be the leader of the group. It was Joe Sharples, father of John. Titus had looked away quickly, so that the man wouldn't notice him. He wasn't in the mood for trouble, though it seemed that Joe was set on making trouble of his own. Titus had picked up a copy of the *Northern Star* that another customer had tossed down on the table and held it up in front of him to hide his face. But he needn't have worried. The men had drained their cups and left, probably to see if they could round up support for their scheme. They'd seemed unsteady, as though they'd been in the beerhouse a long time. It was the likes of them that were getting the Chartists a bad name.

'There's trouble brewin',' warned Titus, when Tom, another of the Chartists, came in.

'Aye, I've seen it,' he replied. 'It were supposed to be a peaceful protest but there's fightin' breakin' out around the market place between them as want to work and them as are determined to stop 'em.' He frowned. 'Once they resort to violence it does the cause no good, but there's always them as think throwin' stones and punches is the best way to get what they want.'

Although he was afraid of getting caught up in the violence, Titus knew that he couldn't hide away in the Dog and Duck and not try to appeal for calm.

'Come on,' he said to Tom. 'Let's see what's happenin'.'

When they reached Radcliffe's mill yard, Titus saw that a large group had gathered. Many were armed with sticks and stones and they seemed intent on breaking down the gates that had been shut against them.

'Lads! Lads!' he called. 'This is no way to win justice!' But the men ignored him. They began to hammer on the gates with their sticks and one was being helped to climb up and over the top.

'Soldiers are comin'!' shouted Tom.

'I wish they'd listen to reason,' replied Titus. 'This'll not end well.'

As he spoke they heard the bugles of the approaching militia.

'They're not Blackburn lads, most of 'em,' said Tom. 'They don't know thee, so there's no reason for 'em to heed thee.'

Although Titus knew it was his duty as a Chartist leader to try to do something to prevent what seemed to be inevitable bloodshed, the memories of that other night, that other riot, flooded back. He'd taken no part in it, had simply been trying to make his way home, but he now found himself running a finger around the inside of his collar as he remembered how he'd been hauled up by the scruff and bludgeoned over the head before being locked in the cellar of the Old Bull.

One of the local magistrates was reading the Riot Act and appealing for the men to disperse to their homes, but none would heed him. They shouted and jeered and told him they were intent on stopping all the engines until they received a fair wage for their day's work. Titus spotted Joe

Sharples amongst them. The man held half a paving stone in his hand.

'Let any man come near me and I'll send this stone at him!' he shouted. He looked fearless, but Titus knew that he was drunk and given to violence even when he was sober.

Titus watched as some of the constables moved forward. True to his word, Joe lobbed the stone. It hit one on the head and he fell to the ground, bleeding and seemingly rendered unconscious by the blow. The crowd fell silent for just an instant, but then their attack on the mill renewed and after a moment the gates flew open under the pressure and the rioters stormed into the yard and in through the doors of the engine house.

Titus shrank back against the wall as the militia galloped into the street. Joe Sharples was still struggling with the constables, but broke free and began to run. Then a noise made Titus jump. His ears rang and he saw Joe lying face down. Blood was spreading across the back of his shirt. The soldier who was looking down at him from horseback held a musket in his hand. There was smoke coming from the barrel.

'Come on,' said Tom, grabbing Titus by the sleeve. 'We'd best get out of here.' Titus followed him away from the crush. He saw nothing but the image of Joe Sharples on the ground. He remembered all the times he'd wished him dead, but he hadn't really meant it, he thought as he walked, head down, allowing his friend to lead him to safety. He wouldn't have wished that on any man – friend or foe – not when he was fighting for justice for the working man.

'What's happened?' demanded Jennet when he got home.

'They're rioting,' he told her.

'Thank goodness tha's home safe!'

He saw that she'd been fretting and felt guilty all over again. He knew that he'd caused her so much worry over the years, and that she didn't deserve it. He wanted to put his arms around her and reassure her, but he didn't think his embrace would be welcome.

'Where are t' lasses?' he asked. 'Dost tha know? Our Peggy should be safe enough in the school. But Bessie?'

'She went to meet George. He'll look after her.'

Titus hoped it was true. Even though Jennet probably wouldn't believe him, he was concerned about Bessie. The centre of the town was no place to be this afternoon and he hoped that George Anderton had enough sense to keep the lass safe.

Bessie was relieved to get away from Blackburn. As she and Joshua climbed the hill, they paused to look back at the town in the valley below them and she saw that there was no smoke coming from any of the mill chimneys. The boilers must have been shut down.

Joshua looked a little shaken.

'It isn't what you expected when you came here, is it?' she asked him.

'No, miss. Mr Anderton told me that this was a free country, that I'd be safe here, but when I look at the workin' folk I wonder if they're any better off than slaves – made to work all hours and live in poverty.'

Bessie wondered if he had a point. Her father – Titus – was always telling them that people had been enslaved when they left their own looms and came to work in the factories. He said they would never be free until they had the vote and could force the factory owners to pay them a fair wage and give them better conditions. But she was sure that violence wouldn't change a thing. It would set the gentry against them even more. They would say that working men weren't fit to have the vote.

She gasped as she heard gunfire ring out across the valley. Surely the soldiers weren't shooting at the rioters? She knew that it had happened before, but she never thought she'd witness it in her own town.

'Come on,' said Joshua. 'Show me where your grandparents lived.'

They turned their backs on the trouble below and walked on towards Ramsgreave. The sounds faded behind them and were replaced by birdsong and the gentle baaing of sheep. They walked in silence for a while, both a little shy, but every so often they would glance at one another and smile.

'Here we are,' said Bessie at last as they reached the cottage near the top of the hill. The garden was even more overgrown than the last time she'd visited and the windows were covered in cobwebs. She wiped some away and looked longingly inside.

'I remember being happy here,' she said as she watched Joshua try the door and find it locked against them.

'It's a sturdy house,' he said. 'Why does no one want to live in it?'

'People need to live where the work is,' said Bessie. 'No one can live the kind of life my grandparents had, not any more. Things have changed too much.'

'I never thought it would be like this,' said Joshua. 'When I was toiling away in the baking sun on that plantation, I damned the folks over the seas who wanted the cotton I was picking. I thought you were all rich, all living in great mansions like the plantation owners. I never knew that folks were suffering here as well.'

'How could you have known?' asked Bessie, seeing the anguish on his face, as if he thought it was his curse that had brought them all this trouble. 'It's greed that's to blame. Some have made money, but it's come at a cost.' She prayed that no one had been harmed. Part of her wanted to hurry back to check that her father was safe – and Titus. He was the one more likely to be in that crowd. What would her mother do if something happened to him?

Joshua had sat down on the crumbling remains of the garden wall and was looking down the valley. 'It sure is pretty around here,' he said.

'But America sounds so beautiful, the way George described it to me.'

Joshua nodded. 'It is,' he said, and she thought he sounded sad.

Chapter Twenty-Eight

When Bessie woke early on the Sunday morning, she was surprised to find that she was alone in the bed. She wondered if Peggy had gone down the yard, but when she tiptoed down the stairs there was no sign of her. Her sister had become increasingly secretive lately and she wondered if she was seeing John Sharples again, even though she'd sworn both to her and to their mother that she wasn't. But if she was, it would account for her adamant refusal to come with her on the railway excursion today. She hadn't even seemed to consider it when Bessie had asked her, but had said straight away that it was of no interest to her and Bessie should go alone. It had almost upset the plans and Bessie had had to ask George to plead with her mother to let her go. She'd relented after speaking to him, but said that she'd have been happier if Peggy had been going too because whilst she had no objection to Bessie being seen with George, she was uneasy about Joshua accompanying them.

Bessie had decided it was wiser not to comment, and she'd held her tongue about Joshua walking with her to Ramsgreave. There'd been nothing wrong in it, she knew, otherwise George would never have allowed it. He seemed quite happy for her to be friends with Joshua, but her mother seemed to have become more anxious about her since the revelation that George was her father. It was as if she was terrified of letting her out of her sight.

Still, thought Bessie, she wasn't going to wake her mother to tell her that Peggy had gone out. She didn't want her suddenly changing her mind about letting her go to Fleetwood.

Bessie washed herself in cold water, shivering a little in the chill of the early morning in the stone-floored kitchen. Then she went back upstairs and dressed in clean underwear and the new frock and bonnet that George had bought for her. She took her precious gloves from the drawer and put them on, wrapped a little pink shawl around her shoulders and let herself out on to the deserted street to meet George.

When she reached the end of Water Street she saw Joshua waiting for her. The sight of him thrilled her and she smiled as he came towards her.

'Good mornin', miss!' Mr Anderton said to come and fetch you, but I didn't want to knock on your door and wake your folks.'

'You don't have to keep calling me *miss*,' she told him. 'Call me Bessie.'

'Would that be all right?' he asked. He seemed unsure about being so familiar with her.

'Of course it would! We're friends, aren't we?' she asked, glancing up at him.

He smiled. 'We sure are ... Bessie,' he replied, as if he enjoyed the sound of her name.

He offered her his arm. 'You're lookin' mighty fine this morning,' he told her and Bessie glowed with pleasure. She was looking forward to the day and she was glad that he was coming with them. He looked quite fine himself, she thought as they walked along. He always looked well turned out and she was proud to walk beside him.

The carriage was waiting for them. The two bay horses shone in the early sunshine. One was pawing at the cobbles, and George was talking with the driver. He smiled when he saw them coming. He opened the door and pulled down the steps, but it was Joshua who offered his hand to help her in.

'We've been blessed with fine weather,' said George as they turned for the Preston road, joining others who were heading in the same direction.

There was a crowd when they reached the station at Preston. Joshua helped her down and stayed close to her as George went to check which of the train compartments was theirs. Bessie had never seen a train before and it wasn't anything like she'd imagined. It was as if someone had taken the huge steam boiler from the mill and set it on wheels. The engine had a tall chimney that was puffing out smoke. Behind the engine were the carriages, but longer than the ones the horses pulled. Some were open just like the wagons that came to the mills with the cotton, only with wooden benches to sit on, whilst others were covered, more like the horse-drawn carriage they had arrived in.

'This way,' said George, leading them to one of the covered carriages near the front. 'First class for my lass,' he told Bessie as he took her hand to help her board.

It was very much like the carriage she'd just left, but everything seemed brand-new. The blue upholstery was spotless and the brass fittings shone. An oil lamp was suspended from the ceiling and on the floor were blankets and hot-water bottles in case the day turned chilly. George slammed the door closed but lowered the sash window so he could put out his head and watch proceedings. Bessie sat down beside Joshua, excited and apprehensive about the journey. Then there was what sounded like a huge explosion of steam. Something whistled piercingly and George closed the window to prevent their compartment from being filled with smoke. There was a shudder and a jerk and they began to move, slowly at first as they rolled past the few remaining people on the platform and then out into the sunlight and the countryside, where they gathered speed until the fields were rushing past at an amazing rate.

Peggy had hardly slept. She was so afraid of oversleeping that she'd woken up every hour or so until she heard a clock strike five and decided that she would slip out of bed and out of the house before anyone could stop her. She dressed downstairs so as not to wake her sister and crept down the street on tiptoe until she reached the corner.

The coach was already waiting at the Eagle and Child and it was filling up. Professor Samuel was looking out for her, his topcoat opened to show off his silk waistcoat and his silver watch chain. He put a foot on the bottom step of the carriage and held out an arm, blocking the ascent of an elderly lady as he called to Peggy to be quick. 'I've been trying to save an inside seat,' he said as he helped her aboard and followed her in, squeezing up the other passengers and closing the door so that everyone else would have to go on the outside. Peggy could feel his leg pressed against hers through the thin fabric of her summer frock. He was warm and solid.

The driver climbed up to his seat, gave a quick blast on his bugle and shook the reins. Peggy watched the familiar streets disappear behind them as they let fly through the countryside towards the railway station in Preston.

There were crowds of people milling about when they got there and Professor Samuel held her arm firmly under his as they walked down the ramp and on to the platform under a canopy held up by brightly coloured pillars and arches. He pushed a way through the milling mass to the carriages. Peggy held on to the brim of her bonnet, trying to keep it low over her face. She knew that Bessie was somewhere in the crowd and she was glad that it seemed so chaotic as it meant there was less chance of being recognised. She was worried that she might bump into her sister and George Anderton later in the day though. She'd been beside herself with fury when Bessie had come home and said that she'd been invited on this excursion as well. She'd even wanted her to go with them, but Peggy had been quick to refuse. It was Professor Samuel who'd asked her first, and he was the one she was determined to go with.

'Here we are,' he said, wrenching open the door of a compartment and handing her in.

'Is this just for us?' asked Peggy as she spread herself across the plush seat. At least she would be able to relax here, she thought, with no worries about being discovered.

'It is indeed. I'm sorry the coach was such a squash but this part of the journey will be much more pleasant.' He took off his hat and sat opposite her, running a hand through his hair with a smile. 'We should be off soon,' he said. 'This'll be something to tell your pupils about tomorrow.'

'I'm not sure Miss Parkinson would approve,' replied Peggy, thinking of the schoolmistress and her Bible stories – none of them mentioned railways.

The engine hissed and the carriages jerked and began to move forwards. The few remaining people on the platform waved them off and there was a cheer from somewhere – probably the third-class carriages, thought Peggy as she unfastened the ribbons on her bonnet, thankful that she was travelling with someone who could afford to pay for better accommodation than those ranks of wooden benches with little protection from the weather.

As they raced through the countryside, Professor Samuel came to sit beside her and pointed out places of interest along the way. Peggy marvelled at how much he knew. He seemed to be very familiar with the area considering that he was from the south, but then she supposed that travelling doctors had been all over.

The rhythm of the train was pleasant and the sky was a clear blue. She wouldn't have missed it for the world and was almost sorry when they drew into the station at Fleetwood and the engine hissed to a stop. Professor Samuel lowered the window and opened the door.

'Shall we let the crowd go first?' she suggested, taking time to fasten up her bonnet again.

'If you like. We don't want to miss the steamer though.'

Once the crowd had thinned and Peggy could see no sign of her sister, they got down from the train. She took the professor's arm and walked out from under the canopy into the glaring sunlight. The scent of the sea met her and she felt her stomach suddenly flutter as she recalled her dip the previous week. There were bathing machines here too, but Professor Samuel urged her not to linger.

'Come on,' he said. 'We don't want the boat to sail without us!'

She almost had to run to keep up with him as he hurried her past the grand hotel and the light-house towards the steamer that was puffing impatiently at the quayside.

'All aboard!' called a man. 'Quickly now, sir, madam. Only just in time!'

Professor Samuel more or less pushed Peggy up the short ramp, which was then wheeled away and the gateway closed. She could already feel the uneven motion of the swell under them and she held the rail firmly as they moved away from the land. The waves were slapping against the hull and Peggy felt a moment of unease as the shoreline receded.

'I hope it doesn't sink,' she said, thinking about the water closing over her head at Lytham.

'You're quite safe,' said the professor, covering her hand with his. 'Look.' He pointed towards another shore some way off. 'That's where we're going.'

The ribbons on Peggy's bonnet fluttered as they sailed further out. Seabirds wheeled and called overhead and a band began to play on the other side of the deck. Peggy began to relax and enjoy the voyage. This was what she wanted from life, she thought, not days spent in the dust-filled classroom with girls writing squeakily on their slates, setting her teeth on edge.

Bessie stood on the deck of the *Orion* between George and Joshua and watched the waves.

'Is this what it's like sailing to America?' she asked them.

'A bit,' George told her, 'except the steamers that go across the ocean are a lot bigger than this, and the seas are much rougher. Poor Joshua was sick for a week until he got his sea-legs.'

'Were you?' she asked, glancing up at Joshua's anxious face.

'Aye, but this is like a mill pond today,' said George. 'I've never seen the sea so calm.'

'Is it far?' asked Joshua as the men on the quayside began to untie the ropes and toss them aboard.

George laughed. 'Only to yon shore,' he said, pointing. 'We'll be there afore tha knows it. Come on, we'll take a stroll around the deck and listen to yon band.'

Bessie took Joshua's arm and George walked beside them. The deck was crowded and everyone was in a holiday mood, their troubles forgotten for a day at least. The three of them stood for a while, listening to the band; then they decided to stroll right around the ship. There were fewer people leaning on the rails at the far side and as Bessie glanced at them she saw a bonnet that looked remarkably like the one Peggy had, with the yellow and pink ribbons that had been a gift from John Sharples threatening to come loose in the breeze. But it couldn't possibly be her sister, she thought. Or could it? She recalled that Peggy had been up and out of the house before her. Bessie looked at the man standing beside her. It wasn't John Sharples. He looked familiar but she couldn't place where she'd seen him before.

'Isn't that Professor Samuel, the phrenologist?' asked Joshua.

'I do believe it is,' said George. He stopped walking and looked again before turning to Bessie. 'Is that thy sister, Peggy, who's with him?' he asked.

'I thought it was when I first saw her, but it can't be,' said Bessie, still reluctant to believe that Peggy refused to come with them but had accepted the invitation of a man they barely knew.

'I think it is.' George sounded concerned. 'What's she doing with him?'

'I don't know. She never said anything.'

'So thy parents know nowt about it?'

'No. She never said a word. But she was out of the house before me this morning,' Bessie told him. 'What should we do?' she asked.

'There's not much we can do,' said George. 'Let's walk back the other way before they see us. I'll not spoil the day by causing a scene, but I'll certainly have a word with thy mother tomorrow,' he said. 'Yon chap's not the type for a decent lass to be seeing.'

'Do you think she's in any danger?' asked Bessie, glancing back over her shoulder. She wasn't convinced that walking away was the right thing to do.

'Probably not. But it's not something to be encouraged.'

When the steamer docked Professor Samuel hurried Peggy off so that they would be one of the first to find seats on the train for the journey up to the ruins.

'We don't want to end up in a queue for something to eat,' he told her. 'We'll go straight in for some dinner and then we'll walk around the abbey.'

Peggy agreed. Her stomach was growling with hunger. It was a long time since she'd gobbled down a few oatcakes for her breakfast and she envied the people who'd had the forethought to bring a picnic with them.

They soon arrived at Furness Station and as Professor Samuel helped her down from the carriage Peggy saw the huge sandstone arches of the ruins. She was amazed by the redness of the stones. The old abbey at Whalley had similar ruins, but they were drab and grey. This place was like something out of a fairy tale, she thought.

They made their way up to the hotel that stood within the grounds of the abbey and the professor secured them a table and ordered food. Peggy ate hungrily, although her meal was rather spoiled by having to constantly glance around the dining room hoping that her sister and George Anderton wouldn't come in.

'Is something wrong?' asked Professor Samuel. 'You seem preoccupied.'

'I thought I caught a glimpse of a woman I'd rather not speak to,' she told him.

'Someone you don't like?'

'She's a gossip,' replied Peggy.

'You're not afraid of being seen with me, are you?' He sounded hurt.

'No. Of course not.' She helped herself to more potatoes.

'What did you tell your parents? You did tell them that you were coming?' he asked.

'I said I was having a day out with a friend.'

'They didn't object?'

'I'm not a child,' she told him. 'I'm eighteen.'

'Still, I wouldn't like to think that you'd deceived them. I'm sure they're good people. Perhaps I could meet them?' he suggested.

'I don't know.'

'Why? I know they're only ordinary working people, but you needn't have concerns about me coming to your house. It may only be a simple place, but I'm not a person who judges others for being poor. I know how hard it is for people when the mill owners keep wanting to cut wages. I know there are those who want the rioters punished, but I don't think it's right to punish them for being hungry. I know what that's like.'

'Do you?' asked Peggy. She was surprised. She'd never thought that the son of a doctor would go without anything.

'Well, not personally,' he said, keen to explain himself. 'No, not hungry like that, of course. But I have sympathy with them. Anyway,' he said. 'If you've eaten your fill I think we should go to look at the ruins.'

They walked along the gravel paths and stared up at the intricate carvings on the high arches.

'I can't believe how long they've been here,' said Peggy.

'It would have been spectacular when it was whole, when it had a roof and the monks were here,' said Professor Samuel, gazing around. 'It seems a shame that it's all becoming overgrown with weeds now.'

'But it makes it so romantic,' said Peggy as they looked inside abandoned doorways and climbed steps that led to nowhere. 'It's all so beautiful.'

'I wonder what the monks would have made of it. They could never have imagined anything like the railway,' said the professor, hearing the train hoot as it came into the station to disgorge another load of passengers.

They turned a corner and Peggy saw her sister. She was standing between George and Joshua, staring up at the stones.

'Let's go the other way,' she said, quickly turning back. 'The person I don't want to speak to is over there.'

Peggy tucked her arm under Professor Samuel's and they walked in the opposite direction, but she felt compelled to keep looking about to make sure they didn't come face to face with Bessie. It made her cross, as if her sister had set out to spoil her day on purpose, and it was with an element of relief that she finally relaxed into the seat of their private compartment on the train as they steamed back to Preston.

*

'We saw you!' Bessie told Peggy later that evening when they had both gone up to bed. Peggy went to shut the bedroom door so their parents wouldn't overhear. 'We saw you,' repeated Bessie. 'You were with that wizard who does the phrenology readings. No wonder you wouldn't come with us.'

'Have you said anything?' she asked.

'No. I'll not tell tales. But I think George is minded to. He said he'll call on our mam tomorrow.'

'It's nothing to do with him!' said Peggy. 'He should mind his own business.'

'He was worried. He said that chap's no good.'

'What does he know about him?'

'He doesn't trust him.'

'Am I not allowed to see anyone without people spying on me and disapproving?' demanded Peggy.

'He's only thinking of you.'

'No he isn't,' said Peggy, putting her bonnet away in its box. 'And he's not my father. I don't have to do what he says.'

'Well, don't say I didn't warn you,' said Bessie.

'And what about you?' asked Peggy.

'What about me?'

'Does our mam know how cosy you are with that black man?'

'His name is Joshua,' she told her sister, angry at the disrespect she was showing towards her friend.

'Aye. Joshua. What do you think they'll say about that?'

'There's nothing to say,' protested Bessie.

'Maybe so, but I've seen how he looks at you,' Peggy told her. 'I wouldn't be surprised if this father of yours isn't trying to pair you off with him.'

'Don't talk daft,' said Bessie, lying down and pulling the blanket around her. She was cross with her sister. Peggy had spoiled her day. She'd spent most of it looking out for her to try to make sure it really was her that she'd seen and not just someone who looked like her. She'd hardly looked at the ruins at all.

But what her sister had said about Joshua was true. He did seem to like her, and she liked him. She'd begun to like him quite a lot since she'd had the opportunity to spend more time with him, and now it wasn't just being parted from George that was bothering her, it was the thought that she might never see Joshua again as well. But there was a plan forming in her head. A plan that might solve all her dilemmas, and it didn't involve setting up a shop. The outing today had helped her to decide. Travelling was nothing to be frightened of. She'd enjoyed the train and she'd loved the steamer. Even if the waves had been bigger, she was sure that she would still have enjoyed it. She wouldn't be seasick, she was sure, so there was absolutely nothing preventing her telling George that she had come to a decision about what she wanted.

Chapter Twenty-Nine

The next morning Jennet answered the door to George.

'I don't think it's a good idea for you to call again ...' she began. 'What's wrong?' she asked when she noticed his grim expression. 'It's not Bessie, is it?' She was suddenly afraid that some harm had befallen her daughter.

'No, not Bessie,' he said. 'Let me come in for a moment, Jennet. This isn't something you want to hear on the doorstep.'

'What on earth's the matter?' she asked after he'd stepped inside.

'It's about Peggy.'

'Peggy?' She wondered what bother her daughter had got into now. The lass seemed to be out of control lately. Ever since John Sharples had told her that tale about them harbouring a criminal it was as if she'd lost all respect for them.

She refused to tell them where she was going and who she was with. She'd been out all day again the day before and hadn't arrived home until after Bessie had got back. It was worrying Jennet to death, but short of chaining her to her bed, she was at her wits' end to know what to do – and George's grim expression made her fear that things were even worse than she'd suspected.

'Aye, Peggy,' he repeated. 'We saw her yesterday. She were on th' excursion with that phrenologist chap – the one whose exhibition I took 'em to. Didst tha know owt about it?'

Jennet shook her head, bewildered by what she was being told. 'She said she was going out with a friend. I was worried that she were seeing that John Sharples again, I'd no idea she was with that chap.'

'I don't think he's fit company for her, Jennet,' said George. 'He's a trickster. I'm right sorry I took the lasses to see his show, I really am. I thought it would be some harmless entertainment, but that chap's no good, I'm sure of it. And I didn't think it were right for Peggy to be with him.'

'And tha's sure it were her?' asked Jennet.

'Aye. There's no mistake,' he said. 'We saw her plain enough although she didn't see us. I almost went and spoke my mind to him, but it weren't my place, so I decided it were best to say nowt but tell thee about it instead. Besides, I didn't want there to be a scene. It would have spoiled Bessie's day.'

Jennet pulled out a chair and sat down. She could barely comprehend what she was hearing.

'I don't know what to do with her,' she confessed. 'She always used to be such a good lass, but I don't know what's got into her lately ...' Jennet shook her head. 'I don't know what Titus will say. She were always his special lass. Not that he didn't care for Bessie,' she added, 'but t' truth is that Peggy always were his favourite and maybe he spoiled her. Perhaps that's why she's like she is now. I'm grateful to thee for coming to tell me. Tha's always been a good friend to me.'

'Aye.' He glanced across at Grandma Chadwick, who was dozing by the fire. 'I wish tha'd made a different choice, Jennet,' he said quietly. 'We could have had a good life together.' He reached across the table for her hand, but she pulled it away.

'It's too late now.'

'It isn't, Jennet. It's not too late.' She saw the familiar pleading look in his eyes. 'There's nowt for thee here. Look at thee,' he said, waving a hand at the wet washing steaming on the rack above them. 'It breaks my heart to see thee strugglin' like this. I want thee to have a better life, Bessie too, and if Peggy came an' all I'd make sure that she stayed out of trouble. There's need for schoolteachers in America too. Come back with me,' he urged. 'Leave all this and come back to America with me. Tha'll never need to wash a shirt again. Tha can live like a lady, like tha deserves.'

'No, George,' she said. 'It's not possible.'

'It is, Jennet. Titus doesn't deserve thee. Tha's too good for him, always have been, despite what I wrote in that letter I left for thee. It broke my heart gettin' on that boat without thee. I couldn't get the thought of thee strugglin' alone with little Peggy out of my head all the time we were sailin' further and further away. And if I'd known about Bessie … well, I don't know how I would have coped with that.'

Jennet laid a hand on his arm. 'We did all right,' she told him. 'Titus is a good man at heart. And he means well.'

'But things are better in America …'

'No,' said Jennet firmly. 'No, George. Tha mustn't ask me again. It's impossible.' She looked at her mother sitting by the fire. 'I can't leave her. She's no one else to care for her and I'll not see her go into yon workhouse. And before tha even suggests it, take a look at her and consider. She'd not survive a sea voyage and a trek across lakes and mountains, would she? It'd kill her, and I'll not have that on my conscience.'

He stood in silence, not knowing what else to say but reluctant to leave.

'I'd better go,' he said at last.

After George had gone, Jennet sat and wondered what she was going to do about her daughters. Bessie had hardly spoken a word to her since she'd found out that George was her real father and she seemed to be spending all her time out of the house. And Peggy as well. What was she thinking? Taking up with John Sharples had been bad enough, but going off to the seaside with some travelling showman? That was too much. She would have to speak to Titus about it and they would have to sit Peggy down and make it absolutely clear that she was never to do anything like it again.

'I need to talk to thee about our Peggy,' Jennet told Titus when he came in. 'She's been to the seaside with that phrenologist chap. Tha needs to put a stop to it.'

'Well, at least it wasn't John Sharples.'

'Titus! That isn't the point. We've no idea who this chap is and she's been all the way to Furness

Abbey with him. George Anderton called round to tell me that they'd seen her.' Jennet stood with her hands on her hips and glared at him as he made himself comfortable in his chair. 'Tha needs to talk some sense into her. She'll take no notice of me these days. I'm at my wits' end with the pair of 'em!'

Jennet had thought that once she'd got her lasses nursed through childhood illness and grown up, once they were old enough to earn their own livings and look after themselves a bit, her role as a mother would be easier. But she was having more trouble with them now than she'd ever had. And it didn't help that Grandma Chadwick was growing more childlike by the day either. Jennet was angry with Titus. He really needed to give her more support or goodness only knows where it would all end. She thought about Mary Sharples, John's sister. She'd been best friends with Hannah for a long time, but then she'd got herself into trouble and nearly died after taking Ma Critchley's little women's pills because she'd got herself with a child. She was determined not to let anything like that happen to her lasses, but Peggy was that headstrong she was terrified for her.

'Tha needs to talk to her,' she said again. 'It's important. We don't want her getting in bother.'

'Aye. I'll tell her,' he agreed. 'But she's become that set against us since she got friendly with John Sharples I don't know if there's owt I can say that'll make any difference.'

'It doesn't help that what he told her were true,' said Jennet, reaching for the towel to lift the pie dish out of the oven.

'It were a long time ago.'

'Aye, but that doesn't make it less true,' said Jennet. 'Perhaps we should be straight with 'em, get 'em both sat around the table and explain it. I know we said we'd never talk about it, but happen they deserve to know all of it.'

Before they could agree anything there was a knock on the door. Jennet wondered if it was George again. She let Titus go to see who it was. If it was George she knew that he'd send him away.

She listened to see if she recognised the voice of their visitor.

'Is it really thee, lad?' asked Titus. He sounded amazed and she craned her neck to see who was standing there. 'Come in!' said Titus.

Jennet watched as a man stepped inside. He was of medium build and dressed in expensive clothes – a silk cravat and embroidered waistcoat, with a shiny top hat in his hand along with kid gloves. He stared at her and then at Titus as if he couldn't believe his eyes.

'I've been looking for you for weeks,' he told them. 'I went to the house on Paradise Lane but they couldn't tell me where you'd gone.'

It was a minute or two before Jennet recognised him. It was years since he'd last stood in her parlour and then he'd been a skinny, frightened little lad.

'Sam?' she asked, still not certain that it was really him.

He nodded. 'Aye, it's me.'

'Sit thee down,' said Titus. 'Get him a cup of tea, Jennet. It's good to see thee, lad, and lookin' right gradely! Tha's done all right for thyself and no mistake.'

'Aye, I've done all right.'

Jennet began to make a fresh pot of tea and wondered how on earth Sam Proctor had managed to come back looking so prosperous. She hoped that what money he'd come by had been honestly earned and that he hadn't broken his promise to her not to fall back into bad ways.

'What's tha been up to?' asked Titus.

'So tha doesn't know?'

'No. Why would we know?'

'I thought you might have been to see my show.'

'Show?' repeated Titus, looking puzzled.

'Tha's not that phrenologist, is tha?' asked Jennet, suddenly putting two and two together.

'That's right! I am!' He grinned at her, the same disarming grin that she remembered from years ago. 'It's a lucrative trade is reading the heads of the gentry. As long as I tell 'em what they want to hear they pay generously!' He paused as he caught sight of Jennet's face. 'What's wrong?' he asked.

'Our Peggy! That's what's wrong,' she told him, slamming the pot down on the table. 'Tha's been carryin' on with our Peggy, taking her off on a day trip without a word to us!'

'Peggy?' He sounded puzzled and seemed to be about to deny it, when realisation dawned on his face too. 'Margaret,' he said. 'Margaret is never your Peggy?'

'She certainly is!' responded Jennet, glaring at him. 'A friend of mine told us that she'd been seen with thee on yon day trip to Furness Abbey of all places.'

'I didn't know. I swear I didn't know!'

'If tha's laid a finger on my lass then tha'll be answerable to me,' Jennet warned him.

'I've done nowt. I swear. I had no idea.'

'So this chap tha were just tellin' me about was Sam?' Titus asked her, looking perplexed. 'I thought tha said he were a bad 'un.'

'Well, George certainly seems to think he's a bad 'un. A *trickster*, he called him.' She ought to have known, thought Jennet as she watched Sam turn to appeal to Titus to help him clear himself of any wrongdoing. She ought to have known that Sam would never have taken that ten-pound note and used it to earn an honest living.

'I'm no trickster,' he protested. 'I swear I'm not, Mrs Eastwood. Phrenology is a science. I've studied it. I'm almost like a doctor,' he told Titus. 'Folk respect me.' He turned back to Jennet. 'Who is this George anyway?' he asked. 'Can *he* be trusted?'

'He most certainly can! Dost tha want to know where that ten-pound note came from? That ten-pound note I agreed to give thee to help thee evade the constable? Well, it came from George Anderton. He give it to me to help me take care of Peggy, but it were never spent. And thee!' She included Titus in her furious tirade. 'Tha persuaded me to give it up to him. Said he'd hang if we didn't help him. And if tha remembers,' she said, turning back to Sam, 'tha promised me that tha'd take ship to America and earn an honest living.'

'I never went.'

'Well, that much is clear!'

'I ran. Like you told me,' said Sam to Titus. 'I ran and ran, and I didn't dare get on a coach in case I was recognised. Then this carter gave me a lift. He persuaded me that it was a fool's game going off over the sea and I ended up in London. He told me that was the place to get on. Magnificent it was as well. I'd never seen owt like it.'

'And did tha go back to pickin' pockets?' demanded Jennet.

'No. I didn't. I swear I didn't. I saw this doctor giving an exhibition of phrenology and it were that fascinating, I knew it was what I wanted to study. I talked him into taking me on as his apprentice, and when I'd learned enough, I branched out on my own, taking my show all around the country. And then it occurred to me that I should come back and show you how well I'd done – and thank you for the help. I've been searchin' for you ever since I got back ...'

Jennet watched his earnest face as he gave his explanation. She wasn't at all sure she believed him. He'd always been clever at spinning a good tale and she'd fallen for his lies too many times in the past to trust what he said now.

'It doesn't matter whether tha went to America or not,' Titus told him. 'It looks like this phrenol-ogy's better money than weavin'.'

'It is,' said Sam. 'But it needs careful study – it's a science.'

'Well, I always knew tha were a clever lad. I told thee, didn't I, Jennet? I told thee he were

286

clever and that he'd be all right. As long as he used t' money well and made summat of himself, that's all that matters. Isn't it, Jennet?' he asked her. 'Look at the lad. He's done well. What more could tha have wanted?'

'I'd have preferred to have seen him in an honest trade,' she replied.

'I know him!' said Grandma Chadwick, having been woken from her nap by the raised voices. 'Hast tha brought me a brown bottle?' she asked Sam.

'See?' said Jennet. 'Even she takes him for one of them travellin' doctors.'

'But there's nothin' wrong in it,' said Titus.

'Dost tha think not? Anyone with an ha'pence of common sense knows that all they peddle is coloured water, and they knows how to charge for it. They've not studied proper medicine like Dr Scaife and Dr Barlow!'

'Phrenology is a science,' protested Sam again. 'It really is. I can show you. Let me read your head and I'll reveal your character.'

'I don't need the likes of thee feelin' my head to know that I can tell a charlatan from an honest man!'

'Jennet, Jennet!' Titus appealed for calm. 'Sit thee down. The whole street can hear thee. An' thee sit down an all, Sam,' he said. 'This fratchin' is gettin' us nowhere. I'm sure Sam's done nowt wrong. And if he did take our Peggy out then I'm sure he were a perfect gentleman.'

'Then why didn't she tell us where she'd been?'

'Did you not know where she was?' asked Sam.

'No, we did not!' Jennet rounded on him again. 'What sort of *gentleman* takes a lass all that way without sayin' owt to her parents?'

'But she told me you knew. I'd never have taken her otherwise.'

'She said nowt to us,' Jennet told him.

As she was glaring at him she heard the door open and Peggy came in.

'Tha'd better go!' she told Sam as her daughter stared at them. 'Go on! Get on thy way!'

'Professor Samuel?' said Peggy, looking horrified. 'What are you doing here?'

'Just a courtesy visit to your parents.'

'But how did you know where I lived?' She looked from her mother to her father and back to the phrenologist. 'What's wrong?'

'What's wrong is tha's been found out!' Jennet told her. 'George saw thee yesterday with this chap and came to warn me about it. What were tha thinkin' of? Going off out all day with some chap tha knows nowt about and never sayin' a word to us? Tha'd better get up them stairs. Thy father'll speak to thee later!'

'Please,' appealed Sam. 'Don't blame her. If anyone's to blame it's me. And I apologise for taking Margaret out without your knowledge. But she was quite safe.'

'Aye, I'm sure she was, lad,' agreed Titus and Jennet realised that he would never take their daughter to task over this. Sam had never been able to do wrong in her husband's eyes, despite plenty of evidence to the contrary, and she was afraid that he might even agree to him seeing Peggy again.

Peggy fled up the stairs to the safety of her bedroom. How on earth had Professor Samuel found out where she lived? And why had he come to see her parents without telling her? It didn't seem to have gone well, she realised as she listened to the raised voices downstairs followed by the shutting of the front door. She tiptoed to the head of the stairs to see if she could hear what they were saying now, but their voices were inaudible to her and she worried about what could possibly have happened to make them so angry. It was even worse than when they'd found out about John Sharples.

After what seemed to be an age, her mother called her down and she found them both stony-faced in the front parlour.

'Tha's to have nothing more to do with him,' her mother told her. 'I'm that vexed at thee for going off with him yesterday without saying a word. And it's not as if tha couldn't have gone with Bessie and George. I don't know what tha were thinking of, our Peggy. I really don't.'

Peggy expected her father to be equally angry, but he seemed more cross with her mother than with her.

'It's a bit harsh, Jennet,' he said. 'There were no harm in it. I don't see why she can't see him again if she wants, now that we know.'

'Titus Eastwood! Tha promised to back me up on this!'

Her father shrugged. 'It's not as if she's been seein' that Sharples lad behind our backs,' he reminded her. 'I would have had summat to say if that were the case. But there's no harm in Sam. He's a good lad at heart and I'm pleased to see him lookin' so prosperous.'

'Titus! We agreed tha'd not mention that!'

Her mother looked furious and Peggy tried to make sense of what was going on. It was clear that there was much more to it than her going out for the day with Professor Samuel. Besides, her father had called him Sam, as if he knew him. Then a horrible thought occurred to her.

'Is he the pickpocket?' she asked, scarcely able to believe that such an important man as the professor could ever have been a common criminal. It was a silly idea, she thought as she waited for them to reassure her that of course he wasn't. But they remained silent. Her mother glared at her father and he looked uncomfortable, realising that he'd said more than he should have. 'Is he?' she asked her mother, not wanting to hear her affirm her suspicions but desperately needing to know.

'It was a long time ago. He's made summat of himself and that's a good thing,' said her father. 'He were only a child. People change.'

'Sam Proctor'll never change!' said her mother. 'Oh, he's charming enough, always was, but he's never done an honest day's work in his life.'

'Well, look where honest work has got us,' protested her father. 'Tha can hardly blame him for seizin' an opportunity.'

'But John Sharples went to prison because of him!' Peggy told them, her anger rising at the injustice of it.

'Well, that couldn't be helped. He's out now,' said Titus, picking up a pamphlet to read.

'Where's tha goin'?' asked her mother as Peggy wrenched the door open. 'Thy tea'll be on the table in a minute!' she called as Peggy went out.

Peggy slammed the door behind her and began to walk with no clear idea of where she was going. She knew that she couldn't spend another minute in that house. And neither did she want to see the wizard ever again. If George had been right about one thing it was that Professor Samuel, as he called himself, was a liar and a trickster.

She walked on and on. It grew dark. It was too late for her to be out on her own and she cringed away from the leering, shouting lads who lingered on the street corners, the worse for drink, and called out lewd comments as she passed.

She wondered where she could go to get away from them. She was cold. The heat of the day had faded since the sun had set and the breeze was chilly. She'd come out bareheaded and without her shawl, she realised. No wonder men were calling after her. She shivered. She needed to get somewhere safe. She didn't want them to think that she was a prostitute.

She turned towards the Old Bull. Should she go and look for George Anderton? she wondered. No. This was partly his fault. If he hadn't taken them to see the phrenology exhibition none of this would ever have happened, and she couldn't forgive him for telling tales to her mother behind her back.

Perhaps she should go to look for John, she thought as she turned into Northgate, keeping to the shadow of the walls. She knew that he lodged here, although she wasn't sure exactly where. But it should be easy enough to find him if she asked.

With her arms folded across her chest she approached the first lodging house and knocked timidly on the door. A scrawny woman with her hair pulled tightly back opened it a crack.

'What dost tha want?' she demanded.

'I'm looking for John Sharples. Does he lodge here?'

'Not any more,' said the woman and shut the door firmly. Peggy turned away and began to walk again, tears of anger and frustration streaming down her face. If her parents hadn't stopped her seeing John none of this would ever have happened.

She wondered whether to go to her Auntie Hannah, but she couldn't face her either. Besides, Uncle James would just insist that she go home and she wasn't ready to do that yet.

With her arms wrapped around herself against the cold, she walked away from the streets and the pubs and the gaslights to where it was quiet, to where she could be alone and think about what had happened. She wasn't even aware of the cobbles giving way to grassland or the path beginning to rise steeply as she walked on. She stumbled in the darkness, tripped over something and fell full length. She banged her head against something hard and it felt wet against her hand when she touched her temple. But she got up and walked on. Just needing to get away, needing to be alone.

After a while she sat down. She wasn't sure where she was, but she felt tired and she needed to rest. It was cold too, so cold. She shivered. She would have to go back soon. She couldn't stay out all night, no matter how angry she was.

Peggy shivered again. Her skirt was damp from the wet grass and she knew that she ought to get up and start heading back. She wouldn't need to speak to them. She could go straight up to bed. Her bed would be warm, she thought, though it seemed warmer here now. The wind had lessened and the clouds were clearing. There was a bit of moonlight and it would help her to find her way back down. But she felt tired, very tired. She was tempted to lie down and have a nap. She'd go back when she felt better, she thought. If she just closed her eyes for a few minutes, she would feel better.

Chapter Thirty

Bessie had gone to find George that morning, to tell him about her decision, but she'd missed him. Neither he nor Joshua was at the hotel. She didn't want to go back and help with the laundry so she went to call for her friend Ruth and they spent the morning browsing around the market, Bessie urging her friend to choose whatever she liked, saying that she would buy it for her.

'Did tha know as Joe Sharples were shot dead in that rioting?' asked Ruth as they sat on a wall and shared a pie between them. 'And lots of 'em were rounded up and taken afore the magistrate. Folk say as they'll be sent to the penal colony. My father were there. I'm just glad as he got away.'

'Aye, mine too,' said Bessie. 'Though, as it turns out, he isn't really my father.'

Ruth dropped a piece of pie into her lap as she missed her mouth in her astonishment. It rolled on to the floor, steaming as it cooled, but she didn't even notice.

'What's tha mean – not thy father?' she asked.

'That chap that's staying at the hotel – the well-to-do one? He's my father. That's why I have some money,' she explained.

'The one with the black servant?'

'He's not a servant! He's a friend. But aye, that chap. He's my father and I've decided to go back to America with him.'

'Tha's not serious?'

'I am,' Bessie said, brushing crumbs from her skirt. 'I'm going to see him this afternoon and tell him.'

Now that she'd told Ruth what she meant to do, Bessie felt compelled to go through with it, and, after her friend had left her to go home, she crossed the street to the Old Bull and asked if Mr Anderton had returned.

'Is everything all right?' George asked when he saw her.

'Of course.'

'Right. It's just that I were talkin' to thy mother earlier ...'

'Were you? I came to look for you. I've something I want to tell you.'

'Well, tha looks like tha's about to tell me good news.' He smiled at her. 'Come and sit down,' he said. 'What is it?'

'I've decided what it is I want,' she told him. 'And it's not a shop.'

'Oh aye. What then?' He smiled at her indulgently.

'I want to go with you. Back to America.'

For a moment he said nothing, then his smile widened and he reached for her hand. 'Really?' he said. 'Is tha sure? Does tha really want to come back with me?'

Bessie nodded. 'Is that all right?' she asked.

'All right? It's more than all right. It's t' best news I've ever had! Come here, lass.' He pulled her to her feet and hugged her to him. 'Best news ever,' he repeated as he held her at arm's length and studied her face. 'But tha's sure? Really sure?'

'I am. It was the train and the steamer yesterday that made me think about it. And I promise I won't be seasick!'

'And what does thy mother say?' he asked.

'I haven't told her yet,' admitted Bessie. 'I wanted to tell you first. In case you said no.'

'I'd never say no to thee,' he told her. 'Tha's given me such joy wi' this. We'll talk to thy mother together, quell her doubts.' Bessie thought that he was going to cry. 'Tha's made me that happy,' he said, hugging her again whilst people passed by and cast glances in their direction, wondering what good news they'd had that was making them so joyful.

George insisted that they celebrate. He ordered tea and cakes, and they ate in the dining room whilst he told her all about the plans he had for a bedroom for her, a room all of her own, and the things they would do and see together.

'Tha'll want for nowt. I promise,' he told her.

They talked all afternoon and into the evening. Bessie hoped that her mother wouldn't worry about where she was and would guess that she was with her father, *her real father*. Besides, George had told her that he'd spoken to her mother about Peggy that morning and told her it wasn't right that she should be out with the phrenologist without them knowing. There was sure to have been trouble at home when Peggy got in from school and Bessie hated arguments.

Joshua joined them in the dining room for supper. He said that he'd been at a meeting with the railway investors and he was keen to talk about tracks, stations, engines and carriages until he realised that he was probably boring Bessie.

'I'm sorry.' He grinned. 'But it excites me.'

'Well, we've had a bit of excitement an' all,' George said and told him about Bessie's decision to go with him back to America. Bessie had thought that Joshua would be enthusiastic about that too, but he looked disappointed, as if he didn't like the idea at all, and she wondered if she'd read the situation wrong.

When they'd finished their meal, George asked Joshua to walk her home. He still seemed quiet as they left the Old Bull and headed towards Water Street. Something was definitely troubling him, thought Bessie. If he wasn't keen on the idea of her going back to America with them she wished he would tell her why.

'Will you come in?' she asked when they reached the bridge. 'Just to say hello.' She didn't want them to part just yet, with things unsaid.

'Just for a moment,' he agreed.

As they approached the door, Bessie saw her mother lift the curtain to look out.

'Hast tha seen thy sister?' she asked Bessie before she was even over the doorstep. She looked worried sick.

'No. What's wrong?' asked Bessie. 'Has she not been home?'

'Aye, she came home. But she's run off somewhere in a temper after she found she were in trouble for going off with that phrenologist chap. We thought she'd come back but it's getting late. Titus has gone out to look for her.'

'Is she not at Auntie Hannah's?'

'No. They've not seen her.'

'You don't think she's run away with *him* – the phrenologist?' asked Bessie.

Her mother shook her head. 'No. She's not with him.'

'How can you be so sure?' asked Bessie. She saw her mother glance at Joshua. It was as if she didn't want to say too much in front of him, but gradually the whole tale came out about Professor Samuel being the pickpocket they'd helped.

'So he's the last person she'd be with,' concluded her mother. 'Hast tha any idea where she might be?'

'No,' said Bessie. 'Unless she's gone to find John Sharples.'

'Where? On Paradise Lane?'

'No. She told me he hasn't lived there for a long time. She said he lived in a lodging house, but I don't know which one.'

'His mother might know.'

'Peggy said he doesn't have anything to do with his family.'

'But it's worth a try,' insisted Jennet. 'Will tha go? She'll not answer the door to me.'

'Aye, I'll go,' said Bessie. 'Joshua will come with me, won't you?'

'Of course I will. And I'm sure Mr Anderton will help to look for her as well.'

'Yes,' said Bessie. 'I'm sure he will. Shall we go back to the Old Bull first?'

'I'd go myself,' said her mother, 'but I want to stay here in case she comes back. And I don't want to leave thy grandma. If she wakes up and finds herself alone there's no knowing what she might do – and the last thing we want is to be looking for her as well.'

Bessie and Joshua hurried back to the Old Bull to tell George what had happened. His face darkened as Bessie told him who the phrenologist was and he went to look for him to ask if he'd seen Peggy. But there was no sign of him. One of his clients was waiting in the lobby, but the landlord hinted that he might have packed his bag and left on the evening coach.

'Go on to Paradise Lane,' George told Bessie. 'I'll walk down to Water Street and check on thy mother. If Peggy doesn't turn up soon I'll get a horse and see if I can find her on any of the roads out of town.'

'It's this one,' said Bessie to Joshua when they reached Nan Sharples' house. She knocked on the door. Then knocked again, more insistently, when no one came.

'Who's there?' called a man's voice. Bessie was taken aback. She'd thought that only Mrs Sharples was living there now since Joe Sharples had been killed in the rioting.

'It's Bessie Eastwood,' she said. 'We're looking for John.'

The door scraped open and she saw that it was him.

'Oh, thank goodness!' she said.

He looked at her suspiciously and then noticed Joshua.

'What dost tha want?' he asked.

'Have you seen our Peggy? She's missing.'

'Missing?'

'Aye. She had a falling-out at home and she's run off somewhere. My mam's that worried. We thought she might be with you.'

'No.' He glanced behind him and then pulled the door wider. 'Come in,' he said.

Mrs Sharples was sitting by the fire and Bessie felt unnerved at the sight of the woman who had glared at her so fiercely in the market place. But Nan Sharples seemed diminished by the death of her husband. The way she sat beside her hearth reminded Bessie of Grandma Chadwick.

'I'm sorry to bother you,' said Bessie. 'We're looking for our Peggy.'

'How long has she been gone?' asked John. He reached for his boots and began to put them on.

'I'm not sure. A few hours.'

'I'll come and help thee look,' he said, pulling on his cap and reaching to get his jacket down from the peg. 'Will tha be all right, Mother?' he asked.

'Aye. Go and help find t' lass,' she said. 'I hope tha finds her soon,' she added to Bessie.

'Have you any idea where she might be?' Bessie asked John once they were out of the house.

'Hast tha tried the Temperance Hotel? We used to meet up there sometimes.'

They asked at the hotel and John went to Northgate to the house where he used to lodge.

'There were a lass asking for me earlier on,' he told them after he'd spoken briefly with the land-lady. 'From her description it could have been Peggy. She said t' lass seemed a bit wild-eyed and had no bonnet or shawl.'

'Where could she be now?' asked Bessie. 'Is there anywhere else you used to go?'

'We used to walk up by the Big Can. But she'll never have gone up there at this time of night.'

'But maybe we should look? Just in case?'

'We'll need lanterns.'

Joshua went back to the Old Bull and got a couple of lanterns then they set off, glad that the skies had cleared and there were a few glimmers of moonlight to help them on their way. Joshua took hold of Bessie's hand to help guide her and make sure she didn't fall and they followed John, who was more familiar with the path, across the Preston road and up on to the moorland.

'Peggy! Peggy!' they called as they climbed.

'She could be anywhere,' said Joshua. 'We could walk right by her and not see her. It's a pity we don't have dogs. Dogs will always find you.' He sounded as if he was speaking from experience.

'There's a place we used to sit and watch the birds over the water,' said John. 'She could be there. It's this way.'

They followed him across rougher ground towards the lake. The moonlight was glimmering on its still surface. Bessie stumbled on the uneven grassland and Joshua pulled her arm through his to give her more support. They'd strayed far from the path now. She had no idea where she was and began to worry that they would all be lost up here until morning.

'Peggy! Peggy!' she called again. They listened but all they heard was a rustling of the wind through the gorse and the distant hoot of a tawny owl.

'Why did she run away?' asked John.

'It's complicated,' said Bessie. 'It was over a man she's been seeing.' Even in the dark she sensed John bristle at her words.

'She's been seein' someone?' he asked.

'It was nothing serious.'

'Serious enough for her to run off.'

'That's because she was angry at my mam and Titus,' said Bessie. 'It turned out that this chap she's been seeing was the pickpocket that they once helped.'

She bumped into John as he stopped dead.

'Sam Proctor? She's been seeing Sam Proctor?' She sensed his hands curling into fists and reached out to put a hand on his arm.

'He's the phrenologist, the one who's been giving demonstrations and seeing clients privately at the Old Bull ...'

'Is tha sure?' John sounded incredulous.

'Aye. He came to see Titus. There's no doubt it's him. And Peggy was so upset that she just ran away.'

'I can't say as I blame her. I'll kill him!' he added. 'If any harm's come to Peggy, I'll kill him!'

Bessie could feel the anger seething out of him and Joshua felt it too.

'Best concentrate on finding her first,' he advised. 'We can deal with the rest later.'

'It's all right for thee!' John rounded on him. 'I spent years in prison because of him. I were only a child. He tricked me and used me and I were left to take all the blame. Tha's no idea what it were like!'

'Oh, I know, friend,' Joshua told him. 'But this isn't finding Peggy.'

Bessie could hear John's breathing as he struggled to contain himself. After a minute or two he seemed to be calmer. 'This way,' he said, and they followed him, blindly, into the night.

Peggy dreamt that someone was calling her name. She rolled over to find her bed was hard and lumpy, and damp. It was a moment before she realised that she wasn't in her bed and even longer before she remembered that she'd come up on to the moorland. She sat up, wincing as a pain stabbed through her head where she'd bumped it. In the distance she could see two lights moving and she heard her name again. She tried to call back, but her voice cracked and came out as a squeak. She waved a hand as a shaft of moonlight shone through a gap in the clouds and the lights seemed to begin to move towards her.

'Peggy! What on earth are you doing up here? Are you all right?' Her sister, Bessie, was on the ground beside her and had her in her arms.

'You're making my head ache,' protested Peggy.

'Have you hurt it? What happened?'

'I think I fell. I can't really remember.'

'Come on. Get up. We need to get you home.'

306

Peggy wanted to protest that she didn't want to go home, but she was too tired to argue. Bessie was wrapping a shawl around her and rubbing her hands to warm them. 'Can you get up? We may need to carry her,' said Bessie to someone behind her in the dark, someone on the other side of the lantern. Peggy couldn't see who it was. The light was hurting her eyes.

Then whoever it was put the lantern down on the ground and put a hand under her arm whilst Bessie lifted her from the other side.

'Whatever were tha thinkin' to come up here in the dark, and all alone?'

'John?'

'Aye, it's me,' he said. 'Canst tha walk?'

'Yes, of course. There's nothing wrong with me,' she told him. What was he doing here? There was someone else as well, but she couldn't see who. She knew it wasn't her father because he would have been shouting if he'd had to walk all this way to find her.

'Let me guide thee down at least,' said John. 'Let me take thy arm.'

She allowed him to tuck her arm firmly under his and he picked up the lantern again. When he swung it around she saw that it was Joshua who had come with her sister.

'I wasn't lost,' she told them. 'I just sat down for a moment. I must have fallen asleep.'

'Aye, well, tha's safe now,' John told her and she was tempted to reply that if he'd been where he should have been when she looked for him she'd never have come up here in the first place.

'Have you moved lodgings?' she asked him.

'Aye. I'm back livin' at home,' he said as they walked slowly down the hill. 'My mam won't be able to earn enough to pay the rent now my father's been killed, so I need to help out.'

'But you said you'd never go back.'

'It's different now that my father's not there. My mam ... she's different. It were a shock for her. She needs time to adjust.'

He was a good man, thought Peggy as she leaned on him. She didn't care what her father thought. In fact, she didn't care what her father thought about anything. Not now. He was the one to blame for all this and she was never going to listen to anything he said ever again.

'Put this on,' said Joshua, taking off his jacket and giving it to Bessie. She pulled it around her, grateful for its warmth after giving her shawl to Peggy.

'Aren't you cold?' she asked him.

'Freezing.' He laughed. 'I'll survive. It isn't far.'

They seemed to get back down the hill in far less time than it had taken them to trudge up. It was easier going and they soon found the path as the lanterns and the moonlight guided them towards the town below.

'She was very near the water's edge,' said Joshua.

'I know.' Bessie didn't want to dwell on what could have happened if Peggy had lost her footing and fallen into the Can.

'What's the story about the phrenologist and John?' he asked and Bessie related as much as she knew of it to him.

'Do you think he came back here deliberately?' asked Joshua.

'Yes. I think he came to look for Titus. But when he met Peggy he had no idea who she was, even though he'd known her when she was a child.'

'So that part was pure chance?'

'I think so,' said Bessie as they reached the road.

'I'll let thee take her home,' said John when they neared the market place. 'I'd best get back.'

'Come in, just for a minute,' pleaded Bessie. 'Mam will want to thank you. We'd never have found her on our own.'

'Not now,' he said as he took Peggy's arm from his. 'I'm right glad no harm came to thee,' he told her. Then he bent and brushed her cheek with his lips before hurrying away towards Paradise Lane.

Bessie thought that her sister would call after him, but she just looked stunned.

'Let's get her in,' she said to Joshua. 'She's exhausted.'

Jennet felt the relief flood through her when the door was pushed open and Bessie and Joshua brought Peggy in.

'Tha's found her! Where were she? Is she hurt? Oh, Peggy, where's tha been? I could slap thee for what tha's put me through,' she said as she gathered her daughter into her arms and hugged her tightly.

Peggy wriggled away from her and Jennet felt that her heart would break. She loved the lass so much and couldn't bear to see the look on her face as she turned away.

'I don't know why you're all making so much fuss. I only went out for a walk.'

Jennet wanted to tell her that flouncing out of the house wearing only a blouse and skirt at that time of night was not just going for a walk, but she held her tongue. 'Let me bathe that cut on thy head,' she told her, wondering where on earth she'd been. 'Then tha'd best get to bed. I'll bring thee up a cup o' tea.'

She watched as Peggy went up the stairs without another word. What was she going to do to make things right with her? she wondered. This was going to take some mending. 'George and Titus are still out lookin',' she said to Bessie, noticing that she was wearing a man's jacket and that the young lad was shivering in his shirt sleeves. 'Come nearer to t' fire,' she invited him.

'Thank you, but I'd best go,' he said as he took his jacket from Bessie and put it on. 'I'll find your husband and Mr Anderton and tell them she's home.'

'Aye, I'd be grateful for that,' said Jennet and he nodded as he let himself out of the door, closing it gently behind him.

'Where was she?' Jennet asked Bessie.

'Up near the Big Can.'

'Dear Lord! What on earth possessed her to go up there?'

'It was where she used to go with John Sharples on a Sunday afternoon. We found him living back on Paradise Lane and it was his idea to look there. We'd never have found her without him. We've reason to be grateful to him, though he wouldn't come by to hear your thanks. He's not a bad person,' Bessie told her.

'I know.' She began to pour the tea that had been keeping warm, waiting for them to come back.

Bessie sat by the fire and Jennet carried a cup up to Peggy. Her daughter was sitting on the bed, still dressed.

'Let's get thee out of them damp clothes,' she said, setting the cup down. Peggy didn't resist when she helped her change into a clean night-dress and tucked her into bed. Jennet handed her the tea and watched as she drank it down. How many times had she nursed this child of hers like this? She'd nursed her through scarlatina, cholera, the measles and the chickenpox, but this was far harder than any of them. This wasn't something that could be cured with the doctor's potions.

'I've been beside myself with worry,' she told her as she sat on the edge of the bed. 'I don't know what I'd do if any harm came to thee. I'm only strivin' to keep thee safe,' she added as Peggy traced a pattern with her finger on the counter-pane. 'Why did tha do it, Peg? Why did tha run off like that? I know tha's angry at me and thy father, but tha doesn't know the whole story.'

Jennet sighed when Peggy didn't respond, but she knew that she might never get a better chance to tell her side of it – at least Peggy was quiet whilst she was sulking and so she would have to listen.

'Thy father said we could all go to prison if we were found out,' explained Jennet after telling her daughter what had happened, 'and what with thee and Bessie only being babies I couldn't risk it. Thy father suggested we give him money and let him get away. I didn't want to. That ten pounds were what George had given me and I wanted to keep it for Bessie, but I knew I'd done wrong there an' all. I were filled with guilt because Dr Barlow had told me I'd never have another child and thy father were longin' for a son. It were guilt that made me agree,' she told Peggy. 'I knew it were wrong and I were sorry for young John Sharples, but there was nowt I could do about it. He'd been caught fair and square. Thy father spoke up for John and told t' magistrate the boy had been led astray and pleaded for him to show some mercy. But he wouldn't listen. He sent John to prison and he didn't deserve that. I know he's not a bad lad,' she said. 'That Sharples family are a bad lot, but young John's all right. I remember the day he had his accident. It were a mess.'

She looked at her daughter. Peggy remained silent and still wouldn't meet her eye. 'I wish it could have been different,' she said as she picked up the empty cup, said goodnight and went back downstairs.

'Give her a while,' she said to Bessie, although the lass looked tired out and ready for her bed. 'She'll soon be asleep and then tha can go up without wakin' her.'

The door opened and Titus came in. 'She's back?'

'Aye. She's back. I've put her to bed. There's things that'll have to be said, but they'll wait until morning,' she told him. He looked tired out too and she poured him tea with plenty of sugar.

'I even knocked on Nan Sharples' door,' he said as he took off his boots and put them to keep warm near the hearth. 'She said as John were out lookin' for her.'

'Aye. It were him as found her. Up at t' Can.' She hesitated. 'He's not a bad lad,' she repeated as Titus frowned. 'We've reason to be grateful to him this night. I don't suppose that Sam came out to help.'

'I think he's gone,' said Titus. 'I were told he was seen loading his bags on to the late coach.' He sounded sad and Jennet saw that he still thought a lot of the lad.

'Well, at least tha knows he's done all right for himself,' she told him, secretly hoping that they would never see Sam Proctor ever again.

Chapter Thirty-One

The mill hooters were sounding again all over the town by the end of August. Titus reached for his cap and settled it on to his head. It pained him to go back after all these months without their demands being met, but folk had grown tired of being pushed to the brink of starvation. What money had been paid into the Friendly Society had all been handed out and, little by little, those who needed wages the most had begun to trickle back. Others had gone back long enough to get a wage to ease their hunger and pay their rent and then come out on strike again, but in the end it had been hopeless. The mill owners knew they had the upper hand. They knew the workers would give in eventually. Although Mr Hornby had refused to put their wages back to the level they had once been, he had at least promised there would be no more cuts and now that the summer was over and the prospect of a cold, hungry winter was in sight, the workers had decided that there was little choice but to capitulate.

'I'll see thee later,' said Titus as he let himself out of the door.

He wasn't happy, thought Jennet as she watched him go. He didn't like to fail and she knew that he felt like a failure: the long march to London, the petition and the general strike had done little to change their situation.

'Tha's goin' to be late,' she told Bessie. 'They'll dock thy wage if tha's not through that gate by the stroke of six.'

'I'm not going,' she said.

Jennet looked at her younger daughter, still sitting at the breakfast table. She wasn't dressed for work either. She was wearing one of the fancy new frocks that George had bought for her and she was spreading far too much of their precious butter on to a slice of the loaf that she'd brought home yesterday – bread that had probably been paid for by George as well.

'What dost tha mean, tha's not goin'?' she asked.

'I'm meeting my father,' Bessie told her. 'We're going to Preston. He has a meeting, then we're going to get our tickets.'

Jennet's heart sank. Bessie had told her weeks ago that she'd decided to go with George when he went back to America, but it hadn't been mentioned again and Jennet had been hoping that it was just a passing fancy and that Bessie would change her mind when the time came. But it seemed not.

'So tha still means to go?' she asked, turning away so that her daughter wouldn't see the anguish on her face. 'I'll miss thee,' she added, wondering how she would face saying goodbye.

'George wants you to come as well. You could, you know,' said Bessie.

Jennet shook her head. 'I can't leave thy grandma.'

'But she ...' Bessie looked at the old woman, still snoring in her bed. 'She's old,' she said.

'Aye, I know what tha's saying. She'll not live for ever,' replied Jennet. 'But whilst she lives I'll stay and care for her. Tha wouldn't want me to send her to yon workhouse, would tha?'

'No.' Bessie shook her head. 'But you could come ... later.'

'Aye, 'appen so,' said Jennet, 'though I'm gettin' a bit long in t' tooth now to be journeyin' all that way. Besides, I've our Peggy to think of.'

Her elder daughter was still poorly. She'd caught a chill the night when she'd run away and it had settled on her chest. Nothing had seemed to improve it and in the end Jennet had taken her to the Dispensary and got a bottle of medicine. It had stopped her coughing, but she still didn't seem better in herself. The bright, lively lass who'd had such zest for life seemed to have disappeared. It was as though she'd turned inwards on herself. She'd hardly spoken a word in the weeks since that night, hardly eaten owt either and Jennet was worried that she might just fade away from them if nothing could be done to rouse her.

'Peggy'll come round,' Bessie told her.

'Has she said owt to thee?' asked Jennet, hoping that the sisters might have confided in one another.

Bessie shook her head. 'No. She's not spoken of it at all. But I think she's sad because of her falling-out with John Sharples. I think she was hoping he'd come and ask after her. But he's not been near, so she thinks he doesn't care.'

Jennet didn't reply. The truth was that John Sharples *had* come the morning after Peggy's disappearance to ask after her. Titus had sent him away, telling him that he wasn't welcome and he'd have no member of the Sharples family cross their threshold again. He'd not even troubled to thank him for what he'd done. It was as if he blamed John when it was Sam Proctor who'd been to blame. It was the past repeating itself all over again. Jennet had said nothing about it to Peggy.

It hadn't seemed important because she'd thought that the falling-out between her and John had been mutual. Now it seemed she was still pining for him.

Jennet took Peggy some breakfast upstairs.

'Here's some bread and butter if tha fancies it,' she said. Peggy took a slice and bit into it. Jennet hoped it was a good sign. 'Is tha goin' to get up and come down for a while?' she asked. 'It'll do thee good.'

'Mam,' said Peggy as Jennet turned to go.

'What is it, love?'

'Did you mean it when you said that you don't think John Sharples is a bad person?'

'Aye. I meant it.'

'He's never been round to ask after me though.'

'He did,' admitted Jennet. 'Thy father sent him away.'

Peggy continued to nibble on the bread after her mother had gone back downstairs. So he had come after all, she thought, and it gave her a warm feeling inside. He was different from that so-called Professor Samuel – she was angry with herself for having been taken in by him. She'd believed everything he'd told her – the story about his father being a doctor – it was all lies. She knew that now. He'd been convincing, but she was to blame as well. It had been obvious that his story hadn't always added up, such as when he knew the names of all the streets in town, but she'd made excuses to herself rather than face the idea that he wasn't being entirely honest with her.

But if John Sharples hadn't been so weak and capitulated to her father, she'd never have got involved with the pickpocket. She found that she partly blamed John, although maybe it was really her own fault for giving in too easily when he said they shouldn't see each other again. She hadn't wanted to defy her father, and she'd been afraid of getting too close to John when she'd thought she would be going away to study for her teaching certificate. It was what she'd always wanted, except that now she wasn't sure it was. The decision had been made for her years ago, and it had been so far in the future then that it had never seemed real. Staying on at school when Bessie had to go and work in the mill had made her feel special, and better than Bessie. But that had all changed since George Anderton had come. Now Bessie was the one who seemed important and she admitted to herself that she was jealous of her sister's good fortune.

She'd been too quick to fall out with John. She realised that now. She couldn't blame him for not wanting trouble, especially when he knew that she was only looking for a friendship that was bound to end when she went away. Why would he take the risk of confronting her father about something that could only end in separation? She'd been foolish. She hadn't been entirely honest with him, and she hadn't been honest with herself. Had she ever really intended to take the scholarship? Maybe she had. But that was before she'd met John and begun to think about all the things she would miss out on if she went through with it. Being a schoolmistress was a lonely life. She knew that Miss Parkinson was alone in her little house after the girls had all gone home. She would never have a husband or children around her hearth. But Peggy wanted a family. She wanted a family more than she wanted the wages and security of a teaching job. She'd thought that John was being weak, but now she saw that she had been unfair to think that. He had done what he thought was best for both of them and in her anger and frustration she'd allowed herself to be duped by Sam Proctor, the very man she had thought she would hate if she ever met him.

When Peggy was sure that Bessie had gone out, she got up and pulled a shawl over her nightgown and went downstairs. Her mother was in the washhouse putting some things to soak. Peggy stood in the doorway and watched her.

'Tha'd best get dressed,' said her mother. 'We don't want folk callin' round and seein' thee in thy nightie at this time of day.'

Jennet was glad that Peggy had got up. She still looked poorly, but it was a step in the right direction and Jennet thought her daughter would feel better if she gave herself a good wash and put some clothes on.

'Can I talk to you first?' asked Peggy.

'Aye, of course. Let's go in.'

Jennet brewed some tea whilst Peggy sat at the table. Her face was almost white and her hair hung limply around her shoulders. Jennet wished that she could simply kiss away her cares like she had when she was a child.

'What's to do?' she asked her when she sat down.

'Do you think Father would be very disappointed if I didn't become a teacher?' asked Peggy.

Jennet didn't answer immediately. The truth was that he would. He'd had his heart set on Peggy making something of herself ever since she'd taken to reading and writing so easily. He was the one who'd decided she could be a teacher. It had been talked about since she was little and Peggy had always seemed keen, but she'd been too young to decide for herself. And Jennet had always had doubts. They'd been selfish doubts because she knew that it meant Peggy would have to stay a spinster to get a job in one of the national schools. It meant she would never see her daughter wed, never see her with childer of her own – grandchildren to spoil and dote on. She'd always thought that she'd have to rely on Bessie for that, but now that dream had been shaken with Bessie's decision to go off to America.

'It's a big thing, but tha mustn't let fears get in the way if it's what tha wants to do,' Jennet told Peggy, wondering how she would cope if both of her daughters left home for far-flung places.

'I don't think it *is* what I want to do,' Peggy replied. 'I've always thought it was because it was just how things were. It was expected of me and I never thought to question it. I don't want to disappoint my father,' she said, 'but those lasses at the school get on my nerves most of the time. I'm not sure how Miss Parkinson manages it.'

'Is that what's making thee so miserable?' asked Jennet.

'I'm not sure. I think it might be.'

'Tha's not still frettin' about that Sam Proctor?'

'No.' Peggy shook her head. 'I think I feel tricked more than anything. I don't know how my father can keep making excuses for him.'

'He can do no wrong as far as thy father's concerned,' said Jennet. 'He thinks Sam's the son he never had. I ... I had a boy – before you were born. He came too soon. He's buried in the church-yard at Pleck Gate. There's no marked grave. There were no funeral. He never counted as a person, but I think of him often and wonder what sort of a grand lad he would have been. I don't think thy father would be so preoccupied wi' Sam if that baby had lived.'

She wiped away a stray tear with her cloth. Even now the thought of that little life could stir such feelings of love and sorrow in her. She still mourned him.

'Don't fret about what thy father'll say,' Jennet went on. 'I'll not see thee unhappy over it. If tha doesn't want to go, then no one's goin' to force thee against thy will. I'll talk to thy father. I can't promise there won't be ructions, but he'll get over it once he realises it's really not what tha wants.' She got up to continue with her work. 'Go and get dressed,' she told Peggy again, 'and brush thy hair. It'll turn out all right, tha'll see.'

Jennet went back into the washhouse. If this was all that was bothering Peggy it was easily resolved, though what sort of a job the lass was going to do was a problem that would take more thought. Titus would never allow her to go into the mill, and she didn't want her here learning how to wash. She was a clever lass, but there weren't that many opportunities for clever lasses in a town like this.

Bessie put on her bonnet and buttoned up the kid gloves. George had hired a carriage and they were going to see some plans for the new railway that was to be built to join Blackburn and Preston. Then they were going to get the tickets for their voyage. She could feel the excitement fluttering in her stomach at the thought of it.

Joshua came with them to the meeting in Preston. He was wearing the same coat that he'd given her to wear the night they were looking for Peggy. She could still imagine the feel of it against her arms. But Joshua had been cold with her recently and Bessie thought it was connected to her decision to go to America with them. She still hadn't found the courage to ask him about it, but she knew she must. She needed to make things right between them before they sailed.

She waited whilst the men studied the plans in the solicitor's offices on Winckley Square. When George was sure that Joshua had understood everything that had been agreed, he promised to pay the company what seemed to Bessie to be an extraordinary amount of money and the men all shook hands.

Then they went to a nearby inn, the Grey Horse, and George ordered them dinner.

'Tha looks worried,' he said to Joshua. 'Is owt wrong? Tha's happy with the arrangements? Or is there summat tha doesn't understand?'

'No. It's all very clear,' he replied. 'Of course I'm happy with it. You've been very generous. It's more than I deserve.'

'Well, there's no one I'd trust as much as thee to oversee my investments,' said George.

Joshua nodded. 'I am grateful,' he said.

'Then what's on thy mind?' asked George.

Bessie saw Joshua glance at her and then look away.

'I suppose I'm just worried about managing when you go back,' he said.

'Nonsense,' replied George, filling up Joshua's glass. 'Tha's a shrewd businessman. That's why I've chosen thee.'

'Then it's not just because . . .' As Bessie watched, he hesitated.

'Because tha needed to get away? No,' said George. 'I wouldn't risk this much money if I didn't think tha were the best man for the job.'

'Well, I am grateful for the opportunity.'

'Cheer up then,' George told him. 'This is supposed to be a celebration!'

Bessie found herself puzzled by the conversation. Puzzled and alarmed. 'So is Joshua going to oversee your investment in the railway?' she asked.

'That's right,' said George. 'I need someone here who's honest and reliable to keep an eye on my affairs. Someone who'll make sure I don't get cheated by unscrupulous men whilst I'm far away. And I know as Joshua will do a champion job.'

'So you mean that Joshua will stay here when we go back to America?'

'That's the plan,' said George. 'He'll have a house to live in, and maybe a servant to do his cooking and such. He'll be such a gentleman as he'll never recognise himself!' George laughed and raised a glass to celebrate; then he lowered it again when neither Joshua nor Bessie joined him.

'I thought he was coming back with us,' whispered Bessie, suddenly realising why Joshua had been so offhand with her. He must have thought that she wanted to get away from him, when the opposite was true. He'd been the main reason she'd decided to go.

'I can never go back, Bessie,' he told her. 'I thought you knew that.'

George frowned. 'Did Joshua not tell thee about his background?' he asked.

'He told me he'd been a slave, but that he was a free man now.'

'So he is,' said George, 'as long as he remains here. The trouble is that even though the northern states did away with slavery years ago, there's still slavery in the south. Runaways aren't safe in Wisconsin because there's a law that allows fugitives to be recaptured and taken back to their owners. I wasn't willing to let Joshua take that risk any longer,' he explained. 'I bought him a ticket and got him on a boat and he saw the last of America. This is his home now.'

Bessie didn't know what to say. What could she do? She'd told George that she wanted to go with him and he'd been so pleased by it. She'd told her mother as well, and Ruth. She'd been so sure that she was making the right decision, but now she was faced with a dilemma she could see no solution to.

'Can he never go back?' she asked George.

'No. Not unless there are changes, and I'm not sure that will happen anytime soon. America's a great country to make money and do well,' he told her, 'but not so great for folks like Joshua.'

Bessie stared at the food on her plate, her appetite gone. How was she going to tell her father that she'd changed her mind? He was going to buy the tickets that very afternoon – just two tickets.

Chapter Thirty-Two

Peggy poured the last of the medicine on to a teaspoon and swallowed it down. It tasted bad and she would have given it up long since if her mother hadn't stood over her and insisted that she take every drop.

'I want to be sure tha's better,' she said.

Peggy's cough was long gone, although she was reluctant to admit that she was completely well because that would mean going back to school when the term began. She couldn't bear the thought of it.

Her mother had mentioned to her father that she was having second thoughts about taking the scholarship exam when he came in for his dinner, but he'd become angry about it.

'Tha's being ungrateful!' he'd told her. 'We've all done without so that tha can stay on at the school and now tha's the opportunity to do summat with thy life, I'll not see thee throw it away! I'll not see thee workin' a twelve-hour day in yon mill when tha's a clever lass and has the chance to better thyself!'

Peggy hadn't argued back. She'd gone up to the bedroom and cried, glad that Bessie was out so that she could be alone. It was rare for her father to be angry with her. She knew it was because he cared about her and wanted her to do well, but she wished he would listen to what she wanted for once rather than making all her decisions for her.

'I think I might go out for a bit,' she said to her mother as she watched her wash the medicine bottle out and put it to dry.

'Fresh air'll put some roses in thy cheeks,' agreed her mother. 'It'll do thee good.'

Peggy went to fetch her bonnet and shawl. Although it was warm she didn't want to get a reputation as a lass who went about without being properly dressed.

She walked down Water Street slowly. Everything seemed the same. It was market day and she browsed amongst the stalls for a while, wishing that she had some money in her purse to treat herself to something nice. She avoided Thunder Alley in case Miss Parkinson saw her. Instead she walked up Church Street and paused outside Miss Cross's hat shop where John Sharples used to wait for her in the mornings. The window display seemed depleted. It was too late in the season for summer hats and soon they would be replaced by the autumn fashions. Peggy wished that she could afford a new hat for each season, like the wives of the gentry could. Her bonnet had become even shabbier as the summer had worn on with only the thunderstorms to wash the smoke from the air – and the ribbons that John had given her to trim it at Easter were starting to fray.

At first she wondered if it was her imagination that had conjured up his reflection in the window. She'd had such vivid dreams about him whilst she'd been poorly and she thought she might be dreaming now.

Slowly she turned, half expecting him to have disappeared. But no. He was standing there with his hat in his hand and his fingers covered in ink smudges.

'I hear as Miss Cross is sellin' up,' he said.

'Is she?' It would account for the scanty display of hats in her window, thought Peggy.

'Is tha feelin' better?' he asked.

'I am, thank you,' she said. 'I had a bad cough, but I'm over it now.'

'I'm pleased to hear it.'

She half expected him to walk away, but he didn't. 'My mother told me that you'd called round, but that my father sent you away,' she said.

'Aye,' he said. 'He made his feelings very clear.'

'He doesn't speak for me,' Peggy told him.

'No, but I suppose he has reason to hate me and my family.'

'He has no reason to hate you,' said Peggy. She noticed him glance across at the church clock. 'Do you need to get home? Please don't let me keep you.'

'No. No, it's not that.' He hesitated. 'Would tha like a sup o' summat cool, with it being such a warm day?'

Peggy was surprised by the invitation but accepted it eagerly. When they reached the hotel he bought her a dandelion and burdock. She drank it, enjoying the sweet taste that washed away the remains of the bitter tang of her medicine.

'Did you know about the phrenologist?' she asked him.

'Aye. Your Bessie told me.'

'I didn't know who he was until he showed up at home looking for my mam and dad. I had no idea before, I swear,' she told him. 'I would have warned you if I'd known.'

John's face darkened and he set down his cup with a thud. 'It's perhaps best I didn't know before,' he told her. 'I went looking for him after they'd taken thee home that night, but he'd gone, scarpered as soon as he knew there were trouble.'

Peggy was glad that John hadn't found him. She didn't think he would have been able to get the better of Sam Proctor, either in an argument or a fist fight.

'Why did tha let thyself get mixed up with him?' John asked her.

'He seemed nice. He was very charming. But it was all lies.'

'Aye, that sounds like Sam,' muttered John. 'He could charm birds from the trees, that one. Tha's well rid of him.'

'I know that now,' she said.

'So, will tha be going back to school, now that tha's feelin' better?' he asked her.

'I suppose I'll have to.'

'Tha doesn't sound too keen.'

'I'm not,' she admitted. 'I'm not sure it's what I want to do. I sometimes hate it at that school,' she told him. 'I don't think I have the patience to be a schoolmistress.'

'It's no use doin' summat as'll make thee unhappy,' he agreed, 'but t' truth is tha probably would be better off being a teacher. Tha doesn't want to be stuck in this filthy town for the rest of thy life when there's such an opportunity.'

'You sound like you want to be rid of me.'

'That's not true, Peggy. Tha knows I'd be sad to see thee go. But I'd not try to persuade thee against it.'

'It isn't what I want though,' she said. 'I don't want to end up an old maid like Miss Parkinson.'

'But what work would tha do instead?' he asked.

'I don't know. That's part of the problem. I've learned no other trade. I don't want to work in the mill and I don't want to take in washing, like my mother. It's a pity I couldn't be like Miss Cross,' she said. 'I can see myself sorting out the post and selling hats and gloves.'

'Aye. But tha needs money to get a shop,' he said.

'I know. It's only a dream.'

John drained his cup. 'I'd best be gettin' on my way,' he said. 'My mother'll be expectin' me.'

'I'll walk back with you,' said Peggy and was pleased when he offered her his arm.

The clock began to chime as they reached Church Street.

'Can I see thee again?' he asked.

'You know my father still won't approve of it,' she said. 'You'll have to be prepared to stand up to him. Will you?' she asked. She hoped that he would. She knew there was no future for them if he didn't.

'I don't want any trouble.'

'I can't promise there won't be trouble.'

He scratched his head and looked worried. 'I know,' he said. 'But if it's what tha wants then I promise I'll tell him straight that I'm serious and I mean well. Does tha feel strong enough to take a walk?' he asked.

'I think so.'

'Meet me on Sunday afternoon then. Usual place.'

She nodded in agreement. She'd been stupid, she thought, stupid to think that she could find a better man.

Chapter Thirty-Three

Bessie stood beside George as he enquired about steamers, berths, times and prices. She'd set something in motion that she didn't know how to stop. Joshua was waiting for them outside and all she wanted to do was run out and tell him that she didn't want to go if he wasn't going too. But she didn't want to disappoint her father who was trying to interest her in the different ships and asking which one she preferred.

'This one sails Saturday week,' he told her. 'Is that too soon? We'll have to get some trunks for thee to pack up. It's best if tha gets new clothes and whatever else tha needs now. There's not many shops in Wisconsin.' He looked at her. 'What's to do?' he asked. 'Is tha feelin' badly? Dost tha need to sit down?'

Someone hurried forward with a chair for her and then brought her a drink of water.

'What is it?' he asked. 'What's to do?'

'It's Joshua,' she said.

'Aw, Bessie. Tha doesn't need to worry about him. He'll do just fine.'

She was shaking her head. 'You don't understand,' she said. 'I like him.' Her father stared at her. 'It's not that I don't want to come with you, I do. I'm so glad to have found you and I don't want to lose you again. But I don't want to leave Joshua behind.' She began to cry and fumbled for her embroidered handkerchief. 'I don't know what to do.'

'I think I'd best leave this for now,' George told the ticket clerk. 'Come on,' he said to Bessie. 'Let's go somewhere where we can talk about this properly.'

She followed him out of the door into the bright sunlight, still wiping her eyes. She wasn't sure if he was angry. He said nothing except to ask Joshua to fetch the carriage round so that they could go home.

When it came he handed her in and he and Joshua followed. Bessie could see that Joshua was wondering what was wrong, but he didn't ask.

'Did you get tickets?' he ventured after a while, breaking the uncomfortable silence.

'No, not today,' George told him. 'Bessie has some more thinking to do.'

She saw Joshua glance at her.

'Have you changed your mind?' he asked. She thought he sounded hopeful, but it might have been wishful thinking.

'Not entirely,' George answered for her. 'But there's things that need to be talked about,' he said, 'before I go buying tickets.'

They rode the rest of the way in silence and when they arrived outside the Old Bull, George helped Bessie down.

'Go home,' he said. 'Have a think about what tha's told me because I want tha to be sure of any decision tha makes. I want thee to be happy. I truly do. It's important.' He kissed her cheek and she clung to him for a moment, desperately worried that she'd offended him. 'See her safe home, Joshua,' he said and strode up the steps two at a time.

She and Joshua looked at one another.

'What happened?' he asked. 'I've never known him so quiet.'

'I've upset him,' said Bessie. 'When I told him I wanted to go back with him he was so pleased, but now I'm having second thoughts, and I've hurt him. I never meant to,' she said. 'I thought we would all go.'

Joshua offered her his arm and they walked towards Water Street.

'I didn't know that you could be sent back to the slave owner,' she told him. 'What a horrible thing. It never occurred to me.'

'It's true,' said Joshua. 'Escaping wasn't enough. I have to stay out of America if I'm to be safe. Here, I'm a free man. I don't need to watch out for the slave hunters. That's why Mr Anderton has been making investments. It's to give me a job and a wage. I'll never be able to repay him for what he's done for me,' he added.

'I do want to go with him,' said Bessie. 'I don't think I could bear to wave him goodbye and go back to working in the mill and living at home with my mam and Titus. Now I know he's my father I want to get to know him better. You don't suppose I could persuade him to stay on?' she asked.

'No.' Joshua dashed her hopes. 'He has his farm and his property back there. He needs to go back.'

They turned into Water Street and Joshua hesitated.

'Come to the door,' Bessie told him. 'Come and say hello to my mam. She'll be glad to see you.'

'Not today,' he said. 'I think I'd better go straight back.'

Her mother came through from the washhouse when she heard the front door open.

'What's to do?' she asked. 'Tha looks like tha's been cryin'.'

'It's nothing. Just a bit of grit in my eye. I'll go and get changed.'

In the bedroom, Bessie took off her gloves and bonnet and put them away. She slipped out of the frock, hung it up and put on an old skirt and blouse. Then she sat down on the edge of the bed and wondered what she was going to do. She wanted to be with both her father and Joshua, and she'd thought that was how it was going to be. But now she needed to make a choice, and whatever choice she made she was going to hurt somebody. Her father would be hurt if she didn't go with him, and she thought, or at least hoped, the reason Joshua had been so cool with her was because he was hurt that she wasn't going to stay.

She didn't know what to do. Her father had been right when he'd said it needed to be thought about, but no matter how hard she thought, she could see no solution. All she could see was a choice – an impossible choice.

After a while, she heard her mother's footsteps on the stairs.

'Summat's to do,' she told her. 'Hast tha had a fallin'-out with George?'

'No. Not really,' said Bessie as her mother sat down on the bed beside her. 'We went to get the tickets for our passage, but I had second thoughts.'

She began to cry and it all came tumbling out about Joshua not being able to go back. 'It's impossible,' she said, shaking her head. 'I can't bear the thought of hurting either of them.'

'But there's no future for thee with Joshua,' said her mother. 'He's a nice lad and he has lovely manners, but he's ...'

Bessie looked up as her mother hesitated. 'Black,' she finished for her.

'Not that there's owt wrong with it,' said her mother. 'He's got lovely skin and beautiful teeth an' all, but George told me that he were a ...'

'Slave? Yes, that's true as well. But he's a free man now. Or he is so long as he doesn't go back to Wisconsin. There are men there who are hunting for him, like you'd hunt a wild animal!'

'Aye, it's wrong,' she agreed. 'But it's not like tha could ever marry him.'

'Why not?' demanded Bessie.

'Well, would it be allowed? Is he even a Christian?' asked her mother uncertainly.

'I've no idea,' said Bessie. 'You'd have to ask him.'

'Aye, I suppose so.'

*

Jennet thought her heart would break as she watched Bessie sitting on the edge of the bed looking so miserable. She didn't think she'd ever known both her daughters to be so unhappy at the same time. She'd always striven so hard to give them some happiness, but now she was at a loss to know what to do to help. How she missed the two little lasses who were always so full of laughter and smiles, even when times were hard.

They both had a big decision to make and there was little she could do to help them except offer sympathy. She was loath to offer too much advice because she didn't want to sway them with her own desires. The truth was that she didn't want either of them to go away. She would miss them too much. She'd tried not to show that she was glad when Peggy had said she was thinking of not taking the scholarship, but she had to acknowledge that she would much prefer her to stay in Blackburn, get wed to a nice lad and give her the grandchildren she craved. Titus would like it too, she thought, if he was presented with a little grandson. And she'd been heartbroken when Bessie had first told her that she was going to America with George. If she stayed, this passion she had for Joshua would fade. Young lasses were like that, she thought. In time, she'd meet somebody suitable. But in the meantime she just wished that she could make her younger daughter happy again. She wished that George had never come back. Nor Sam. The past should have been finished with long ago, not come around again to trouble them with their mistakes.

Chapter Thirty-Four

'I'll not keep it secret from thy father. It's not fair to ask me to,' Jennet told Peggy when she said that she was going to meet John Sharples on Sunday afternoon. Her daughter shrugged and said that she didn't care what her father thought any more. Jennet wondered how it had come to this. A few months ago, she'd never have thought that Peggy would turn against her father. She could have understood it if it had been Bessie, but not Peggy.

She didn't try to stop her going though. She was relieved that her elder daughter had begun to look happier, more like herself, and if making up with John was what it had taken then she was glad of it. Not that Titus would agree, she knew. But he was out and didn't need to know until later.

'Peggy gone out?' he asked when he came in from his meeting.

'Aye.'

'Gone to study?' He sounded hopeful. He still maintained that Peggy was just being stubborn about the scholarship and would change her mind when the time came.

'No. She's gone walking.'

'Who with?'

Jennet knew she would have to tell him. 'John Sharples,' she said. 'And afore tha gets into a lather about it tha can sit down and listen, because I have summat I want to say to thee!'

It was rare that Jennet spoke her mind to her husband, but she was so fed up with this feud against the Sharples family, especially now Joe had been shot dead in such a horrible way, that she'd decided it was time to put it behind them, and she needed to tell him so.

Titus sank down on to his chair. He looked stunned.

'I'm right worried about our Peggy,' she told him. 'We could have lost her that night when she went wandering. Owt could have happened to her, and we've John Sharples to thank for bringing her home safe. I don't think it's fair to stop her seeing him. He's done nowt to hurt this family. And the truth is that if we hadn't taken Sam Proctor in when he came out of prison, John would never have got into any bother.'

'So tha thinks we should have turned the lad away when he had nowhere else to go?'

'As it turns out, I wonder whether we should,' she told him. 'He brought nowt but trouble the first time and nowt but trouble when he came back.'

'From what he said he treated our Peggy like a lady.'

'I can't understand thee, Titus, I really can't,' Jennet told him. 'Tha's dead set against her seein' John, but tha's happy that she went off on a train and a boat to goodness knows where with a man she'd hardly known for two minutes. It doesn't matter that it turned out to be Sam. She'd no business going off like that and I've told her so. At least this time she's been honest and said who she's with.'

'Aye, well … 'appen so … but I still don't want her seeing that Sharples lad. He's set her against us.'

'He hasn't told her anything that isn't true,' said Jennet, sitting down herself. She felt tired, so tired of trying to sort out the mess. 'We should have known when we said we'd never speak of it that it would all come out in the end. As far as Peggy's concerned, we're the ones who did wrong – and if tha thinks about it, she has a point.'

'It'll all blow over when she gets her scholarship and goes off to school.'

'She'll not go, Titus. I really don't think she will. It's time as tha faced facts. I know tha's always wanted her to be a schoolteacher, but if it's not what the lass wants then it's wrong to force her.'

'She'll change her mind after a twelve-hour shift in yon mill.'

'She doesn't have to go into the mill. There's other things she could do.'

'Washin'?' he asked.

Jennet lost her temper with him. 'There's nowt wrong with washin'! It's kept this family fed and clothed on more than one occasion when tha were too busy with thy meetings and thy petitions to put money on the table!'

She glared at him and he looked shamefaced.

'I'm sorry, Jennet,' he said. 'It were a stupid thing to say, but I'll not see our Peggy throw her life away when she could better herself.'

Jennet sighed and went through to the back kitchen. It was useless, she thought. He'd never see reason. She just hoped that George would be more realistic when she went to speak to him about Bessie and Joshua.

*

John was waiting for Peggy in the churchyard, dressed in his Sunday best. He smiled when he saw her.

'I wasn't sure tha'd come,' he said. 'Dost tha want to walk up th' ill? Or is it too far? I don't want to tire thee out.'

'We'll walk a bit and see how I feel,' she suggested, taking his arm.

'Tha doesn't mind going back up there?'

'No,' she said. 'It'll be different in the daytime, and you'll be with me.'

They walked on until they'd crossed the Preston road and began to climb the track towards the Can. Peggy could hardly believe that she'd found her way up here in the dark. She couldn't remember much about that night, except that she'd needed to get away from home, away from Sam Proctor.

'It must have been about here that you found me,' she said at last. Everything looked different in the daylight.

'It were over there,' said John, pointing towards the edge of the lake. 'Tha were lucky not to stumble into the water.'

Peggy looked towards where he pointed. She had no idea that she'd been in such danger.

'I'm glad you found me,' she said. It had been bad enough when the water closed over her head at Lytham, but if she'd gone under here she knew she'd never have managed to get out. The thought made her heart race with fear and she tightened her grip on his arm.

'Promise me as tha'll never do anything like that again,' he said. 'I don't know what I'd do if anything happened to thee. Look!' he said, pointing. 'Swallows. They'll be off on their travels soon, back to Africa.' They watched as the birds swept low over the water, taking the insects. 'We'd best go back,' he said after a while. 'Tha looks tired.'

'Will you come back to Water Street and speak to my father? Tell him that you want to keep company with me?' asked Peggy.

'Dost tha want to keep company with me?' He pulled her around to face him, his hands on her arms and his expression a mixture of earnestness and wonder. 'Is tha sure?'

'I am,' she said. 'I've been thinking about it and I'm sure it's what I want – if it's what you want.'

'Of course it is,' he said. 'I'd like nothin' better.'

'Then will you come back and speak to him?' She saw his hesitation. 'He's all talk,' she said. 'I'm sure he'll come round when he sees you're serious. Don't look so worried,' she told him. 'Come on.' She got hold of his arm and tugged, hoping that her father wouldn't be too difficult about it.

Jennet was sitting at the fireside with Titus opposite her, reading one of his pamphlets. They hadn't spoken since she'd shouted at him, but at least he hadn't gone out again and there was an uneasy truce between them.

She glanced up as she heard voices outside and Peggy came in, more or less dragging a reluctant John Sharples behind her. The lad looked terrified, thought Jennet as she watched him take off his hat and clutch it in front of his chest as if it would give him protection. She gave Titus a warning look as he thrust the pamphlet aside and got to his feet.

'Come and sit thee down,' she told John. 'I'll put t' kettle on.' She waved to the chair opposite Titus and watched as John sidled towards it and sat on the edge, all the while keeping a wary eye on her husband.

She raised an eyebrow at Peggy who gave a half-smile. The lass looked worried too and Jennet knew it had taken courage for them to come like this to speak to her father.

John broke the silence first as he turned his hat in his hands. 'I've come to ask permission to keep company with Peggy,' he blurted out.

Jennet watched as Titus glared at him. She didn't even dare go to fetch water for the tea until she was sure he wasn't going to do something stupid.

'I told thee not to come back 'ere,' grumbled Titus.

'I know,' said John. 'But I ... We ...' He glanced at Peggy. 'We don't want to do owt behind thy back.'

'She'll not be here long. She's goin' away to school.'

'I'm not!' said Peggy. 'I'm not going. I've already told you.'

'And tha thinks tha'd be better off keeping company with this lad than learnin' to be a school-teacher?'

'It's what I want,' Peggy told him.

'Aye. Maybe it's what tha wants now, but will tha still want it when tha's livin' in poverty with 'im? Tha could have a good life, but tha's intent on throwing it away.'

'She'll not live in poverty. I'll make sure she's taken care of,' said John.

'And where would tha live if tha were wed?' asked Titus. 'I don't know as a clerk's wage will pay for much of a house.' He turned to Peggy. 'Dost tha really want to live back on Paradise Lane wi' 'is mother?'

351

Peggy looked doubtful. 'He's not askin' to wed me,' she said, 'only to keep company.'

'One leads to t' other in my experience.'

Jennet slipped out to fill the kettle. No fists were flying and although Titus could be stubborn she doubted it would come to blows.

She came back to put the kettle on the hob to boil and got out the best cups and saucers. At least they were all still sitting down. Peggy looked pale, but Jennet could see that she was determined, as determined as her father. And Titus hadn't totally lost his temper and told John to go.

'If it's what she really wants...' ventured Jennet as she poured milk into the cups. 'And it's good that John doesn't want to go behind our backs. Not like Sam.'

'At least he had money.'

'And what sort of a life would she have had with him, travellin' all over the place, takin' advantage of folk?'

'He were a doctor – a scientist.'

'He were a trickster, Titus, as tha knows full well. John here's a decent lad. And we owe him,' she reminded him. 'He's done well to get a good job after what happened. There's many in his position as wouldn't. And he'll be good and kind to Peggy. Tha knows that.'

'Aye, but she could do better.'

'As a schoolteacher? Maybe so. But it's not much of a life for a lass, is it? Look at Miss Parkinson. She might have a nice little house to live in and money enough to feed and clothe herself, but she's alone. Dost tha want Peggy to be alone like that for the rest of her life?'

'Miss Parkinson has respect.'

'Aye, but it's a high price to pay,' said Jennet.

'I want to be married and have a family,' said Peggy. 'I can't do that and be a schoolteacher, so it would be a waste of time going.'

'And what'll tha do for a job instead?' asked Titus.

'I'll find something. I can work in a shop.'

'It's not what I wanted for thee,' said Titus. 'I wanted better.'

'I know tha did,' said Jennet as she poured the tea. 'But things don't always turn out the way we want 'em to. Look at thee and me,' she reminded him. 'When we were their age we'd never have dreamt we'd end up like this. Let 'em keep company for a while,' she told him. 'There's no harm in it.'

'Tha'll have to tell Miss Parkinson,' Titus warned Peggy. 'And speak to thy auntie and uncle. Tha's goin' to disappoint a lot of folk with this notion.' He shook his head as he accepted the cup that Jennet handed to him. 'I did my best,' he said. 'It's not my fault t' lass is so ungrateful for everything I've done for her.'

Jennet offered tea to John but he shook his head. 'I'd best go,' he said.

'Don't take it as a refusal,' Jennet told him. 'Tha's welcome to call again.'

He nodded and, with a glance at Peggy, he left.

'If you've spoiled this for me I'll never speak to you again,' she told her father and went up to her bedroom, slamming the door shut behind her.

'I don't know what's got into her,' grumbled Titus.

'It's called being in love,' Jennet told him. 'Canst tha not remember what that was like?'

Titus could remember what it was like to be in love even if Jennet doubted it. He could remember how he'd hurried to meet her on a Sunday afternoon, before they were wed, and how happy he'd been the day he'd plucked up the courage to ask her to marry him and she'd said yes. But he'd had plans for Peggy. He wanted her to have a better life. It was a shame that Sam had gone off like he had. He'd managed to make something of himself, despite Jennet's doubts. It would have been different if Peggy had wanted to marry him. But not John Sharples. Never in a million years would he have thought that a daughter of his would have been set on marrying into that family.

And how would they keep themselves? The lad had work, but he doubted it was enough to keep a family. Peggy would have to work, and it would break his heart to see her in clogs and shawls, answering to the whims of the mill owners.

Chapter Thirty-Five

'I'm coming with thee,' said Jennet, reaching for her shawl when she saw Bessie getting ready to leave. 'I need to have a word with George.'

They walked up to the Old Bull in silence. Jennet knew that Bessie thought she was interfering, but now that she'd had time to think about it properly she'd come to the conclusion that it might be for the best if Bessie did go with her father. George was obviously wealthy. He could offer her a good life and maybe it was a good thing that Joshua wouldn't be going back with them. There was no future for Bessie with him. She was sure of that, and she knew that if Bessie stayed she would only have her heart broken.

George met them in the lobby. Although he looked surprised to see Jennet with their daughter, he didn't comment on it and ordered chocolate for all of them.

Jennet sipped on the sweet drink. She knew it was going to be hard for her if Bessie went away, but she wanted her daughter to be happy and she knew she must put the lass's best interests before her own wishes.

'Bessie says she's had second thoughts about goin' with thee,' she told George.

'Aye, I know. I never tried to persuade her to come,' George told Jennet. 'I'd said nowt about it until she came to me and said it were what she wanted. She seemed very keen on it.'

Jennet glanced at her daughter, who was folding and refolding a corner of the tablecloth between her fingers. She looked sullen.

'Aye. Well, she were under a misapprehension,' Jennet replied. 'She thought as young Joshua would be going back with thee, and that were where the main attraction lay.'

Jennet thought that it would have been easier to have this conversation without her daughter present, but she was hesitant to send her away when it was her future that was being discussed. 'She tells me as she's fond of Joshua,' Jennet said to George, 'but there's no future in it. I don't want to be parted from her, but I'm wonderin' if it might be for the best if she does go with thee.'

She looked from George's concerned face to the miserable face of their daughter and wished that there was something she could do that would make them both happy.

'I knew tha were friendly with Joshua,' George said to Bessie, 'but I didn't realise it were owt more.'

'Tha's not used to young lasses,' Jennet told him. 'But there can't be any future in it, can there?'

'How dost tha mean?' he asked.

'Well, she can't be wed to him, can she?'

'He's not a slave here,' George told her. 'He's as free as any man. He can wed who he chooses.'

'But how can he be wed in a Christian church when he's ...' She hesitated, not sure how to describe the lad.

'He's as good a Christian man as any I've met,' said George.

'But has he been baptised?'

'I've no idea. I'd have to ask him, but I don't see as it's a problem. I'm sure he'd get himself baptised if it were necessary and it was what he wanted.' He turned to Bessie. 'Tha's very quiet,' he told her. 'What's tha got to say about this?'

She looked close to tears, thought Jennet.

'Is there an understandin' between thee and Joshua?' George asked. 'Has he said summat to thee about marriage?'

'No,' whispered Bessie, 'but I like him and I know he likes me too. You're just set against him

358

because he looks different,' she accused her mother.

'No, it isn't that,' protested Jennet, although she knew deep down that what Bessie was saying was true. Although she liked Joshua and acknowledged that he was attractive and had perfect manners, she'd seen the way that folk stared at him on the street and she'd heard them whispering about him behind his back. She didn't want them talking about Bessie like that, but she knew that some would and they could be cruel. She would have preferred her daughter to take up with a local Lancashire lad whose family she knew.

'I think I need to speak to Joshua about it,' George said to Jennet. 'It may be that it's all a misunderstanding. He's said nowt to me about the lass.'

'Well, he wouldn't, would he?' Jennet told him. 'He'll not risk upsetting thee in case tha changes thy mind about helpin' him.'

'I'd never do that, and he knows it.'

'But they could never marry,' protested Jennet again. 'Besides, she's too young to know what she wants. It'll be better if she goes with thee. I think tha should go, Bessie,' she said to her daughter. 'I think it's for the best.'

'I don't care what you think!'

Jennet's cup rattled on its saucer under the sudden onslaught of her daughter's anger.

'I've always done what you've told me up until now,' she went on. 'But this is different. I'm old enough to make up my own mind!'

'Hush, Bessie.' George put his hand over his daughter's to calm her. 'Don't fret,' he told her. 'I promise I'll do everything I can to see thee happy. We'll get it sorted out. Don't thee worry.'

Jennet felt angry with George. She'd thought that he would agree with her when she said it was for the best if Bessie went with him. She knew it was what he really wanted, but instead he seemed more intent on ensuring that Bessie had her own way.

'I'll speak to Joshua,' he repeated, 'and see what he has to say. Then I think he should talk to Bessie. But if it's what they both want then I'll not object to it,' he told Jennet. 'She'll not find a better man,' he said.

Bessie had been so angry when her mother insisted on going with her to see her father. It had been excruciating to have to sit there whilst they talked about her as if she was a child. But now she was glad that it was all out in the open because after George had suggested that she and Joshua needed to talk to one another, he'd booked them a table for dinner so that they could do it in style.

Joshua was waiting for her at the front door of the Old Bull. His face lit up with a huge smile when he saw her coming and he hurried out on to the street to escort her inside. Bessie felt flustered. She'd been so apprehensive about this meeting in case she'd made a terrible mistake. She'd been afraid that he would explain he'd only been polite and there was no more to it than that.

In the dining room he held the chair for her as she sat down and waited until the jug of water had been brought before he said anything. But she could see from his face that he was eager to speak.

'Mr Anderton explained it all,' he said. 'When you said you were going back to America with him I was so sad, but I thought it was because you didn't want to be parted from your father.'

'I don't,' Bessie told him. 'It'll break my heart to say goodbye to him. But I don't want to say goodbye to you either. I'd never have said I wanted to go if I'd known you weren't coming with us. The trouble is that if I change my mind now, my father will be disappointed. He's trying to be brave and he says that it has to be my decision, but I know I've upset him.'

Joshua nodded. 'It has to be your decision, Bessie. I'd like you to stay, but if you decide to go ... well, then I'll try to understand.'

'Could you not come later?' she asked him. 'Surely things will change?'

'Maybe, but I'm not anticipating it. This will be my home now.'

'Does it make you sad, not being able to go back?' she asked him.

He shook his head. 'No. I wasn't sorry to leave that place. There are too many bad memories for me to want to go back there. Here, I'm a free man.'

'So, I'm forced to make a choice,' she said as a variety of dishes were laid out on the table in front of them.

'Ain't nobody forcing you to do anything, Bessie,' he said. 'But it sure would be nice if I could begin my new life here with you to help me.'

'What if it doesn't work out?' she asked. 'What if we don't get along?'

'Well, I suppose you could always go to America if you changed your mind. You'd have to travel alone. It wouldn't be easy, but it would be possible.' He fell silent for a moment. 'Let's eat the food before it goes cold,' he said at last and they busied themselves filling their plates. 'If things work out ... between us, I mean ... I could offer you a good life here,' he went on after a moment. 'You'll not want for a thing.'

Bessie and Joshua had finished eating by the time George got back. He came into the dining room, pulled up a chair and looked at them enquiringly.

'So, what's been decided?' he asked them.

Bessie reached out and put her hand on his. She'd grown to love this man so much in the few months that she'd known him. She'd felt an almost instant bond with him, which, she supposed, wasn't surprising. He'd been so happy when she'd asked if he would take her back to America with him and she hated to disappoint him. When he'd told her that his farm in Wisconsin was in a wild place and the only neighbours were miles away so she might find it lonely, she'd brushed his concerns aside, thinking that Joshua would be there and that they might one day become a family.

'I don't want to be parted from you, I really don't,' she told him.

George grasped Bessie's hand in his. 'When I came back I'd no idea what joy were waiting for me,' he told her. 'I'd only two things on my mind – to see my Lizzie's grave marked with a proper stone, and to get Joshua safe. I had no idea that tha existed, but now tha's the most important thing in the world to me, and I only want to see thee happy.'

'Then stay here,' pleaded Bessie, still hoping that she could have both of them.

He shook his head. 'I've got to go back. I have folk out there depending on me and, besides, it's my home now.'

'But this was your home once,' she told him. 'And now that you've made investments in the railway couldn't you make a life here again?'

'I don't think so,' he said. 'I like the wide open country too much.'

'I don't know what to do,' Bessie told him. She felt as if she was being torn apart between the two of them.

'Thy decision doesn't need to be final,' he told her. 'I'll be there if tha ever changes thy mind. And if things change, and Joshua can come back, then maybe tha both could come.'

'You sound like you're telling me to stay,' she said quietly.

'Aye.' His blue eyes were sad and Bessie thought she'd never bear it. 'Happen it's best for a young lass like thee to be with a lad, rather than with an old chap like me.'

Jennet couldn't settle to anything after Bessie had gone to meet up with Joshua. By the time the door opened and her daughter came in with George, she'd decided she would be glad of any decision that put an end to her worrying.

Bessie's face was glowing with excitement, but that didn't tell Jennet anything. Her daughter had been changing her mind about what to do more often than the wind shifted.

'She's decided to stay,' said George. He looked sad and Jennet felt for him. It seemed he was destined to be alone. 'She'll want for nothing,' he added. 'She'll never need to darken the doors of that mill ever again. I'll get 'em a house and furniture and everything they need. If the railway shares do well there might even be money for a housemaid ...'

'But they can't get married straight away!' protested Jennet. 'She's too young and they barely know one another.'

'Tha doesn't have to know someone long to know that they're the right one,' he told her and Jennet knew that he meant her. 'Besides,' he said. 'I'd like to see it all settled afore I go back.'

'She'll have to get Titus's permission,' Jennet warned him. 'It's his name on her birth record. He's her father in the eyes of the law.'

'He'll not make difficulties, will he?'

Jennet shook her head. 'I don't know,' she said. 'I feel like I barely know him these days.' She wondered if Titus might refuse out of spite, to get his own back on George.

'She can't marry him,' said Titus when Jennet told him what had been decided.

'Why not?'

'Well … it's not right,' he said.

'George has no objection,' Jennet told him. 'He's set the lad up in business and he's buying a house on King Street for them to live in. That's not summat to be sniffed at. Besides, he's a nice lad, even if he is … black.'

Titus shook his head. 'I wouldn't allow it if it were our Peggy,' he grumbled.

'But it isn't Peggy. It's Bessie. And she wants to marry him. And,' said Jennet, 'tha must remember that she's not thy daughter.'

'My name's in the register as her father,' he reminded her. 'And she'll need my name on her marriage certificate.'

'Please don't be difficult about it,' said Jennet. 'I'm not entirely happy about it myself,' she confessed. 'I think she's too young and I would have been happier if they'd waited a while and got to know one another better. But George wants to see them married before he goes back to America. He wants to see her settled and provided for – and it's what she wants. Don't spoil it for her out of spite.'

'Aye, well. I suppose it's none of my concern,' he grumbled. 'It's only me that fed and clothed her all these years.'

'I'm sure George would pay thee back the money! Dost tha want me to ask him?'

'Don't talk daft, our Jennet.'

'Then agree to the wedding with good grace.'

'Aye. I suppose as there's no choice. And to be honest it's our Peggy that I'm most concerned about. I'll not be givin' her permission to wed that Sharples lad.'

'I don't see why tha's bein' stubborn about that,' Jennet told him. 'If tha thinks she'll change her mind about the scholarship I can tell thee now that she won't. She can match thee for stubbornness,' she said.

'What did Titus say?' asked George when he called round the next morning.

'He wasn't keen on the idea, but he'll come round. It's Peggy that's concerning him.'

'Is she still refusing to take the scholarship?'

Jennet nodded. 'She's like him. Once she's set her mind to summat there's no changing it.'

'Young John Sharples seems a decent lad though.'

'Aye. He is. His sister, Mary, were best friends with our Hannah. His other sisters are nice enough lasses too, and Nan's changed since Joe were killed. It's taken t' wind out of her sails. She barely speaks to anyone now.'

'So could tha make things up with her?'

'It's too late for that,' Jennet told him. 'I'll never like the woman, but as long as Peggy's happy I'm willing to try to rub along with her – as long as she keeps a civil tongue in her head.'

'What will Peggy do – if she gives up teaching?'

'I don't rightly know. I'm beginning to think I were foolish in encouraging Titus to set his heart on it. It seemed a long way off when she were a child. But I should have realised that she'd meet some lad and that would put paid to any talk of being a schoolteacher.'

'Aye. Even if she'd got the scholarship it were probably only a matter of time afore she gave it up to get wed,' agreed George.

'I think Titus might have accepted it if it had been anyone but a Sharples,' said Jennet.

'I've been thinking,' said George. 'I saw yon hat and glove shop on Church Street's for sale.'

'Aye. Miss Cross is retiring. She's postmistress an' all. It's a good little business for somebody.'

'I thought I might buy it,' said George.

'For Joshua?'

'No, he'll have plenty to do with the railway investments. I thought I could offer it out for rent. Dost tha think John Sharples might be interested?'

'I can't see him sellin' ladies' hats and gloves.'

'No, but he could take on the post office part. It's a growing opportunity now that there's the penny post and folk are sending more letters. And 'appen Peggy might like to sell the hats. She likes hats, doesn't she?'

'Show me a lass as doesn't like hats,' said Jennet. 'Though she knows nowt about buyin' and sellin' 'em.'

'She could learn. I could ask Miss Cross to show 'em both what's what for a week or two. And best thing is there's rooms up above where they could live. I thought Titus might be more amenable if he knew Peggy weren't going back to Paradise Lane.'

Jennet could hardly believe his offer.

'Joshua would be in charge of collectin' the rent and makin' sure it was all done proper,' he told her. 'He'd be sending t' profits back to me, so I wouldn't be losing out. I've been looking out for some other investments and this seems a good one, especially now that I know I can rent it out to a couple who'll work hard.'

'Well, that's generous,' Jennet told him, wondering why it was that George always seemed to come up with a solution to her problems when she needed one most.

'Tha knows that I'm doing it for thee,' he told her. 'More than anything I want to see thee happy and if it means getting the lasses settled and secure then it's what I'll do.'

'I know,' she told him. 'But tha knows I can't repay thee. I can't go with thee.'

'Aye, I know,' he said. 'But I'll never give up hope that tha might change thy mind one day.'

When Jennet looked at him she could see his love for her in his eyes. Titus had once looked at her like that, a long, long time ago.

'George,' she whispered. She wanted to reach out and put her arms around him. She wanted to kiss him, as she had done that night so long ago in the little attic room overlooking the quay in Lancaster. She wondered if she would have been better off if Titus had been transported and she'd gone with George whilst she was still young, before her mother needed her. 'I can't leave them,' she said, wiping tears from her eyes.

'Aye, I know,' he replied.

Bessie gazed up at the house. There were four steps up to the front door, which was black with a polished doorknocker. The man with the key unlocked it and they went inside. The hall floor was tiled and a staircase with a mahogany rail curved to the upper floor.

'There's a drawing room at the front here,' he told them, 'and there's also a dining room and a morning room. The kitchens are down below in the basement and there are four bedrooms in total and a room in the attic if you should require accommodation for a maidservant.'

'Can we really have all this?' Bessie asked George. It was a palace by comparison with the little two-up two-down on Water Street. They would be the neighbours of a mill owner on one side and a doctor on the other.

'Aye. If tha likes it then consider it my wedding gift to thee,' he told her.

Bessie walked into the morning room. It was bright in the sunshine. It would make a wonderful sewing room, she thought. And now that she didn't have to work in the mill she would have plenty of time to sew. She might even begin a little business making dresses, she thought. She would need something to occupy her days and she had no intention of sitting doing nothing whilst Joshua worked.

'What dost tha think, Joshua?' asked George. 'Will it suit thee? Tha could use one of the rooms upstairs for an office.'

Joshua seemed as overwhelmed as she was, thought Bessie as she watched him stare up at the intricately plastered cornicing.

'It'll do just fine,' he said.

'Then we'll take it,' George told the agent. 'I'll go to sign the papers,' he said to them, 'whilst tha goes down to yon furniture shop and picks out a few pieces. Get what tha likes,' he told them when they were back out on the street. 'Chairs, lamps, rugs, whatever tha needs. Tell 'em to send the bill to me.'

Joshua offered Bessie his arm and they walked to the shop.

'I never expected anything like that,' said Bessie. 'I hope he can afford it.'

'We could live on the street if it turns out he can't. It's a mighty fine street,' replied Joshua. 'But don't you worry. Mr Anderton wouldn't show it to you if he couldn't afford it – although it makes me think I'm going to have to work extra hard to meet his expectations!'

Peggy knew that she would have to tell Miss Parkinson that she'd decided not to take the scholarship exam and she wasn't looking forward to it.

'Margaret,' said the schoolmistress when she went to call on her. 'Are you feeling better?'

'I am, thank you.'

'And when can I expect you back?' She seemed pleased and Peggy was hesitant to disappoint her.

'I'm not coming back,' she blurted out. 'I'm not taking the scholarship.'

Miss Parkinson stared at her. 'I don't understand,' she said. 'I've told the inspectors that you're a candidate.'

'I've decided it's not for me.'

'But I thought being a schoolteacher was what you wanted. You'd be a good teacher, Margaret. Don't miss out on this chance,' Miss Parkinson implored her. Peggy was shaking her head. 'What will you do instead?' asked the schoolmistress.

'I'm thinking of being married,' Peggy told her.

'Are you sure? It seems very sudden.' She stopped and looked at Peggy. 'You're not ... you know ... having a baby?'

'No! Of course not.' Peggy was insulted by the suggestion.

'Then why decide so suddenly?'

'It's what I want.'

'You can never have a second chance at this if you marry,' Miss Parkinson warned her.

'I know,' said Peggy. 'And I have thought about it.'

'Well, I can't say I'm not disappointed. I had such high hopes for you.'

Peggy hung her head. She felt sad to be disappointing so many people, but deep down she knew it was the right decision, and she was glad to escape the schoolroom for the very last time.

When she got home, Bessie was in the bedroom with a parcel open on the bed.

'Do you like these?' she asked, spreading out some lengths of fabrics. 'They're for soft furnishings for my new house. You should see it, Peg! It's on King Street and it's huge! There are so many rooms I don't know how I'll ever fill them. Joshua and I have been to choose furniture and George says we can have whatever we want!'

Being jealous of her younger sister was still a new emotion for Peggy. She'd rarely felt it in her life before. Bessie had always been the one who was second best. But now Bessie had a father who could and would give her anything she wanted, whilst her own father seemed set on making her miserable and denying her the only thing that would make her happy – his permission for her to marry John.

She sat down on the bed and fingered one of the silky fabrics. It would make beautiful cushions, she thought, and Bessie could sew so neatly.

'I told Miss Parkinson I wasn't going back. He can't make me take the scholarship now,' she said.

'But that doesn't mean he'll agree to you marrying John. It just means you'll have to get work,' Bessie told her. 'But George says he has an idea. He wants to talk to you and John.'

'What about?'

'I don't know. He was a bit secretive. I think he has an idea about one of his investments. I think he might be able to help you.'

'George Anderton wants to talk to us,' Peggy told John later when she met him at the Temperance Hotel after he'd finished work. 'Bessie said we're to call on him at the Old Bull.'

'What does he want?' asked John. He sounded suspicious.

'I don't know, but Bessie thinks it's something to do with a job.'

'I have a job.'

'I know, but there's no harm in going to see what he has to say,' replied Peggy. 'Bessie says he can help us.'

She watched as John finished his drink and set his cup down on the table. She hoped he wasn't going to refuse to come with her. She was curious to hear what George had to say, even if she was still angry with him for telling tales about her to her mother. As it turned out, Sam Proctor had been a fraud and a cheat, but George hadn't known that and it had been none of his business who she went out with. He wasn't her father.

'Let's just go and hear what he has to say,' she said to John. 'It doesn't commit us to anything.'

They walked down to the Old Bull arm in arm. It was more lively in there than it had been in the Temperance Hotel and George ushered them into a fairly quiet corner and offered John a beer, which he declined, telling George that he had signed the pledge.

'Good lad,' replied George. 'I'm after someone who's sober and reliable.'

'What for?' asked Peggy when John didn't reply.

'Tha knows Miss Cross's shop?'

'Yes, of course.'

'Dost tha fancy takin' it on?' he asked. 'Tha'd have to pay a fair rent, of course, and it wouldn't be easy. It's a fair responsibility running a post office and then there's the hats and gloves.'

For once Peggy was lost for words. It would be a solution to her worries about what work she could do and she knew that John would be much happier being his own boss. She glanced at him. He was watching George carefully, probably wondering if he was serious.

'I'm doing this for Peggy,' George told him. 'It's on condition that you marry her. And I expect thee to work hard. My manager, Joshua, will be keeping an eye on things and collecting the rent. He'll report back to me.'

Peggy stared at George. Those vague memories she had, the ones of being bounced on a man's knee, being tossed in the air, laughing and squealing with delight: they had been of him. She was sure now. He'd been kind to her then, and he was being kind to her now. She wasn't sure she deserved it. She knew she'd acted very rudely when he first arrived, thinking that he was a criminal. But he wasn't doing this for her sake, she realised. He was doing it for her mother. He loved her mother. And her mother had loved him. She could remember her crying and she'd always thought she was crying for her husband. Now she knew that she'd cried for George.

'Well, ye're both very quiet,' he said. 'What dost ye think?'

'It would be wonderful,' said Peggy. 'Wouldn't it, John?'

'Aye,' he said. 'But we still need thy father's permission to marry.'

'Happen he'll come round if he knows tha has th' opportunity to run thy own business. And there's rooms upstairs,' George told them. 'Tha could live up there. There'd be no need to go back to Paradise Lane.'

'You're not going to refuse it, are you?' Peggy asked John, worried that he didn't look as enthusiastic as she felt.

'No,' he said. 'No, of course not. It's just a bit of a surprise, that's all.'

Titus came home from work, hungry for his tea, to find the parlour crowded with folk. He scowled at them all. That George Anderton was there. He'd brought the black lad with him too, the one he wanted to marry young Bessie. And, worse, John Sharples was there, sitting beside Peggy and both of them with great grins on their faces.

They were all sitting around the table, drinking tea out of the best cups and saucers, and eatin' some fancy food.

Jennet got up and went to fetch another cup.

'Sit down and have some of this ham that George has brought,' she said.

Titus saw that there was fresh bread too and fruit. He felt like saying he wasn't hungry but his mouth was watering at the sight of it and he couldn't resist.

'We're havin' a bit of a celebration,' Jennet told him.

'Oh, aye,' said Titus, making a sandwich with the meat. The bread was buttered too and he relished it for a moment before taking a long drink of his tea.

'George is going to buy Miss Cross's shop and John and I are going to rent it from him,' Peggy told him. 'John's going to run the post office and I'll sell the hats.'

'Is that right?' Titus replied, putting the rest of the sandwich down on his plate. He glared across the table at George Anderton. He was sick of the man interfering in his family, making decisions for them without ever asking him.

'Tha's no objection, hast tha?' asked George. 'It's a good opportunity for them.'

'George says there's room above the shop where we can live,' Peggy told him. She looked so happy, happier than she'd been for a long time, thought Titus, and he couldn't bring himself to spoil her mood even if George Anderton seemed to be forcing his hand towards agreeing to this marriage. It was bad enough him coming in and saying what Bessie could and couldn't do. She was his daughter. But he resented the man offering things to Peggy even more. She should have been a schoolteacher. He could have been proud of that.

'It doesn't seem as I have much say in the matter,' he grumbled.

'Please don't be difficult,' said Jennet. Her face held a pleading look and Titus could see that it was what she wanted too. He didn't reply straight away. He knew that although all these arrangements for Peggy had been made behind his back they needed him to agree. She couldn't be wed without his permission and he wasn't sure he wanted to give it. If anyone had asked him who was the worst possible choice of husband for Peggy, he couldn't have picked anyone worse than John Sharples. He glared at the lad across the table.

'Titus?' asked Jennet. 'It's such a good opportunity for Peggy. I know tha had thy heart set on her being a teacher, but would tha really want her to do it if it would make her miserable?'

He shook his head. They would all hate him if he didn't agree to their plans. None of them would ever forgive him. He was beginning to wonder if it was worth making a fuss over, or whether he should just agree and let them face the consequences – because there would be consequences, he was sure. None of it would turn out well. It never did where the Sharples family was concerned.

He looked at young Bessie, holding hands with the black lad. They couldn't be married either, unless he agreed to it.

'I've asked George to give me away,' said Bessie. Titus didn't reply. That would be the final insult, he thought. Everyone would remark on it. 'He is my father,' she added.

'Aye. I know,' said Titus. 'I were in t' prison when tha were conceived. I got arrested after this man abandoned me to the mob.'

'I never abandoned thee, Titus,' said George. 'I lost sight of thee in t' crush, but it were never my intention that tha should be arrested.'

'Aye, well tha didn't lose any time takin' up with our Jennet – and thy Lizzie barely cold in her grave.'

George at least had the grace to look shamefaced. 'I could say as I'm sorry,' he replied, 'but truth is I'm not. I wouldn't have had this lass otherwise.'

'She's too young to be wed,' said Titus. 'She's not old enough to know her own mind.'

'I am!' protested Bessie.

'I'd agree to a longer engagement,' George told him, 'but I want to see them settled before I go back – and I can't delay much longer.'

'Titus,' said Jennet again, 'please don't be difficult.'

'I'm not being difficult. I'm pointing out the truth of it,' he said. 'Marriage isn't something to be rushed into.'

It seemed as if no one ever listened to him, thought Titus. First it was the Parliament who refused to listen to the demands of the Chartists, and now even his own family wouldn't listen to him. He pushed the remains of the bread on the plate aside. He picked up his cup, but the tea had grown cold and he put it down. These fancy cups were no use either. He wanted a proper drink from his pint pot.

He knew that they were all looking at him, waiting for him to give his agreement. He knew that if he refused he would lose what little regard Jennet had left for him, and he couldn't bring himself to fall out with her again.

'Aye, all right,' he said after a moment.

Chapter Thirty-Six

Bessie woke early on the morning of her wedding day. It was just coming light and she could hear the knocker-up making his way down the next street. The mills were all working. The pay hadn't been increased and although there was talk of more parliamentary reform, none of the Chartists' demands had been met. The vote was still denied to the ordinary working man. She was glad that she didn't have to go to work in the mill again. She wouldn't miss it and she had a mind to spending her time fighting for Reform to make things better for people.

Peggy was still sleeping beside her, one hand tucked under the bolster and the other curled into a tight fist. Titus had reluctantly agreed to her marriage too, although he'd said that they would have to wait a few months. John was going to take over the shop on Church Street and live upstairs; Peggy would help him, but would live at home for the time being. Bessie thought that Titus was still secretly hoping that her sister would change her mind about the scholarship exam. Bessie doubted that she would.

She pushed back the covers and felt for her clogs. She pulled her shawl around her shoulders and crept down the stairs to let herself out of the back door to go down the yard. The late September morning was chilly, but it looked like it was going to be fine.

When she got back to the kitchen her mother had the kettle on. She didn't remark on Bessie being outside in her night clothes.

'Happy?' she asked her.

'Yes. Of course I am.'

'No second thoughts?'

'No, none. He'll come, won't he?' she asked. 'Titus, I mean. He needs to sign the papers.'

'Aye, he'll come,' her mother reassured her. 'He does care about thee,' she told her. 'I know he doesn't often show it, but he does love thee, and he's been a good father to thee all these years.'

'I know,' said Bessie as she watched her mother hand a cup of tea to Grandma Chadwick.

'Are you still in love with George?' she asked her. Her mother didn't reply straight away. She began to slice a loaf of bread.

'Love's a funny thing,' she said after a moment. 'Just because tha loves one person, it doesn't mean tha can't love another one as well.'

'Do you ever regret not going with him?'

'Sometimes,' she admitted. She finished cutting the bread. 'Come and get some breakfast,' she said. 'Then tha can go and put on thy fancy frock.'

Peggy came down whilst they were eating. Bessie knew that her sister was jealous that she was marrying before her. As the firstborn, she thought that she should have been the first to wed. She would have preferred to wear her new frock for the first time to her own wedding. But she'd given Bessie a new bonnet to wear from the shop and chosen one for herself as well. They were straw, with blue ribbons and white flowers.

'No one will want these,' she'd said. 'All the ladies are asking for autumn fashions now and it would be a shame to let them go to waste.'

John had told her that they would never turn a profit if she pilfered the stock, but he hadn't taken much persuading. Peggy could twist him around her little finger, thought Bessie, just as she'd always done with her father.

Once they were all dressed up they left Grandma Chadwick with Molly next door and walked to the church. Titus had grudgingly taken the morning off work and he'd put on his best clothes.

Her mother took his arm as they walked and Bessie walked arm in arm between Peggy and her friend Ruth, who had agreed to be a witness.

George was waiting for them at the church door. He kissed Bessie and told her she looked beautiful. He said the same to Peggy and to her mother. Bessie saw him exchange a look with her that was filled with regret. Then George held out his hand to Titus. There was a tense moment before he took it and shook it. Her mother and Titus went to take their places in the pews and Bessie took George's arm. He walked her up the aisle with Peggy and Ruth following. Joshua was waiting. He looked handsome and she thought he seemed relieved when he saw her. She wondered if he'd been afraid that something would go wrong. He smiled at her and George put her hand into his and went to sit down. Then the Reverend Whittaker cleared his throat, raised his open prayer book and began the ceremony.

After the wedding they all went to the house on King Street. George had employed a maid for them and she was waiting at the door to welcome them home. There were flowers in the hallway and the dining table was spread with food. Bessie knew that she should have been completely happy, but she couldn't shake off the sadness she felt at the thought of George leaving. He'd booked his ticket, he'd told her, and would sail the next Friday. But she had Joshua and she would never be sorry about that. Her new husband smiled down at her and bent to kiss her cheek.

Her mother was wiping away a tear as she sat down. She couldn't stop telling her how lucky she was to begin her married life in such a beautiful house, and Bessie knew that it was true. They'd brought Grandma Chadwick from Molly's house to join the celebrations. She didn't understand what was happening, but she knew she was in a fancy house with plenty to eat and a roaring fire, and it pleased her.

Only Titus was scowling. Bessie went to lay a hand on his shoulder. She leaned towards him and kissed his cheek. The smell of him was familiar and comforting.

'Thank you,' she said. 'Thank you for everything.'

'Aye, lass.' He patted her hand and the scowl was replaced by a smile.

Peggy reached for John's hand as she sat beside him at the table. She'd found it hard not to cry as she'd listened to her little sister making her marriage vows. She hoped that Bessie would be happy. But who wouldn't be happy beginning their married life in a house like this? Peggy looked around the room scarcely able to comprehend that it would be her sister's home.

John's fingers tightened around hers. 'We'll be next,' he whispered. 'It won't be long.'

George caught her eye and smiled at her. She had reason to be grateful to him. Without his offer of the shop she didn't think her father would ever have been persuaded to agree to her marrying John. It had worked out so well. John loved sorting out the letters and going out to deliver them to the householders. There seemed to be more arriving each day and he had even mentioned employing an apprentice for the deliveries. Whilst he was out, she stayed behind, accepting any post that was brought in, being careful to cancel the stamps and put the letters into the right bags for the mail coach. And she loved welcoming the ladies who wanted a new hat or a pair of gloves. She tried to emulate Miss Cross by being polite but never servile and she enjoyed discussing the latest colours and fashions with them, pleased when they sought her opinion on which suited them best. She was hoping that she might even get a trip to London in the spring, to choose new stock for the shop.

She saw Bessie lean over to kiss Titus. He patted her sister's hand and smiled. He'd told them that he was going back to work after the wedding, but her mother had persuaded him to come for something to eat first. Peggy hoped that her father would eventually forgive her for not taking the scholarship. She knew it was a disappointment to him, but she needed to live her own life, not the one he'd chosen for her.

George was going around the table filling their glasses. John shook his head. He would stick to his spring water, but he joined them as they raised a toast to the bride and groom, and Peggy saw that her mother could no longer disguise her tears. She hoped that they were tears of happiness.

Epilogue

1843

It was 26 April and, as usual, Jennet had picked bluebells to lay on Lizzie Anderton's grave. No one disturbed her this year as she knelt beside the stone that had Lizzie's name engraved on it. Jennet brushed off some moss that had grown there over the wintertime. She wondered what George was doing. He would be thinking of Lizzie today, that was for sure, but was he thinking of her as well?

It had been so hard to say goodbye to him again. In the market square that Friday morning, seven months ago now, she'd watched as he'd hugged Bessie as if he couldn't bear to let her go. Then he'd shaken Joshua by the hand and given him some last-minute instructions before hugging him as well. The coachman had called to him to get on quickly or he'd have to leave without him. The horses had been pawing restlessly at the cobbles and George had turned to her. They'd simply looked at one another. Nothing had been said. There had been nothing left to say, but Jennet had seen the tears in his eyes.

Grandma Chadwick was growing frailer by the day and Jennet knew that before the year was out she would be laying flowers on another plot. It made her sad, but she knew it was part of the cycle of life. She just hoped that her mother would live long enough to hold at least one of her great-grandchildren in her arms.

Bessie was expecting a baby in July and Peggy had told her only yesterday that she was with child too. It would be strange to take on the name of grandma, thought Jennet. Strange, but wonderful too, and she was looking forward to nursing those new babies in her arms. They would both grow up in better circumstances than the ones in which she'd struggled to raise her own daughters. But she hadn't done a bad job, she thought. And she was glad that they were both settled with good husbands – husbands they loved, and who loved them.

She would have to get home in a minute and start on Titus's tea, she thought as she tidied the flowers once more, got stiffly to her feet and dusted down her skirt with her hands. He'd come to accept Peggy's choice in the end, even though it was a disappointment to him. He'd given Peggy away on her wedding day and managed to stay civil to John, and to Nan as well, who was a changed woman. Jennet almost felt sorry for her.

And she'd accepted her own choice too. She could never have left her mother to go with George, and now she could never leave her daughters. But Titus had promised that, when the summer came, he would take her on one of the carriage excursions to the seaside. She didn't want to bathe, but she wanted to look out over the water and think about George, as she'd thought about those who were being sent to the penal colonies that day in Lancaster – that day so long ago when she'd thought she would never see Titus again.

Jennet walked back through the town to Water Street and let herself in. The house had been quiet since her daughters had left. It had given her and Titus the time they needed to rediscover the reasons they'd fallen in love all those years ago. It could never be the same; Jennet knew that. Too many things had happened along the way. But she and Titus had become a little closer now that there were only the two of them. He still liked his politics, but he didn't go out to his meetings every night. Sometimes they just sat on either side of the fire – her with her sewing and him with his pipe – and they remembered the things they'd done at Pleck Gate when he'd woven at his loom and she'd spun at her wheel. Their lives had turned out very differently from the future that they'd imagined back then. It had been hard at times, but it had brought some joys, and there were more joys to come.

Jennet filled the kettle and put it on to boil. She had a loaf of bread today, and jam and butter. It would make a grand tea, she thought as she listened out for the sound of Titus's clogs coming down the street, coming home.

Welcome to

Penny Street

where your favourite authors and stories live.

Meet casts of characters you'll never forget,
create memories you'll treasure forever,
and discover places that will stay with
you long after the last page.

Turn the page to step into the home of

Libby Ashworth

and discover more about

A
FAMILY
Secret

Dear Reader,

Here we are at the end of the third book in The Mill Town Lasses series. It gives me so much pleasure when you get in touch to say how much you have enjoyed my stories. Even though I love to write them, it's extra-special to be able to share them with such enthusiastic readers. I loved writing about what happened to both George and Sam after we saw them go their separate ways in *The Cotton Spinner*. I hope you enjoyed meeting them, as well as Peggy and Bessie, again now that they've all grown up.

When my editor Jennie read this book, she said straight away that we should have Bessie, with the lavender gloves, on the cover. I thought it was a wonderful idea and was thrilled when the designer and photographer managed to find a pair! I hope you all noticed. So much work goes into designing the delightful covers for my books and I always fall in love with them as soon as I see them.

I'm going to say goodbye to the Eastwood family for a little while now – although, who knows, they may return to my stories in the future. I hope you've enjoyed reading these books; they're so close to my heart, and I've loved watching each character grow and change throughout different time periods.

Much love to you all,

Libby x

Railway Excursions and Sea Bathing

From the 1840s onwards, the growth of the railways meant that day excursions gained popularity. Places that had previously been too far away for the working classes to visit became accessible and Sunday trips were widely advertised – often with a line in the small print to say that there would be ample time to visit a place of worship during the day. Trips to ruins were particularly popular, and Furness Abbey became a major tourist attraction, with the building of its own railway station and the conversion of the manor house into the Furness Abbey Hotel. Not everyone was happy about the development, though. The poet William Wordsworth said: *'many of the trees which embowered the ruin have been felled to make way for this pestilential nuisance'.*

Sea bathing was another popular pastime that was regarded as beneficial for the health. It was said that, off the coast of Lancashire during August and September, there was a special 'physic' in the sea – *'a physic of a most comprehensive description, combining all the virtues of all the drugs in the doctor's shops and of course a cure for all varieties of disease.'*

In the book, I mention a woman who was a 'dipper'. The dippers were there to keep an eye on the bathers in case they got into difficulties, but it was also their job to give the bathers a full immersion in the water!

But even for a dip in the sea, ladies and gentleman remained well covered. Bathing machines provided privacy so bathers could change into their costumes. Similar to a hut on wheels, the bathing machines were drawn, either by a horse or several strongmen, down into the sea so that bathers could open the curtain that protected their modesty and step straight into the water.

Men and women were strictly segregated on different areas of the beach so that the men wouldn't see the women in their costumes. However, the following court case did appear in a local newspaper:

1850
CAUTION TO KEEPERS OF BATHING MACHINES

On Tuesday last at the Kirkham Petty Sessions, the owner of a bathing machine at Lytham, was fined 1s. and costs amounting to 9s.6d. under the Lytham Bye Laws, for taking down three gentlemen to bathe within the limits prescribed by the Bye Laws for females.

Preston Guardian, Saturday July 13, 1850

Phrenology

If you've ever browsed in an antique shop, you may well have seen a ceramic model of a head with the different areas of the skull marked and labelled. These are phrenology heads.

The 'science' of phrenology was very popular in Victorian times. It was first developed by a German physician, Franz Joseph Gall, in 1796, who claimed that the shape of the skull could reveal someone's personality. Phrenologists believed that the brain was made up of different organs, each responsible for different aspects of the mind. They thought that the brain was like a muscle and that the more an area of it was used, the larger it would grow, and that the skull would change its shape to accommodate the growth. Likewise, the lesser-used areas would shrink. Therefore, the shape of the skull could reveal much about a person!

Phrenologists were regarded as experts, and they set up consulting rooms where people could go to discover more about their abilities and aptitudes. People also went to a phrenologist to find answers to their questions about the future, and which path they should take in life. Even children were taken to see what profession they should study for.

Many scientific discoveries were being made at this time, and phrenology was widely accepted as a serious science. Some employers even asked for a phrenological reading before giving someone a job. It reminds me of the vogue for the study of handwriting that was prevalent some years ago.

Even Queen Victoria was an advocate. On at least two occasions she and Prince Albert invited the Scottish phrenologist, George Combe, to read their children's heads.

Towards the beginning of the twentieth century, phrenology fell out of favour, and it is now regarded as a pseudoscience.

Slavery

Slavery was closely linked with the cotton towns of Lancashire. The cotton that was spun and woven in the mills there at the height of the Industrial Revolution was imported via Liverpool from the southern states of America, where it was picked by slaves. The Slave Trade Act of 1807 made it illegal for British ships to carry enslaved people between Africa, the West Indies and America. This was followed in 1833 by The Slavery Abolition Act, which abolished slavery in most of the British Empire. But it wasn't until the end of the American Civil War in 1865 that all the slaves who picked cotton were emancipated.

Prior to the Civil War in America, runaway slaves headed for the northern states where slavery had already been outlawed. They were assisted by people who set up the Underground Railroad – escape routes, safe houses and guides to help them find refuge and safety. Possibly the best-known conductor on this secret network was a woman named Harriet Tubman. She was a former slave herself who had escaped, but she risked returning to the south repeatedly and guided around seventy slaves to freedom. 'I was free, and they should be free,' she said.

But reaching one of the northern states did not ensure safety or complete freedom. The slave owners in the south viewed escaped slaves as property and demanded a law that would see them caught and returned. So thousands of escaped slaves went as far as Canada to ensure they were not caught and returned to their 'owners'.

As I researched this topic, I began to wonder if any fugitive slaves had escaped to England, and that led me to the story of William and Ellen Craft, who escaped from a plantation in Georgia in 1848. Ellen, whose skin was fair, disguised herself as a slave master and William was disguised as a valet. They managed to reach Boston, where they lived in freedom for eighteen months. But the passing of The Fugitive Slave Act in 1850 put them in danger, and when two slave-catchers came looking for them, their friends smuggled them to New Brunswick from where they caught a steamer to Liverpool. They joined British abolitionists on the lecture circuit, speaking in many places about the plight of the southern slaves, and Ellen's appearance as a 'white' woman was particularly shocking to the audiences. You can read their story in the book which was written by William Craft and Ellen Craft and published in 1860 – *Running a Thousand Miles for Freedom*.

Lancashire, 1826

When Jennet and Titus Eastwood are forced to move from
their idyllic cottage into the centre of Blackburn to find
work in the cotton mills, their lives are changed in ways
they could never have imagined and their new home on
Paradise Lane is anything but . . .

Then Titus is arrested and sent to prison for attending a
Reform meeting. Jennet is left to fend for herself and things
go from bad to worse as she finds herself pregnant and
alone – with another man's child . . .

'An engrossing tale of hardship, struggles, love
and family. Well-researched, perfect for fans of
Catherine Cookson.'
Kitty Neale

AVAILABLE NOW

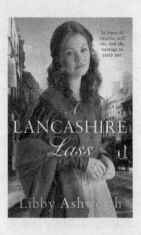

Lancashire, 1832

Maids Hannah and Mary find themselves with no jobs and no home when their employer, Henry Sudell, loses all his money and disappears in the middle of the night. They have no choice but to return to Blackburn where Hannah is lucky to be taken in by her sister Jennet and brother-in-law, Titus, but Mary must seek lodgings in the infamous Star beer house.

Mary tries to get her job back as a weaver, but the influx of workers from the countryside and no support for the working class means that jobs are scarce. With no other choice she remains at the beer house, forced to risk her reputation and even her life.

In the middle of a cholera outbreak and political upheaval, can Mary ever find a way to recover all she's lost?

'Vividly drawn characters . . . gritty and heartfelt.'
Evie Grace

AVAILABLE NOW

Hear more from

Libby Ashworth

SIGN UP TO OUR NEW SAGA NEWSLETTER

Penny Street

Stories You'll Love to Share

Penny Street is a newsletter bringing you the latest book deals, competitions and alerts of new saga series releases.

Read about the research behind your favourite books, try our monthly wordsearch and download your very own Penny Street reading map.

Join today by visiting
www.penguin.co.uk/pennystreet